THE HARD WAY

JILL SANDERS

GRAYTON

DIGITAL ISBN: 978-1-945100-30-7

PRINT ISBN: 979-8-511661-96-4

Copyeditor: Erica Ellis – inkdeepediting.com

SUMMARY

Brent has spent the last few years of his life in denial that his shithead parents had left him and his little sister all alone in the world. Alone and broke. Naturally, after their sudden death, he'd done what any guy would have done. He drank, screwed anything that moved, and let his little sister take care of him. But then, things had changed. He had changed. Now, he knew that it was past time he woke up and grew up. Which meant returning to Haven, Montana, and facing the music.

Mel has been trying hard to leave her past behind her, keeping her head down, working hard, and staying out of sight. She'd already started over once, and she wasn't about to screw up this time. After taking the first job available in a small town, the last thing she'd expected was to fall hard for her new boss.

CHAPTER 1

Brent stood over the grave of his parents on his twenty-first birthday and silently cursed them. Life as he knew it was officially over. When he felt his sister Dylan take his hand, he couldn't help thinking that it felt like a weight, holding him down. He loved Dylan, really, he did. As far as little sisters went, she was cool. But knowing that he would now be responsible for her future caused him to wince.

Why hadn't his parents been more like parents and less like cool older friends who liked to party and hang with their children? They had left their two kids totally unprepared for life and destitute, which made him even more pissed.

Their vacation to Cancun had started out like all their other family vacations. By day two, he was missing his then girlfriend, Tilly. He was horny and had been eyeing a cute girl his age who was staying at the same resort. He didn't want to cheat on Tilly, not really, but if the pretty brunette kept giving him looks, well, he was game.

But when the boat bringing them back from their snorkeling trip that day had blown up, everything had changed.

Thankfully, he and Dylan hadn't been injured too badly, aside from some cuts and burns they'd received when they'd been thrown clear of the explosion.

Their parents and several of the others on the vessel hadn't been so lucky.

"What's going to happen now?" Dylan whispered to him.

He squeezed her hand and looked down at her.

"Now, we go home." He wrapped an arm around her. "Just the two of us. That's how it's going to be."

For the first few months, he did his best, or at least tried. But nothing he did stopped the flow of money out of their accounts. First, there had been the funeral charges. Just having his parents' bodies brought back to the States had drained their savings accounts. Then there were the house payments, insurance payments, and his outstanding college fees. He dropped out quickly after seeing that bill.

Then he'd received the call telling him that his parents had left behind massive debt and, before they'd taken that fateful trip, his mother's car had been repossessed. He'd thought she had left it at her work or at the airport. His father's car was taken away shortly after that.

If they hadn't sold their childhood home, along with several other large items that their father had purchased, such as the boat that sat in storage and the Jet Ski that they'd only taken out on the lake twice, he and Dylan would have been destitute.

But a little over a year later, they were in the same position anyway. Thankfully, he still had his truck. He had gotten a dead-end job and had started to give up on life. Drinking helped him drown his sorrows. So did fucking every pretty woman that batted an eyelash at him. He'd also let his anger loose on any guy that looked at him sideways. Which is how he'd ended up in jail that first time. By the third time, he understood that Dylan had pretty much given up on him.

He still remembered a fight he'd had with her a while back. She'd actually compared him to their father.

Just how the fuck was he like their old man? They were nothing alike. Carl McCaw had been a banker. The son of a banker and grandson of a banker. Brent was pretty sure that if his dad had lived much longer, he would have convinced Brent to go into banking as well.

Not that any of his family had owned their own bank. No, they worked for men or women who had all the money.

The fact that Carl, third generation banker, didn't know how to balance his own personal budget said everything you needed to know about the man. In everything his dad had done, he'd been selfish first and foremost.

He'd push a car payment or two back to take the vacation he wanted, then claim that the trip was well worth it. Bills would pile up, and he'd spend a few months working harder to catch up, only to throw it all away again on the next thing he wanted.

Brent was nothing like that. His bank account had sat empty since the day he'd paid the last cent of his parents' debt off.

In a last-ditch effort to make a living, he'd allowed his sister to talk him into moving to nowheresville Montana for jobs. Dylan had told him that she'd read somewhere that the small town of Haven was desperate for workers.

The moment he'd driven into town, he'd known nothing would change for him there. The first sign was that the small town had almost as many strip clubs as it did gas stations. Then he'd met Darla. From the moment he'd laid eyes on the pretty blonde, he'd been infatuated. Then again, it could have been her double Ds and watching how she worked the pole at the strip club. Plus, some of the draw was the fact that he'd never dated a stripper before.

Months later, he'd caught Darla poking holes in the

condoms in his nightstand. That had been the wake-up call he'd needed to break things off with her.

That hadn't gone over great since Darla had been both drunk and high at the time. Then she'd had the gall to yell at him and say that he didn't know how bad her life was.

But the final thing that had opened his eyes for good was the night of his friend Jake's stag party. He and a bunch of his work buddies had ended up in the drunk tank.

Instead of bailing him out, Dylan had left him in jail all night. Normally, after he called her, she'd come post his bond and take him home. This time, he'd waited the entire night out with his buddies and had to walk to work the next day.

When she'd showed up, he'd grabbed her arm. He knew he was being a little rough with her, but damn it, he was tired and pissed that he didn't get a shower before having to come into work.

"Oh, good, you found your own ride." Dylan had smiled at him as if it was the most natural thing in the world to leave him to rot in a cell.

"Dylan, why the hell did you leave me there?" he'd asked.

Her eyes had narrowed. "I don't know, Brent. Why the hell did you allow two of your idiot friends to break into my place and scare me to death?" Oh, right, he'd forgotten that his buddies had tried to kidnap him the night before for the party. He winced remembering how scared Dylan had been. "Why didn't you give a damn about me when someone broke into the office and knocked me unconscious? You didn't even stop by the clinic to see if I was okay!" she screamed in his face. Over the past few years, she'd yelled at him a lot. He could take that. But then she lowered her voice, took a step back, crossed her arms over her chest, and gave him the look that broke him. "You've been less like a brother to me every year since the accident. I'm tired of playing parent to you. I need to focus on my own life. I don't have the strength anymore to raise you." He felt his heart skip and drop in his chest. "I can't keep caring about someone who doesn't care about me." She turned to go, but once again, he placed a hand on her shoulder to stop her, this time more lightly. Tears stung his eyes, and something came over him. Something surfaced that he'd believed had been long dead, killed the day their parents had been.

Without thinking, he let his heart split open and his mouth for once finally caught up. He loved Dylan. Probably more than anyone else on the planet. She'd been there, by his side, through thick and thin. Not just after their parents had died, but long before.

He remembered the day she was born so well, even though he'd only been three. He'd fallen for her then and still felt the same way. He knew he'd fucked up. It was about damn time he let her be happy, and he could see that the man she was currently dating was making her so. He figured he'd get the hell out of the way, since he was the one thing making her unhappy.

"I'm sorry," he told her softly. "I... didn't know..." He shook his head. "I fucked up. No one asked me if I was prepared to take on such big responsibilities at such a young age." He closed his eyes. "I've been pissed at our folks." His eyes opened, the pain that had built up totally exposed to Dylan. "They should have made better choices. They should have planned for something like this. Instead, they continued living like..."

"Children?" Dylan finished for him. He nodded in agreement.

"I was thrust into adulthood when I was only twenty-one. I didn't know what to do to make house payments. Hell, they didn't either." At this point, he released the secrets that he'd been shielding from her. "They were months behind on the house payment when they died," he admitted.

"What?" Dylan looked at him with surprise.

"One of the cars had already been repossessed before we took the trip." He sighed, really wishing for a shower and some coffee. "Dad's car was next. Thankfully, they had enough life insurance policies to pay his truck off."

"Brent." Dylan reached up and touched his shoulder. He didn't want her pity. Hell, that's why he'd kept most of this from her in the first place. She was the smart one. All his life, he'd known she'd make something of herself. Then his parents had gone and fucked that up.

"I wanted you to go to college." He closed his eyes. He'd always thought she would. "Hell, everyone knew I wasn't smart, but you…" He smiled down at her. "Wile E. Coyote." He smiled at his old nickname for her. "Super genius," he finished. "I had always expected that you'd go to Harvard or Yale. Then… they left us with a mess, and nothing mattered anymore." His shoulders slumped. "I fucked everything up. Just like they did." His stomach twisted, and he knew there was only one thing he could do at this point to make things right.

"Hey." Dylan moved closer. "You've gotten us this far." She wrapped her arms around him for the first time in years, which broke him even more. "You can go the rest of the way. I'll help you."

He swallowed the pain. "No." He took a deep breath. "I don't want to drag you down with me. You've got a fresh start here." He glanced around and saw the big brick building with McGowan Enterprises in fancy letters hanging above the door. "You'll be better off if I leave."

"What about your job?" Dylan asked.

He thought back to a possible job opportunity his buddies had mentioned the night before. "I have a chance to transfer to a job site in North Dakota for the McGowans." Hell, if he had to, he'd beg Trey McGowan, the man Dylan was dating, to transfer him. "I think I'll take it. Jake is heading there after Seth's wedding. I've told him I'll drive. I've already packed," he lied.

So, after work that day, he'd walked home, packed quickly, and within a week, he'd driven to North Dakota to start his new life.

In the first few months, he'd cleaned up, stopped drinking all together, started saving his money, and never looked back. That's all it had taken. Just knowing that he'd hurt his sister as much as his parents had hurt him.

* * *

Two years later...

Brent sat at the table and looked down at the piece of paper sitting in front of him. What the hell had he just done? How the hell had he ended up here?

It was just chance that he'd been there that night. A friend of a friend had gotten the flu, which meant the guy's poker night had been short one person. Since Brent owed that friend, he'd been talked into filling in. This particular group of McGowan Enterprises employees had been gathering since they'd all met up in Haven. And since he was part of that main group, he figured he'd sit in. He didn't have anything better to do that night, anyway.

The last thing he'd expected was to win and win big. Looking down at the deed, he suddenly felt a surge of excitement. He'd been meaning to return to Haven, Montana.

After all, Dylan and Trey's baby was due in a few weeks. It would be nice to be close to his first nephew or niece, right?

Then a spike of adrenaline rushed through him. Here it was, his first chance to be his own boss. He folded the paper up, tucked it into his jacket pocket, and left the tiny hole-in-the-wall bar with a new spring in his step.

The following morning, he waltzed into his boss's office, set down his resignation, and start driving to his new future.

Less than three days later, he was standing on a side street in Haven, Montana, again, in front of an old two-story brick building. The building had obviously had its heyday back in the early eighteen hundreds.

All of the windows were boarded up and several of the outside walls were covered in graffiti. The sign for the place was falling off. Instead of reading Hardwood Way, the sign was down to just saying Hard Way.

He couldn't remember ever seeing the building before, and that somehow caused the scene in front of him to sink in a little further. He'd just given up the steadiest high-paying job he'd ever had for a money pit.

When a car honked, he turned around to see his brother-in-law Trey stop directly behind hm.

"You're back?" Trey jumped out of his truck, leaving it running in the middle of the road—a sure sign of the low traffic the street had—and headed his way. "I didn't know you were back." Trey gave him a one arm man-hug. Then he leaned back and narrowed his eyes. "Does Dylan know you are back?"

"No," he answered quickly. "It was kind of last minute."

Trey chuckled. "Good, because I'm not the one who's going to be murdered today." Trey slapped him on the shoulder, then pulled out his phone.

"Do you have to?" he asked. It wasn't that he didn't want his sister to know that he was back. He'd just hoped he'd have some good news to tell her first. He glanced sideways at his new place and held in a groan.

"Done." Trey stuffed his phone back in his pocket. "So,

what are you doing?" Trey glanced at the building and then back at him.

"I'm…" Maybe if he told Trey first, telling his sister he'd done a stupid thing would come easier. "She's all mine." He motioned to the building.

Trey's eyebrows rose. "You… bought the Hardwood Way Inn?"

"It's an inn?" Brent looked back at the building once more.

"It used to be." Trey laughed. "About a hundred years before we were born. So, does this mean you're back in Haven for good?"

He was so focused on assessing the building that he absently nodded to Trey.

"Your sister is going to be so happy," Trey replied, then he looked at the old building. "She's not much to look at. What are you going to do with her?"

"I thought it was a bar," he answered. "I wouldn't know what to do with an inn. How many rooms are there?"

"Two," Trey said with a chuckle. "The rest of the buildings out back burned down in…"—he tilted his head— "the nineteen eighties."

He turned to Trey, just as his sister's car turned into the parking lot of the building. "So, it's not an inn?"

"Not anymore. But around here, nothing ever changes," he said with a shrug.

Trey walked over and helped his sister out of her car. Dylan looked the same, with the exception of the wide belly and some baby weight.

She walked over to him and, without a word, wrapped her arms around him.

"You're here," she said softly into his chest.

"I am." He closed his eyes. Brent took a moment and held on to the only person in his life that truly loved him.

CHAPTER 2

$\mathcal{M}$el, as she was now calling herself—instead of Melinda Rose Hawk, as her birth certificate said—pulled into the gas station just as steam exploded from the hood of her beat-up pickup truck. She'd paid cash for the thing nearly ten thousand miles ago.

She felt her face heat as she yanked open the hood and glanced around under there. The last thing she wanted to do was to cause a scene.

"Need some help, pretty lady?" a deep voice sounded directly behind her.

She cringed and at the same time rolled her eyes.

"No, thank you," she said without turning around. But the man moved closer until his shadow fell over her. She jerked around as her entire body tensed. "No, thank you," she told the older man, whose belly was as thick as his head. "I've got this." She tried to sound as sweet as she could, but it was obvious annoyance laced her voice.

"Looks like it's your radiator," he said, paying no attention to her.

"Yes," she practically hissed. "I can see that." She slammed the hood and started walking around the truck, only to have the man follow her.

"I'm just trying to help out a pretty lady in need." To her shock, he reached out to take her arm.

It was a gut reaction, the one she'd spent the last year training for. Before she could stop herself, she side-stepped the man's beefy hands, gripped his wrist, and had it behind his back before he could blink.

He smelled of sweat and chew, and she almost gagged. "I said"—she lowered her voice and moved closer to his ear— "I don't need any help."

"You may not need help, but it looks like Jimmy might need some," a rich voice said directly behind Mel. Once again, she held back the urge to roll her eyes. Why were men always trying to assert themselves where they weren't needed?

Mel glanced over her shoulder but the sun blocked her view of her new would-be rescuer. However, she could tell that the man was tall and thin, instead of short and thick, like Jimmy.

"I was just trying to help," Jimmy said again, and hearing the worried tone in the man's voice, she dropped her hold on his wrist. The man stumbled a few steps away from her while rubbing his wrist. "You could have broken it," he barked at her.

"Go on," she said, making a move toward the older man, who quickly scurried away.

She heard a rich deep chuckle and turned to the other man. Lifting her hand to shield the sun, she assessed the new situation.

Around six four, easily one-ninety—most of it muscle—and the kind of dark scraggly beard most men wore in these parts. What stopped her from further assessing the man was his kind green eyes.

"I think you damaged Jimmy's manhood," the man said with a smile that showcased a perfect set of pearly whites. Either he had taken really good care of his teeth or he'd been raised with money.

She felt her guards slip into place again.

"No man should ever grab a woman. Especially one that doesn't know them." She turned back to her truck to reach in and grab her purse through the open window.

"I would agree to that," the man said easily. "It's why I headed over here after seeing him approach you. Most people think Jimmy's harmless, and in the right circumstances, he is. But after a week of binge drinking and who knows what else..." The man shook his head, and Mel got a good look at his face when he turned into the sunlight.

She felt her breath hitch. Was it possible for anyone to be that good-looking naturally? He had perfect skin, high cheekbones, a wide, strong jawline. And that body.

She turned away, tucked her purse under her arm, and headed towards the gas station.

"Well, now that I know you can fend off unwanted creeps..." The man turned to go, and she realized it would be rude not to at least thank him for trying to help out.

"Thanks," she called over her shoulder, expecting him to walk away. Instead, he followed her into the gas station. She narrowed her eyes at him, but he walked over to the beer section and acted like it had been his purpose all along.

Grabbing two containers of antifreeze, she walked up to the counter just before the man. Thankfully, he didn't say another word to her as she paid.

She stepped outside again and quickly glanced around to confirm that Jimmy had moved on. She walked over to the truck, opened the hood again, and filled up her empty radiator. The green neon liquid gushed out from the bottom of the truck as she poured it into the top.

"Damn it," she said, bending further into the engine compartment to get a look at what was going on.

"Looks like you have a hole." The tall sexy man was back.

Jerking to stand up, she almost hit her head on the hood. She glared at the man.

"You think?" It had the opposite effect than she'd intended. Instead of turning and leaving her alone, he smiled.

"Larry down the street might be able to put in a new radiator for you." He motioned down the street.

Instantly, she thought about the cost of the repairs and winced. She'd purchased the antifreeze with some of the last money she had.

How had she sunken this far in life? She was a highly educated woman. A bachelor's in business had to count for something, right?

"If you want, I can call him and have him tow you?" He pulled out his cell phone.

"Why?" she asked quickly. What she'd meant by the single word was, why even bother? There was no way she would be able to pay for it or the repairs. But instead, the man's smile grew.

"Just trying to help out." He held his cell phone up to his ear. "Hey, Larry, it's Brent." The man glanced away. "Yeah, I'm back in town. No, not tonight. We'll chat later." She listened to the man—Brent, apparently—continue talking to Larry. "Yeah, well, I'm down at the gas station. No, the one at the end of your street. Yeah." He shook his head and rolled his eyes at her. "I've got someone here with a busted radiator. Think you can tow it in and take a look? Yeah, okay, see you in five." He hung up. "Sorry, Larry's a talker." The man tucked his phone in his back pocket. "He'll be here in five." He bent down and picked up the case of beer he'd set on the ground and turned to go.

"I can't pay," she blurted out. The man stopped and

glanced back at her. Instead of saying anything, his eyes locked with hers. "That is, I was just... passing through. I was hoping to hit Helena and look for work before doing the repairs on the truck." She felt her face heat. "I don't suppose there's any work around here?"

He turned back towards her. "What kind of work?"

"Office work." She bit her bottom lip. "Marketing, management, accounting." She rattled off her best skills, skills which she hadn't been able to use in the last few jobs she'd been forced to take. The man frowned and her heart sank. Of course there wouldn't be any kind of work in a town like this. It was too small of a town. Too... raw.

She thought about having to settle for a waitressing job again and held in a groan. At this point, she would take anything, just as long as it wasn't in a bar.

"I might know of something." He moved back over to her and set the case of beer back down. "I'm Brent McCaw." He held out his hand.

"Mel Haw... Hawthorn," she improvised quickly. She looked down at his hand before shaking it.

"I'll wait for Larry to tow your truck and then take you over to where there's work. If you trust me. If not, I can get my sister, Dylan, on the phone and have her come pick you up."

She thought about it for a moment. Any man willing to call his sister seemed okay in her book.

"No, I'll ride with you."

"I don't suppose you have a place to stay either?"

She shook her head from side to side. "I literally just rolled into town."

He nodded. "There's a room there. It's not much, but I think it'll work. It's better than nothing."

"Thank you." She leaned against the hood of her truck. "Why are you helping me?"

Brent sighed and glanced away.

"When my sister and I rolled into Haven, a few good people helped us out." He glanced back at her. "I guess I'm just spreading the goodness around."

Something told her that he wasn't giving her the entire story, but she didn't want to push her luck.

"How long ago was that?" she asked.

He tilted his head, as if he was trying to think about it. "About three years ago."

"What does your sister do?"

"Dylan? Well, she works for her husband's family business." He shrugged a little. "His family is pretty much the reason Haven is still around."

Instantly, Mel wondered if that was who he was suggesting she work for. Not wanting to ask, she glanced around.

"Is there more to it? The town, I mean." She motioned to the one gas station she'd pulled into just off the highway.

Brent followed her gaze and then sighed. "Not much. The standard things. You know, grocery store, town hall, etcetera." He looked over at her. "About a half dozen or so strip clubs."

Her eyebrows arched up. "Okay," she said slowly.

"Don't worry, none of them are hiring." He smiled.

She laughed. How long had it been since that sound had escaped her?

"Not that I have the luxury of turning away any job at this point." She smiled and relaxed back as she leaned against the car. Then she remembered part of his conversation with the tow truck guy. "You just returned to town yourself?"

"Two weeks ago." He nodded.

"How long were you away?" she asked, needing to know more for some reason.

"About two years or so." He glanced away.

"What brought you back?"

"Opportunity." He waved to someone, and she turned and watched a tow truck pull up and then back up to her truck.

A man about her age stepped out of the truck and nodded to her. "This the one?" he asked Brent.

"Yeah." Brent motioned to her. "Mel Hawthorn, Larry. He owns the local body shop."

The man, who was a lot skinnier than Brent, held out his hand for her to shake.

"Thank you, Larry. Brent here has offered to help me find work. I'm not sure how long it will take me to work off my bill…"

"You have my number," Brent said to the man. "When you have an estimate for the new radiator, let us know." He turned to her. "Need anything from in there?" He motioned to her truck.

"Yes." She rushed to get the two small bags that held everything she owned and then started towards Brent's newer model truck.

Brent took the bags from her and set them in the back seat, then held the passenger side door open for her.

When she slid onto the leather seats, she suddenly realized she'd forgotten what it was like to sit in a newer car. There was a small computer screen attached to the dashboard. Brent climbed in and turned the truck on, and the air conditioning blasted the heat out of the cabin quickly. How long had it been since she'd sat in a car with AC?

Small luxuries were easily forgotten when you were running for your life.

As Brent drove further into town, she watched the small town roll by them outside the windows. They passed everything from floral shops to animal clinics. It was, outside of the half dozen bars and strip clubs, the perfect small town.

Then he pulled in front of an old rundown brick building and turned off his truck.

"What's this?" she asked, looking up at the fallen sign on the front of the building that read Hard Way. At one point, she could see where the rest of the letters for the Hardwood Way Inn had been.

"This is where the job is." He climbed out of the truck and grabbed her bags. "And where there's free room and board until you make enough to pay for your repairs." He walked towards the doors and she followed slowly, taking in the obvious recent work that had been done to the windows and door.

"Is this even Hardwood Way?" she asked as she stepped inside.

"It used to be. I think the street sign was run over some time back." He shrugged.

She could tell someone was fixing the place up. She'd never really worked at an inn before, but figured it was better than nothing.

When she stepped into the dark place, she had to blink a few times until her eyes adjusted, and she realized that there had been more work done on the inside.

Brent set her bags down at the base of an amazing half-spiral staircase on the opposite wall before walking over to set the case of beer he'd purchased behind a bar that had yet to be stained or painted. There wasn't even a top on it yet.

"Is this your place?" she asked, moving towards him.

"Yeah. I'm hoping to open my doors soon. But before then, she'll need a lot of work." Brent put the beer into a beer fridge on the back wall. "Have you ever worked at a bar before?" he asked her, opening a beer and then pouring it into a glass and holding it out for her.

"A bar," she said, holding in a groan. She took the beer from him since the last time she'd had anything to eat or drink had been about twenty-four hours earlier. "But isn't this an inn?" she asked after taking a sip.

"No, it used to be. All of the rooms burned up years ago. It's been sitting empty for years. I have plans to turn it into a bar and grill." He motioned around him. "Maybe serve some fried foods or chips." He shrugged. "Haven't decided yet. That's where you'd come in."

"Me?" she asked, almost spitting out the sip of beer she'd just taken.

"Sure. I figured opening up a place like this shouldn't be too hard for someone with your skill set." He took a sip of the beer he'd opened for himself.

"Are you..." She took another sip of the beer. "Are you offering me a job as your bar manager?"

Brent shrugged. "I guess I could ask about your references and all."

She felt her heart skip and shook her head. "No!" She realized she'd practically screamed it and sighed. "I mean, if you're offering, I'll take the job. I mean"—she glanced around — "you will have the inside finished first, right?"

He looked around. "Yeah, I'll have it done."

She glanced towards the stairs. "If the rooms burned up years ago..."

"There are two rooms upstairs. I had them furnished with new stuff the day after I moved in." He walked towards the stairs. "We'll have to share a bathroom," he warned as he picked up her bags. "There are two sets of stairs. The front ones lead to the landing, a shared sitting room, an office, and a small kitchen area. Down the hallway are the bedrooms. The back stairs are outside of the bedrooms. Like a fire escape or a deck of sorts."

She swallowed slightly and nodded. At this point, if he didn't look into her past, she was willing to agree to anything.

She followed him up the stairs and through a heavy metal door that he unlocked with a code.

"The code is one-nine-three-three," he said. "These rooms are private rooms, and the door will keep patrons out of the rooms."

She nodded in agreement and followed him through the space, glancing in each room when he pointed them out. There was a small landing that had a few chairs and end tables in it. The sitting room had a flat-screen television, a comfortable-looking sofa and chair, and a bookshelf full of books. The kitchen was very small and only had a half fridge, a sink, a stove, a couple cupboards, and a two-seater table.

"The bathroom is at the end of the hallway between the bedrooms. My room." He motioned to the door on the left, then he opened the door opposite it and waved her inside the room. "Your room."

She stepped in and looked around the large space and was instantly impressed. Not only was the room big, but there was a queen-sized bed, a nightstand, a dresser, and even a sitting area complete with a comfortable-looking chair.

She turned to him. "This is the room?"

He set her bags down. "I was going to rent it out, but since I also need to hire someone…" He shrugged. "It makes sense. It's yours for as long as you want to work."

"Th-thanks," she said swallowing the guilt and worry. Worry because she knew the moment he tried to pay her or run her background check, she was screwed.

"I was going to work for a few hours before I cook up some hamburgers in the kitchen downstairs. I don't really use the one up here since it's so small. You're welcome to join me." He leaned against the doorframe.

She felt tears sting her eyes as her mouth watered at the thought of having a hamburger. Real meat. For the past few months, she'd been stuck going through the cheapest drive-through she could find.

"Thanks," she said again.

He shifted to go but stopped and looked at her. "You're not running from the law or anything like that are you?" he asked.

She felt her heart sink. She hated lying to the man since he was being so kind to her.

"No." She shook her head and avoided his eyes. "I'm not wanted by the law," she said firmly.

"The only requirements are that you don't steal from me and, when you decide to pack up and leave, you give me notice."

"I understand."

He walked out, and she shut the door behind her. She listened as he walked down the hallway and back downstairs.

She leaned against the door, resting her head on the hardwood door, and closed her eyes as she took several deep breaths. Then she turned around and looked at the room with awe. How the hell had she gotten so lucky?

CHAPTER 3

$\mathcal{B}$rent knew he was taking a chance on the pretty brunette with big amber eyes, but hell, he recognized the desperate look in Mel's eyes. He'd had that look a million times before. His life hadn't been a walk in the park, not since his twenty-first birthday when his parents had died.

Whatever or whoever Mel was running from, he figured she could use a break. He'd told her the truth—the McGowans had given him and Dylan a break when they'd first arrived. Thanks to them, they'd both had a shot at happiness.

Even now, he had enough money to fix up this hellhole and make it into something he could be proud of. Turning the old inn into a bar and grill hadn't really been his idea—he had Dylan to thank for that—but still, it was one he could get behind.

Since he hadn't spent a dime on buying the property, other than paying to get some legal papers notarized and filed, he had all of his savings to spend on fixing the place up.

Until he'd run into Mel, he hadn't thought about the business side of running a bar and grill. He knew he'd need to hire employees at some point, but outside of that... He really hoped that Mel had all of that knowledge. He had gotten his business and liquor licenses already, something his sister had helped him apply for. But he didn't want to tax Dylan too much, not when she was getting ready for the baby to come soon.

He glanced up at the ceiling and wondered what Mel was doing up there.

As he sanded the large chunk of walnut he'd purchased for the top of the bar, he thought about Mel. When he'd spotted the brunette being harassed by Jimmy, he'd rushed over there to help out, since he knew how the man could get. He hadn't expected to see her kick the man's ass. Figuratively and physically. The move she'd pulled on the man, who was easily three times her size, had been impressive and sexy as hell.

The next thing he'd noticed about her was that she could hold her own verbally as well. She had guts as well as spit and fire.

Her long dark hair had blonde on its tips, as if she used to dye it and was growing it out to its natural darker color. She'd been wearing cut-off shorts and a tank top with a pair of Chucks. He'd noticed she had a few tattoos on her wrists and ankles. He had a few on his own skin, including a large one across his left pec in honor of the day his life had changed.

He glanced around. He still had several tables to resurface, the floors to seal, and the new kitchen equipment to install. The way he figured it, he could very easily open the doors within the month, if he worked hard enough.

He was having the sign out front repaired. Since nothing else had come to him, he'd decided to keep the name so he could use most of the old letters. He was adding a fancy cursive *The* above the words *Hard Way* and then a straight white bar with black letters underneath it that said *Bar and Grill.*

The Hard Way Bar and Grill would be all his. He'd never expected that he would someday be his own boss. Hell, he'd never expected he'd have enough money saved up to pay for anything.

The first time he'd moved to Haven, he'd screwed things up pretty bad with his sister. Thankfully, over the past couple of years, things had been mended and now their relationship was better than it had ever been.

That included his relationship with the rest of the McGowans. Tyler, Trent, and Trey all thought of him as a brother now and treated him as such. Which meant that when they weren't busy at work or at home with their own families, they were down there helping him fix up the place.

It was thanks to them that he had all that new furniture upstairs. Well, at least new to him. Gail, McGowan, the three brothers' mother, had recently purchased all new furniture for her home and had given him a really good deal on everything.

She'd also helped him find all the furniture for in the main dining room and bar, as well as the new kitchen equipment. The equipment he still had to set up. He knew there would have to be some electric work done to allow for the high voltage equipment. He'd already done plenty of work behind the bar to allow for the refrigerators and blenders.

Since he knew everything there was to know about electric rewiring, he hadn't questioned flipping the breakers and doing the wiring himself.

Right now, he busied himself with sanding and cutting the large chunks of wood that would become the top of the long wide bar.

"You're doing that all by yourself?" He heard a warm sexy

voice behind him. He glanced over his shoulder and saw Mel standing behind him at the base of the stairs. Her long hair was damp, as if she'd just stepped out of a shower.

"Why not?" He shifted the large chunk of wood back to the top of the bar.

She rushed over and lifted the other end and helped him set it down.

"That's why not." She frowned over at him. "You're going to hurt yourself."

"I lifted it half a dozen times before you came down." He shifted the piece and was thankful that he'd cut the end of the wood correctly this time as it slid into place. "There." He dusted his hands off. "How does it look?" He stepped back. He could squint his eyes and see how nice the bar would be with the other two pieces in place and all of it covered with the thick layer of epoxy that he planned on using to seal it and make it all shine.

"It looks unfinished," Mel replied.

He glanced over at her and smiled. "A realist." He nodded and watched her glance over at him.

"What are you? An optimist?" she asked.

He chuckled. "Hell no, I'm a dreamer." He smiled bigger. "I'm dreaming I won't have to finish the last two pieces on my own." He motioned to the other two large pieces of walnut that would finish off the bar.

"What needs to be done to these?" Mel asked.

"Sanding mostly, then I'll have to cut them to the right size." He walked over and pulled out a tape measure and doubled checked the next section. "This one will be next." He toed the wider chunk of the two pieces.

"If you show me what to do, I'll try and help," she offered.

He shook his head. "It looks like you just showered. I can't ask you to get sawdust all over yourself."

"You don't have to ask. I'm offering."

"I can finish these if you want to tackle cleaning the windows." He motioned to a bottle of glass cleaner and a few cleaning rags. "There's a razor blade for scraping the paint off the glass, if you need it." He nodded to the table where a stack of straight blades sat.

For the next hour, he sanded and cut until all three pieces of walnut were in place while Mel scrubbed, scraped, and buffed until the front glass was completely cleaned, letting in more of the late spring evening sun.

"Now what?" she asked when she came back inside.

"Now, it's dinnertime," he said after his stomach growled. She followed him back into the kitchen.

"You're going to cook in all this mess?" she asked looking around.

"No, I have a grill I've been using on the back deck." He grabbed the hamburgers from the large stand-up fridge and walked out back.

Again, she followed him. "This is nice," she said as he started the gas grill.

"I'm hoping to extend the deck to the side door area for the warmer months, so people can sit around a firepit or toss a few horseshoes or play cornhole."

"You could do a sand volleyball court right there," she suggested.

"Not a bad idea," he said. "Want a drink?"

"Sure, whatever you're having." She sat when he motioned for her to take a seat at the picnic table that he'd built a few weeks before.

He walked back inside, grabbed two of the cold beers he'd purchased earlier, popped the tops, then grabbed buns, lettuce, tomatoes, and pickles before heading back outside, balancing everything on a large tray.

"Oh." She started to get up, but he stopped her with a

wave of his hand and set it all down on the table. "I could have helped you."

"I would have asked if I needed it," he said easily as he handed her a beer.

"Thanks." She paused to meet his eyes. "I… thanks for everything." She sighed and glanced out at the scenery. The bar sat on one of the side roads on the very edge of town, and a large grassy field sat directly behind the inn.

"Apparently, there used to be two rows of smaller buildings that that held all the rooms for the inn out there," he told her. "But now they are nothing more than cement foundations with wires and pipes buried in them."

Beyond the field of tall grass was a view of the Northern Rockies. Their high peaks stretched up to the clouds, some still with snow on their tips. A wayward cold breeze sometimes blew down the hills and cooled the town. But as he sat down across from Mel, the breeze was warm and smelled of cut grass.

They remained in silence for a few moments, listening to the sounds of the small town—a dog barking somewhere in the distance, a lawnmower, the call of a bird, and the sizzling of the meat on the grill.

"It's nice here." She took another sip of her beer.

"Yeah," he agreed. "You never did mention where you were heading to," he said, watching her eyes scan the mountainside before she turned to him.

"Helena," she answered.

"Did you have a job lined up?"

"No, but I figured there'd be plenty to choose from." She shrugged.

"Where are you coming from?" He saw her tense, and she averted her eyes from his.

"California," she answered before taking another sip of her beer.

"L.A.?" he asked, and she nodded. Something told him that she would have agreed to whatever he'd suggested. He didn't want to let on, but he could hear a little of north Washington State in her voice. Not much but enough that he understood she'd been there at some point in her life. He'd lived there long enough to recognize one of his own.

"I suspect that it's a lot nicer here than in the city." He knew that he wouldn't get much about her past out of her. Not when they'd only just met.

"Where have you been?" she asked him.

"I was in North Dakota for a while. I transferred there from here. Then when I won this place—"

"Won?" she jumped in. "You won this place?"

He smiled. "Lucky hand with a pair of ladies."

"Do you gamble much?"

"No, I was filling in for a buddy who was sick the night of a poker game." He shrugged.

"So, what? You dropped everything, came back, and decided to open a bar?"

He chuckled. "I thought it was an inn. I'd forgotten that the place had burned down. Haven could have used a good inn. I was going to do the whole B and B thing." He shrugged. "But since it's just this building, a bar and grill will do nicely."

"Do you have any experience running a business?"

"Nope." He stood up and walked over to flip the burgers. "You?"

She tilted her head before shaking it. "I took enough business classes to understand the basics of it, though."

"Back in L.A.?" he asked, sitting back down.

She glanced over at him but didn't answer. "Is your sister older or younger?"

"Dylan's a few years younger." He looked out over the mountains. "Do you have family?"

"No," she said quickly and, once again, he got the hint that she didn't want to talk about it with him.

"What made you pick business?" he asked, hoping for a light subject.

She shrugged. "It's easy and I figured no matter where I went, there would be jobs."

"Well, what do you think about this place? What can you do to help get money through the doors?"

She was silent for a moment as she thought. A small crease formed between her eyes, and she sucked her bottom lip in between her teeth.

"For starters, I'd finish all the work," she said, causing him to chuckle.

"I should be done in a week or so," he agreed.

"Then I'd hire the best chef around. Someone with a reputation. You'll want to spend most of your income on them. Food makes the place. Beer and liquor are cheap. Environment is important, so you'll want the inside decorated in a way that is unique and comfortable. A place people can enjoy coming back to. From the looks of it, you're halfway there."

"Okay," he nodded, wanting her to continue.

"Once all that's in motion, we'll create a big buzz for opening day." She leaned forward slightly.

"How do we do that?"

"What about prizes."

"Prizes?"

"Sure. Each hour, someone will win something grand."

"Such as?" he asked.

"Am I correct in assuming you made this table?" she asked, knocking on the wood.

"Yes," he said, frowning down at the thing.

"I suppose you can make other things, like this and the bar top?" she asked. He nodded again. "People around here probably like this sort of thing. Rocking chairs, picnic tables, maybe even a few bird houses or feeders."

He nodded again. "I suppose I could make a few things like that."

"We could also do gift cards." She glanced around as she thought. "You know, to bring them back. The gift cards will be good on their next visit." She pulled out her cell phone and started punching the screen, taking down notes.

He got up and checked the burgers. Already, she had thought more about it than he had. He doubted he would have come up with the idea of gift cards or prizes, no matter how long and hard he'd thought about it.

"How will they win?" he asked.

She glanced up at him. "Door prizes. Raffles." She narrowed her eyes. "We can have fun events each hour. Maybe a type of bingo game?" She tilted her head again. "I saw an old chalkboard in the hallway upstairs. Any chance you'll hang it downstairs somewhere?"

He nodded. He had planned to put it over by the dartboard he was going to purchase.

She glanced down at her phone again and was quiet for a while. "I'll make up a few options," she said after a moment. "I might need a few things. Paper, pens."

"I have an account at the local market. We can go tomorrow and get you set up on the account."

She looked at him for a second. "I can make a list," she suggested. "For your approval."

He placed the buns down on the top rack to toast them and walked back inside to grab some plates and two more beers.

He pulled the toasted buns and cooked burgers off the heat, and they sat and ate as they continued to talk about the possibilities for the business. She suggested he create a stage area inside and hire a band for opening week. He thought about it and figured there was enough space for a small stage in the far corner of the main room, where he'd planned on having a jukebox.

He had to admit, she had a lot better ideas than he'd had since he'd been working on fixing the place up. He supposed it was because he'd been focused on making sure the building didn't fall in on itself.

The more she talked and plotted, the more he realized that he just didn't have the talent and foresight to think about all the possibilities.

Even though the conversation was one hundred percent focused on the business, he picked up a few of Mel's personal habits. Little things like when she was deep in thought, she tended to tilt her head to one side.

If she liked an idea he had, a small dimple appeared to the right of her mouth. If she didn't like an idea he had, a crease formed between her eyebrows.

She tended to fidget with her fingers as she talked, and her eyes never really stayed in one place. She was always scanning the horizon, as if looking for something or someone.

It wasn't so much that look that concerned him. It was the look of fear and the fact that she jumped at shadows. He hadn't noticed it at first, but when they headed back inside to discuss their ideas, he watched her very closely and saw the fear building.

CHAPTER 4

$\mathcal{I}$t was the night. Her fear always spiked just as the
sun started setting. She had never been afraid of
the darkness when she was a kid. But then Ethan had come
along, and everything had changed.

Now, the moment the sun started to sink, she jumped at
shadows. Even after a full year, she felt her skin crawl at the
thought of being alone in the dark.

"Are you okay?" Brent had asked her when he was
showing her where he planned on building a small stage.

"Yes," she said, trying to fend off the shakes. "I suppose
I'm just chilled." She wrapped her arms around herself. In
truth, if anything, it was overly warm in the building. She
doubted he had the air conditioning on, if there was any
at all.

He surprised her by walking over and grabbing an old
sweatshirt from behind the bar and handing it to her.

"The moment the sun goes down behind the mountains,
it can get chilly. Even in the middle of summer," he said
easily.

She wrapped the hoodie around herself and forced her body to stop shaking.

"Thank you," she said after a moment.

"You're probably tired." He glanced at the clock. "I'm going to finish up a few things down here. Maybe we can pick this conversation up in the morning."

"Yes," she said, feeling relieved that he didn't push her any further. She wasn't tired, not really, but she did want to be alone. The hot shower earlier had been the first she'd taken in days. It had relaxed her enough that she figured she could close her eyes for a few hours. "Thank you, again."

He nodded. "Mel?" he said as she turned to go. "Tomorrow, there's no more need for all the thank-yous. I hired you and after the conversation we just had, it appears it was one of the smartest ideas I've had in years." She smiled. "So, thank you for that. Now, we've both said it enough. Let's get to work tomorrow. Deal?"

"Deal," she said easily. "Night."

"Night." He turned and picked up a block of sandpaper and got back to work. She could hear him sanding the other bar tops as she climbed the stairs. The moment she walked through the hallway door, every sound from below was cut off.

It was obvious the upstairs was highly soundproofed, shielded from the space below. It would help when there were patrons downstairs, she thought as she let herself into her room. Her room.

She stopped just inside the doorway and looked around.

The space was fairly empty and had obviously recently been cleaned out. The back wall was made of old bricks, and the opposite wall was filled with large windows that overlooked the town. Still, earlier in the daylight, the view of the mountains surrounding had taken her breath away.

Exposed wood rafters crossed the large space overhead

and worn oak hardwood covered the floors. There were a few rugs strewn around, as if they were tossed down in no particular place.

A queen-sized bed sat against the brick wall. The soft cream-colored comforter and red pillowcases looked very new and inviting. Two older oak nightstands sat on either side of the bed, matching a dresser that sat off to one side of the bed.

There was a dark blue chair directly in front of the windows, along with another cream-colored chair and ottoman and a large oak coffee table.

The furnishings didn't seem to belong together, as if it was all from different sets, yet they all went well together.

There was a small, unplugged fridge sitting on a wall by itself, as if it was just being stored there. There was also a desk that had stacks of boxes on it.

Her bags sat at the base of the bed. Earlier, she'd showered out of necessity and desire before changing into her last clean clothes.

What she wanted was a few hours of downtime. What she needed was to wash everything she owned, which wouldn't take too long.

She'd seen the stacked washer and dryer in the hallway closet along with the laundry soap. It had been over a week since she'd washed any of her clothes.

Walking over, she dumped everything in the bag out onto the bed. She fumbled through her clothing and found the gun she slept with every night. She tucked it under the pillow before turning back to separate her clothes for washing.

After starting the first load of laundry, she shut herself back up in her room and looked out the windows. Since it was dark, she figured anyone looking up could see her clearly, so she made a point to keep the lights in the room off so that she could look down on the street without being seen.

She stood there until she heard the buzzer on the washing machine signal that her first load was finished. She switched those clothes to the dryer and had just started a load of whites when she heard Brent climbing the stairs. She wanted to hurry up and scamper back to the room before he came into the hallway, but she wasn't quick enough.

His eyes locked with hers as she poured some laundry soap into the machine.

"All done down there for tonight?" she asked, trying not to act like her heart was racing.

"Yeah." He sighed and ran his hands over his face. "Going to hit the shower and then bed." The fact that he half mumbled it told her that he was tired. He looked dirty and exhausted, and sexy as hell. The last part had her turning her eyes away from him. She couldn't afford to fall for anyone. Not again.

"If you need the washing machine…" she started.

"I won't tonight." He opened the bathroom door before nodding into the bathroom. "If you need in here…"

"I'm good." She shut the lid of the machine. "Thanks."

He nodded and then shut the bathroom door, leaving her to return to her own room.

She crawled into bed and closed her eyes. How long had it been since she'd been somewhere that she felt safe?

Pulling her body into a tight ball, she watched the lights of passing cars flash on the ceiling and counted her breaths until she drifted off.

She woke with a start when the machine buzzed outside her door. Instantly, she remembered where she was. She took a moment to glance around the dark room. She'd left a small lamp on since she never liked to be completely in the dark. She relaxed when she confirmed that she was alone.

She climbed out of the bed and stepped out into the hallway to gather her dry clothes.

She had just pulled the warm clean clothes from the dryer when the bathroom door flew open. She jumped and let out a low scream as she dropped her clothes.

"Sorry," Brent said as he stepped out of the bathroom, a white towel tied low around his hips. He had a pile of his soiled clothes in his hands, and she sat on the floor, surrounded by her clean clothes.

"Need any help?" he asked.

"N-no." She took a deep breath and started gathering her things. "I thought you'd gone to bed," she said nervously.

"I fell asleep in the bath." He leaned against the door-frame. "Guess I was more tired than I thought."

Her first thought was to ask him if he even fit in the small bathtub that she'd seen in the bathroom earlier. But then images of him naked surfaced and muddled up her mind.

He set his dirty clothes on top of the dryer and then bent down and placed his hands under her arm pits to help lift her off the ground, clean clothes and all.

She found it very difficult to keep her eyes off his bare chest. He was full of muscles. Every inch of him. Strong, hard. Toned. He had several large tattoos that ran over his left pec and went all the way up his arm. A trail of dark hair ran down the middle of his chest to just below his belly button and disappeared under the white towel. Her mouth watered at the sight.

When she was back on her feet, she dumped her clean clothes in the basket he'd set on top of the washing machine for her.

"Thanks," she said again and then proceeded to unload her wet clothes and put them in the dryer while he picked up his soiled clothes. He paused outside his bedroom door and looked back at her.

"Whoever you're running from, you're safe here. If you ever want to talk about it, to me or someone else..." He stopped for a moment and then shrugged. "Just let me know. Goodnight."

With a lump in her throat, she quickly started the dryer on her last load and took the basket of clean clothes back into her room.

She wondered for a moment if she should pack them back up in her bags but then surprised herself when she started hanging them up in the closet instead.

Did this mean she was planning on sticking around? Could she trust Brent and anyone else in this town? So far, he hadn't done anything to cause her concern. There were even two locks on her door, a deadbolt and a chain lock. He'd given her the keys for her door and the outer door earlier.

It wasn't as if she was worried he was going to sneak into her room in the middle of the night. Something deep down told her that she could trust him. Then again, at one point she'd trusted Ethan as well.

After all of her things were hung up in the closet, she pulled off her clothes and crawled into bed.

She woke to the faint sounds of the saw starting up downstairs. Sunlight was streaming in the large windows, making the entire room bright and cheerful.

She'd slept like she always did, curled up in a tight ball with one hand resting on the loaded gun.

She'd taken three classes at the strip mall after she'd moved that last time: Brazilian jiujitsu, Krav Maga, and a defensive shooting class. She'd spent a total of seven months at the shooting range, learning all about safety and self-defense.

All in all, she felt confident that she could protect herself, one way or another. At least for a while. She remembered how strong Ethan could be and how many friends he had and how long his reach was.

She stretched her arms over her head and took her time getting up. She pulled the rest of her clothes from the dryer and put them away in the closet.

She stood there for a few moments, looking at all her worldly possessions hanging in a strange closet. It seemed to make the entire situation more real.

Finally, after dressing in the only thing resembling business attire that she had, she stepped into the bathroom, combed her hair, and applied what little makeup she had before heading down the stairs to find Brent.

She found him standing over the bar top, frowning down at the new section he'd just put in.

"Morning," she said, trying to add cheer to her tone. He glanced over at her, and his dark eyebrows rose slightly.

"Morning." He turned back to the countertop.

"Problems?" she asked.

"It's boring." He motioned to the wood. "I thought it would be… more."

"It looks absolutely beautiful," she said, taking it all in. The three separate pieces of wood covered the entire bar area, surrounded completely by plywood and pieces that she assumed would hold in the resin once he poured it.

"Yeah, I suppose." He tilted his head and ran his eyes over the area.

She glanced at it from a different angle, thought about how it would look once the bar opened, how it would feel sitting there, sipping a beer.

He was right. The more she thought about it, the more she expected something to look at other than the pretty wood.

"What about adding some bling?" she asked.

He laughed. "I didn't think you were the kind of woman who liked bling."

"Oh, I don't," she assured him. "But people like looking at shiny things." She walked behind the bar and found the bottle caps of the beers they'd had last night and then set them in the cracks of the wood. "I'm not suggesting these, but you could get little trinkets, maybe ask locals to come and donate items?"

His eyebrows shot up again. "That… is a great idea." He nodded and moved around the bar to grab his phone.

She stood there while he sent a few text messages. "Done," he said, looking up from his phone. He laughed after reading a reply text message. "You've earned your breakfast. It should be here shortly. How do you like your coffee?"

"I don't," she answered. "I won't say no to an orange juice."

He nodded and then typed something quickly before looking up at her. "No coffee?" He shook his head. "And yet you are still up at seven o'clock with a smile." He shook his head. "Unnatural."

She smiled. "Some people become dependent on the caffeine and never break free. I was one of the lucky few who never got addicted."

"It's a vice, alright." He picked up a mug and took a sip, then frowned. "It's cold." He set the mug down just as a knock sounded at the back hallway door. "That will be Dylan." He disappeared into the hallway.

Dylan? His sister. She was curious what his family was like. He'd mentioned her a few times and each time she got the hint that Dylan was something amazing.

Whatever Mel had been expecting, it hadn't been the very pregnant woman who stepped into the room, holding a box of donuts. Brent held another box and a container holding a mug of coffee and a large orange juice.

Dylan was taller than Mel's own five six but only by a

little. She had short jet-black hair cut in sharp angles. She wore a bright red maternity shirt with black leggings and flats. Mel could see several brightly colored tattoos on the woman's upper arms and a few on her ankles and feet.

"Salvation has arrived," Brent said cheerfully. "How's my nephew?" he asked, setting the items down on the bar.

"Your niece is angry with me this morning," Dylan answered with her eyes on Mel. "You must be Mel?" She held out her hand after setting the box of sweets down.

"And you must be Dylan," Mel said with a smile.

"Dylan, Mel, Mel, Dylan," Brent said through a mouth full of donut. "Dig in." He motioned to the box. "I didn't know what you'd like, so I had Dylan get you one of everything."

Dylan turned to her and smiled. "That's a ruse. My brother eats like a pig. He ordered one of everything for himself. You'll be lucky to get two of these." She motioned to the box. "Brent tells me he hired you to run and do the marketing for this place?"

"Yes." She took an offered donut, one with chocolate sprinkles and frosting. Then she took the orange juice and sat down next to Dylan, who had plopped down on a barstool.

"Where are you from?" Dylan asked her.

Panic filled her when she completely forgot what she'd told Brent the night before. Her heart started racing, her palms started sweating, and her mind went completely blank.

CHAPTER 5

*B*rent could see the sheer panic in Mel's eyes and knew she was having a difficult time keeping up with the lie she'd told him the night before. Since he figured it was best left between him and Mel, he jumped in.

"L.A.," he answered for her after a sip of his coffee. "Mel mentioned she's from L.A." He turned to get another donut from the box and shoved it in his mouth.

He'd been thankful Dylan had answered his text and had even been more thrilled when she'd mentioned she was at the bakery. Convincing his sister to get them breakfast hadn't been hard. Not after he'd mentioned he'd hired a woman and she was living there with him.

Dylan had been so curious to come over and meet Mel that she'd offered to get him breakfast. He knew how to manipulate his sister. Then again, she'd manipulated him with the promise of food.

"We were originally from the Seattle area," Dylan said, leaning back and rubbing her back slightly.

"Seattle's… nice," Mel responded. He heard the shake of her voice and knew that his sister heard it as well.

"It used to be, when I was a kid. Some parts of it still are, but…" Dylan sighed as her eyes ran over Mel's face. "It's not the same."

"No." Mel shook her head. "The world has changed," she added quietly.

"Why Haven?" Dylan asked Mel. Brent wanted to know the answer as well. He understood she was just passing through, but why? Why move on to Helena? What was there waiting for her? When Mel didn't answer right away, his sister added, "I was asked the same question when I first moved here. My response was it wasn't really my decision." Dylan's eyes narrowed slightly at Mel. "My brother tells me your truck broke down?" Dylan glanced at him.

"It did," Mel answered quickly.

"You either learn to love it here or you don't." Dylan turned to look over at Brent, then back at Mel. "Brent originally didn't take to Haven." She smiled. He wanted to deny it but knew that it was fact. Haven hadn't been right for him back then. "I think he just needed some time."

"Time and a purpose," he added, taking another donut.

"So, do you have a lot of experience?" Dylan asked.

"Experience?" Mel responded with a frown.

"Marketing a business such as this?" Dylan asked.

Mel shook her head. "No, not for a bar and grill."

"Lay off the questions, sister," Brent broke in. He didn't want Dylan to scare Mel away. He was enjoying having her around. "I've hired her, and she's proven her worth with some of the ideas she's come up with so far."

"Ideas?" Dylan turned back to Mel. "I'd love to hear them. I have a few of my own that my brother's too stubborn or stupid to hear."

"Hey," Brent said from behind the bar as he shoved an entire glazed donut in his mouth. He knew his sister could be pushy.

"Oh, go on, do something sweaty with power tools." Dylan waved Brent away. "We brainiacs are working here."

His sister gave him that look, the one that he knew better than to argue with. Shrugging, he took the box of donuts and his coffee back into the kitchen while Dylan turned towards Mel and asked, "So, what are some of these great ideas?"

For the next hour, he busied himself setting up the equipment in the kitchen. For most of it he just had to unpackage it and plug it in, but with the stove, he had to put the gas fittings on and hook it up to the gas pipes that were already in place.

It wasn't as if the kitchen was in desperate shape. Hell, most of the building was in better shape than he'd expected. The plumbing was good, the electric had just needed a little work, and the bones of the place were strong enough. The flooring had needed some sanding, the walls some patching and painting.

The hardest work he'd done thus far was building the bar all by himself. He'd never done anything this big before, but he'd really enjoyed it. He was just moving the fryer into place when he heard his sister squeal and Mel call out.

Dropping everything, he ran out to the front room to see his sister doubled over.

"What happened?" he asked, taking his sister's hand in his.

"She just... doubled over," Mel said, sounding concerned.

"It's nothing, I just..." His sister cried out again. "The baby's just kicking," Dylan said, looking a little pale. "It can't be anything else. I'm not due for four more weeks."

"My phone." He motioned to where his cell phone was sitting, by the new unboxed cash register. "Call Trey."

"No!" Dylan sat up straight. "It's nothing," she said before doubling over again. This time, a gush of water rushed down from between her legs.

"Screw this," he said, hoisting Dylan up in his arms and

marching towards the back, intending on driving her to the hospital himself. He yelled over his shoulder. "Call Trey. Tell him we'll meet him at the hospital. He's having a kid today."

"No," Dylan called out. "I can't give birth today. It's a Friday."

He laughed as he set her gently in the front seat of his truck.

"I'm going to ruin your seats," Dylan said, holding her hands between her legs.

"They're leather." He rushed around to climb in the driver's side, only to realize he'd forgotten his keys inside.

He turned to go back and get them, but Mel rushed out, his keys and his cell phone in her hands.

"Trey says he'll meet you there." She shoved both items into his hands. "Good luck," she said to Dylan.

"Thanks," his sister said back.

While he drove, Dylan started breathing strange and groaning as she gripped her belly.

"Don't you dare have that baby in my truck," he said, almost begging. "Trey will kill me if he's not here with you."

"I...I'm trying not to," she said. "It's too early." He heard the worry in her voice and reached over to take her hand as he hit the main roadway and gassed it. They were ten minutes from the nearest hospital, and he was determined to make it there in half that time. Safely. "I'm scared," Dylan said with a wince as another pain hit her.

"Did you know you were born a month early?" he said, filling the silence. "I can't really remember much, but I know mom always told the story of how you were born early." He glanced over at her and smiled. "That's why you're so short."

She laughed. "I'm five seven."

"See." He shrugged. "Short."

She laughed and then winced again. "Brent." She squeezed his hand tightly causing him to wince.

"I love you," he said suddenly. "Just know that I love you. You're going to be an incredible mother."

Dylan bent over again. "I don't think I can wait any longer." She shifted slightly and he watched in horror as she pulled her yoga pants down.

He pushed the gas even more and silently prayed for his nephew or niece to hold on just a few more minutes.

"Brent!" his sister screamed as he pulled into the parking lot. "Trey!" she cried out when she saw her husband standing at the entrance to the emergency room.

Brent's tires squealed to a halt and then Trey was there, opening the passenger door.

"The baby's coming now!" Dylan cried out. He watched in horror as Trey lifted his sister's shirt and spread her legs just as a little greyish glob of a baby slid out into Trey's waiting hands.

"Holy shit," Trey said and looked up at him.

Then two nurses rushed forward and took over as Dylan was lifted carefully from his truck seat and placed on a gurney while she held the little girl in her arms.

He sat there in his truck, counting his heartbeats, while everyone disappeared inside. He had a niece.

He parked his truck, after a security guard told him to move it, and he got out just as his phone rang. Seeing an unknown number, he answered.

"Did you make it okay?" Mel asked.

"Yes, she had a girl. In my truck. In the parking lot at the hospital. But as far as I can tell, they're doing okay. I'm about to head in and check myself."

"Congratulations," Mel said.

"Thanks." He wiped his hand through his hair as he stepped inside the hospital doors. "I guess I need to get them something." He glanced towards the lobby area.

"Flowers," Mel suggested. "What are your sister's favorite flowers?"

He thought about it and felt his heart sink. "I don't know."

"Carnations are always nice," Mel suggested. "Pink and white if they have them."

"Okay."

"Don't forget a card."

"Right." He walked towards the gift shop.

"I'll let you go. Tell Dylan and Trey congratulations."

"I will. I should be back in a few hours."

"Don't worry. I've got plenty to do."

"You do?" He tucked the phone between his ear and his shoulder.

"Yes, your sister helped me create a list."

"Of course she did." Brent chuckled. "She's good at lists." He pulled a vase of white carnations from the fridge in a pink vase. "Well, have at it. If you need any supplies, there's some cash in the drawer behind the counter." The line was silent for a moment and he thought that he'd lost the connection.

"I will need some office supplies," she finally responded. "I'll make sure to keep the receipts if I go."

"Sounds good." He started looking at cards. "There doesn't seem to be a card for what just happened in my truck," he joked and enjoyed the sound of her laughter.

"I think just a congratulations one will cover it."

He smiled. "Gotcha. See you later."

"Bye," she said and hung up.

Almost fifteen minutes later, he walked into his sister's private room, holding the flowers and the card.

Dylan was sitting up in the bed, holding the baby while Trey sat next to her, watching the pair of them.

"Hey," he said, smiling as he ran his eyes over his sister's face. He needed to know that she was okay and seeing the smile on her face assured him of it.

"There's your uncle now," Dylan said softly to the baby. "She just had her first meal and is sleeping." Dylan looked up at him.

"So, she…" He set the flowers down and walked over to look down at the dark-haired beauty sleeping in Dylan's arms.

"Bella Maria." Dylan smiled up at him. "Maria after mom."

He felt tears sting his eyes as he reached out a hand and gently ran a finger over his niece's dark curls. "All that hair."

Dylan laughed. "No wonder I had heartburn every day."

He looked up at Trey and held out his hand to shake it. "Congratulations."

"Thanks, and thanks for getting them here in time." Trey shook his head. "It's a good thing I played a lot of ball with my brothers." He chuckled. "I never imagined I'd be catching my daughter one day."

"Everyone's alright though, right?" He glanced back at his sister. "I mean, she is early."

"Yes," Trey answered. "Early, but healthy."

"Good." He relaxed. Just then there was a knock on the door, and Trey's brothers rushed in and surrounded Dylan and little Bella. He stood back as the entire McGowan family filled the room.

Over the past few years, he'd grown used to the family. Every single one of them had proven to him at one point or another that they were worthy of his sister's affection. Not to mention his own.

A little over an hour later, he made his way to his sister's side and held his niece for the first time while someone took pictures. He couldn't get over how small Bella was.

"She's so tiny. Are you sure she's fully cooked?" He looked

up to see someone's camera zeroed in on him. He felt embarrassed when the entire room burst out laughing.

"Yes," Dylan said softly as she ran a fingertip down her daughter's tiny nose. "She's fully cooked. Well, a few weeks early, but still fully cooked. The doctors have given her a clean bill of health."

He bent his head down and placed a soft kiss on Bella's forehead, noticing that his mouth covered the entirety of the area.

After he handed Bella back over to his sister, he made his excuses and headed back to work, promising to visit the new family later that week, after they had a chance to settle Bella at home.

His first stop was the carwash where he hosed down the inside of his truck, thankful for the leather seats and the heavy-duty floor mats he'd purchased.

When his truck was clean, he swung by and grabbed a large pizza, some bread sticks, and a couple sodas before heading back to work.

He found Mel in the small office off the kitchen when he arrived. She'd completely cleaned out and organized the space.

"Looks like you got a lot done in here," he said, holding up the pizza box. "Lunch?"

"I think you mean dinner." Mel glanced down at her watch. "It's past six."

"Six?" He frowned and looked down at his own watch. "I guess I spent more time at the hospital than I thought. No wonder I'm starving, and you were able to clean out this entire office. Looks good, by the way."

"Thanks." She stood up and dusted off her pants. He noticed that she'd changed into a pair of jeans and a T-shirt. "I figured we'd need a place to work," Mel said, following him out to the kitchen.

"I hope you like anchovies," he said, setting the pizza box down. At the look on her face, he smiled and lifted the lid to the pepperoni pizza. "Just kidding."

"Good." She rolled her eyes. "I mean, does anyone like anchovies? Why is that even an option on pizza?"

"Right." He motioned with his hand and pulled two stools over to the countertop and handed her a soda. "Hope you like Coke."

"It's the one place I do allow my body to get caffeine," she said before taking a sip.

He tilted his head slightly. "So, instead of talking shop, why don't we get to know one another a little better. How about you tell me a little more about yourself?"

In the blink of an eye, she transformed from being completely relaxed to tense and on edge.

el felt her heart skip several times as another panic attack threatened to consume her.

"I'll start if you want," Brent continued as he took another slice of pizza. "My birthday is October eighth. I was born in Seattle. My parents died on my twenty-first birthday in a boating accident in Mexico. Dylan and I were two of the four survivors. After that, I was given custody of Dylan and for the next few years proceeded to do a shit job of raising her. Then I lucked out by winning this place and am hoping that things have finally turned around for me." He had said all of it in a pleasant tone, but she'd gasped at his story.

"How horrible." She set down her drink.

"Yeah, I know, being born in Seattle." He rolled his eyes, and she couldn't help but smile.

Her smile slipped a little. "How old was Dylan?" she asked, and Brent's eyes turned sober.

"She'd just turned seventeen." He looked down into his pizza.

She thought back to what she'd been doing at seventeen. How her parents had been there, at least back then, supporting her, giving her everything she'd wanted. Even now, all it would take was a phone call to have them send her the money for a plane ticket home. Back into the arms of her husband. Ex, she corrected.

Swallowing, she decided she could tell Brent a few details without giving him the entire story.

"I grew up in the city. I graduated high school and business school top of my class."

"A brainiac," he interrupted with a smile. "Pegged it."

She smiled and then took a deep breath.

"I married my college sweetheart within months of graduating and divorced him less than a year later," she said, avoiding Brent's eyes.

"How long ago was that?" he asked.

She glanced up at him. "A year ago."

His eyes narrowed. "Since then?"

Her eyebrows shot up. "I've been traveling."

"Sabbatical?" he asked.

"Of sorts," she agreed, though it was the farthest thing from the truth. A sabbatical is really a discovering of oneself. She knew who she was. What she wanted.

"I suppose that's what I've spent the last two years doing myself," he said. "The last time I was in Haven, things weren't going so well for me." He leaned back slightly. "I had been with this woman…" He took a deep breath. "She wasn't… good for me. I was in a bad place and surrounded myself with people as damaged as I was. I believed I couldn't do any better. That I wasn't worth anything." He reached for his drink but, instead of taking a sip, he turned the cup several times while he thought. She could see him trying to decide what to say next and waited patiently. After all, the more he talked about himself, the less he would expect her to open up. She just wasn't ready for more at this point. "I guess you could say my eyes were opened when I caught Darla poking holes in my condoms."

"What?" She sat forward. "Seriously?"

He chuckled and nodded. "Yeah. I mean, who does that, right?"

"Yeah." She shook her head in disbelief as she thought of the birth control patches that she'd hidden from Ethan. It wasn't the same thing. Not really. He'd been pushing her to have kids, and she'd known beyond any doubt that if they had children together, she would never be able to escape him. "Children should be a mutually agreed move in any relationship."

"Exactly." He motioned with his drink. "Not that I don't love kids." He pulled out his phone and looked at the image of him holding his new niece. "Bella." He showed her the image. "She's so small. I like them best when they're bigger."

She chuckled. "They don't stay that small for long."

"No." He sighed and looked at the image again. "She has my sister's hair and eyes."

"That's a good thing," she joked.

"Yeah. Not that the McGowans aren't a good-looking group. But I'm thankful she looks like Dylan."

"Babies all look alike to me," Mel admitted. She had a couple cousins that had kids. Each one of them looked like the other until they grew up and started running around. Then she could easily tell them apart.

He turned his phone towards her again, and she took a closer look at the little bundle he was holding wrapped in pink.

"Look at that hair." She grabbed his phone and was shocked to see thick black hair on the little girl. "My god, you could almost braid it."

He chuckled. "Dylan was the same when she was born.

My mother claimed she had to give her a haircut the first week after she was born."

"She is super cute," Mel admitted. "I doubt I would confuse her with any other baby."

"No," he agreed with a chuckle. "Bella is in a league of her own."

"It is a good thing you made it to the hospital in time," she said, thankful that the subject had turned away from her life.

"Just barely. Trey opened the truck door and had to practically dive in to catch his daughter." He smiled. "I had to run the truck through the wash inside and out, twice."

She could see by the smile on his face that he didn't really mind.

"Still, it makes for a good story."

"Yes, it does." His smile grew. "Best story ever."

"What now?" she asked.

"Now"—he took another slice of pizza— "the family goes home, celebrates with a cookout this weekend, and gets started on a little brother for Bella."

She laughed. "No wasted time."

He shook his head. "Trey was already talking about creating an army of dark-haired kids just like Bella."

"Cute," she responded as she thought about her own future. For many years, she'd dreamed of her own family. Kids, house, dogs, a picket fence. Everything. Ethan had taken that away from her.

"Something wrong?" Brent asked her when she stopped talking or responding to him.

"No." She shook off the mood and reached for another slice of pizza. "Just thinking about the marketing plan. I think we can—"

"Nope, no more shop talk tonight. Today is a national holiday." He stood up suddenly and walked to the standing fridge and pulled out a bottle of champagne. He opened it and poured two glasses. "Celebration." He held up the glass for her and then tapped it against his own. "To Bella Maria McGowan."

"To Bella," she said and took a drink.

Then Brent stood up again and walked over to the freezer. "How do you feel about butter rum?" he asked, his head deep in the freezer.

"Not one of my favorites, but it'll go with champagne."

He set a massive container of ice cream in front of her.

"It's my favorite." He moved over to get two bowls and spoons.

They sat in the kitchen, eating butter rum ice cream and drinking champagne, and talked about Haven and everyone in it. He filled her in on a few of the locals, the business the McGowans owned, and how a few years ago things had turned a little scary for McGowan Enterprises.

"So, that's how Trey survived a fire after the explosion." He finished telling the story of how his brother-in-law escaped the sabotage of one of the oil pumps.

"Wow, for such a small town, you really have a lot of crazy things going on around here. Maybe I should have found another town to have my truck break down in?"

He smiled. "Naw, that was a couple years ago. Things have settled down around here since."

"Enough that you decided to come back and open up your own business." She motioned around her. He'd poured her more champagne, her third glass. She didn't mind, since he was currently on his third glass as well.

Could one get drunk off champagne? She'd never really had much of it. Except for the glass at her wedding. It had been expensive and tasted so bad that she'd only had two sips before setting her glass down and leaving it behind.

"It was time. I wanted to be here when my niece was

born." He smiled and held up his glass again. "Guess I made it just in time."

She smiled as he scooped up another spoonful of melted ice cream, not seeming to care that it was now runny.

"What about you? If you had to settle down somewhere, would it be back in L.A.?" he asked.

"No." She shook her head. "I'm done with city life. It's too easy to get lost in the shuffle."

"That's why I like it here in Haven. Not only are the townspeople kind, but they also go out of their way to help one another. You won't find that in the city. Well, not very often, at any rate."

"No," she agreed and set her glass down, done with the drink. "You won't."

"It's obvious you've been hurt." The tone of his voice lowered, and she met his eyes. "It doesn't take a genius to guess that it was at the hands of your ex." She turned her eyes away from him again. "I won't try to guess why you're on the run, nor will I ask." He held up his hand. "What I will ask is that, whatever the reason, if at any point you feel unsafe, you let me know before taking off."

She met his eyes again and nodded. "I can do that."

"Good." He smiled. "Now"—he sighed— "I think I'm going to call it a night." He glanced down at his watch and winced. "Who cares if it's only ten o'clock. I'll get used to bar hours soon enough."

She laughed and helped him clean up the pizza boxes and the ice cream mess. Then she watched as he locked all the doors.

"When do you plan on hiring the kitchen staff?" she asked as they made their way up the stairs. When he gave her a look, she held up her hands. "I know, no shop talk."

"It's okay. I was hoping to hire them after the kitchen was finished getting setup," he answered. "Along with the bar employees and waitstaff." He stopped at the top of the stairs and unlocked the door that led to the private rooms. "Do you have any experience hiring?"

"Some," she told him. She'd spent most of her time in the past few years working as a waitress. She figured the experience would help her here.

"Good, maybe you can take on that task." He turned to her and leaned on his door. "I'll be honest, I've been dreading it."

"Sure," she answered. He'd stuck his neck out for her, so she should be willing to do the same. "If you have a list of potential employees…"

"Nope, I figured we'd just put a sign out in the window." He shrugged.

She held in a chuckle, then realized he was serious. "Oh, right. I'll… come up with something. Does Haven have a local paper?"

"They might. I don't know."

"I guess I'll need to go into town in the morning," she said mostly to herself.

"We can go together. Grab some breakfast at the Dancing Moose."

"The Dancing…" She laughed.

"Moose," he finished with a smile. "It's a diner in town."

She shrugged. "The Dancing Moose it is."

"Great." He opened his door but stopped. "I really appreciate you being here."

"I'm glad everything worked out for Dylan and the baby," she added.

"Me too." He disappeared into his room.

She entered her room, but the sugar from the ice cream and champagne running through her kept her pulse kicking, so she decided to use the energy by pushing the coffee table aside and exercising. She changed into her yoga pants and sports bra and started with some warmup moves. The moves came to her without thinking.

She let her body take over while her mind shut down to anything beyond the movements, clearing everything out until all she was focused on was her heartbeat and her breathing. Sweat dripped down between her breasts, her breathing was shallow, and she believed she'd worked all the sugar out of her system by the time she came to rest.

Deciding she wanted a shower, she grabbed her night clothes and set off across the hallway. She hadn't heard the shower running, but when she stepped in the bathroom, Brent was just getting out of the shower.

"Oh!" She turned around quickly while he wrapped a towel around his hips. "Sorry, I didn't know you were in here."

"No, it's my fault. I guess I got used to not locking the door," Brent said from behind her. "The bathroom's all yours," he said after a moment.

She turned and saw him standing before her with only a white towel resting low on his hips. Damn. She was going to need the cold shower for other reasons now.

Maybe it was the two and a half glasses of champagne, or maybe it was the way he got so excited looking at the picture of his niece. Whatever the reason, it was as if her body had a mind of its own. Suddenly, she moved towards him until her body was pressed up against that wet, hard body of his.

She'd dumped her clothes on the counter and hadn't even noticed she'd done so until her fingers ran over his wet skin. He held still, as if waiting for her next move. Reaching up on her toes, she brushed her lips against his. If she would have known how potent kissing Brent would be, she would have stayed in her room.

CHAPTER 7

*E*very fiber of his body came alive with Mel's gentle touch. The moment her fingers touched his wet skin, it was as if he'd been touched by a live wire. Electricity shot through him. His pulse spiked, and his breathing became erratic.

Then she kissed him, and everything came to a screeching halt.

He would have been perfectly content keeping what was between them as professional if she had wanted. He could have denied himself the pleasure of knowing how her body felt up against his. Or at least he'd told himself that, until this very moment. Now that he'd had a taste of Mel, he doubted he could ever go back to normal.

With her body plastered against his, her hands started roaming his shoulders. They moved to the muscles on his back, and he felt her nails scraping his skin. He hadn't realized his own hands were gripping her hips until she pushed against him a little more, core against heat.

She was wearing a tight pair of grey yoga pants with a

matching sports bra, and he'd never seen anything as sexy in his entire life. Her body was smaller, toner than he knew what to do with. The softness of her skin had him pulling away. They were both breathless, and he needed a moment to think about where this would take them. He took a step back.

He glanced around, anywhere but into her eyes. "I'll let you shower," he said quickly, and he walked out of the room.

He closed his bedroom door behind him. He felt like kicking or punching something. Anything. He'd never had as much pent-up sexual frustration as he was feeling now. He wanted to go back in there and take Mel where she stood. But that's the way the old Brent would have done things.

Instead, he dumped his dirty clothes into the hamper, pulled on a pair of sweat shorts, and climbed into bed, his body still revved up from her kisses.

Ten minutes later, he punched his pillow when he heard the shower turn off. He punched it again when he heard Mel's bedroom door shut.

Why had he fucked that up? Why couldn't he just be happy? Why was it so hard to be a better man than he used to be?

The little voice in his head answered quickly, "Because you don't deserve to be happy." It was so loud. He felt his entire body shake. He was a fuckup. Plain and simple. Whatever he touched ended badly.

The Hard Way wasn't just the name of his bar, it was his mantra. It was the way he did everything in life. Not that he'd set out to do things the difficult way. Somehow, life just always ended up taking him that route.

The two meaningful relationships he'd had in life had ended badly. There was Darla, whom he'd seen on and off again for only a few months. That relationship had left him raw and scared. Maybe because he'd been at a vulnerable place in life?

Then there had been Tilly. Sweet Tilly. His first love. He'd been dating her when his parents had died, leaving him alone to fend for Dylan. One of the first things he'd done after returning home was break it off with the first woman he'd cared for.

Again, he'd done it the hard way, by yelling at her and telling her that he'd never loved her. That he'd only been using her for the sex.

He'd broken her heart that day along with his own. It was years before he realized he'd loved her more than anyone else in the world.

He was pretty sure that if his parents hadn't died, he would have married her. Two years after he broke it off with her, he heard that she'd married her new boyfriend and had a kid. He was happy for her, really, but he knew then that he'd lost his opportunity for happiness.

Maybe that was why he'd chosen a doomed relationship with Darla. Everyone in Haven knew what kind of woman she was. Hell, it was obvious that she was even more damaged than he was.

It could be the reason he had pulled away from Mel. He guessed that she had a dark past. It was obvious from the fear in her eyes that first night.

When she'd mentioned an ex, he'd known then what had happened to her. He'd heard all the statistics before. One in every five women are abused by someone they trust.

Seeing firsthand the aftermath of that abuse pissed him off. What kind of man could terrorize a woman enough that she jumped at shadows, even a year later?

His mind was whirling with these thoughts, and he figured he wasn't going to be able to sleep at all that night.

He was startled when he woke the next morning to his cell phone ringing on his nightstand. Seeing his sister's number, his mind rushed to what had happened yesterday before he fumbled to answer it quickly.

"Is everything okay?" he asked.

"Yes." Dylan's voice was calm, confirming that everything was okay. "I just wanted to let you know that we're heading home in an hour or so."

"So soon?" he asked, frowning at his clock.

"Yes." She chuckled. "We've both been checked out and are healthy. There's no reason to keep us here any longer."

"Okay." He sat up and wiped his hands over his face. "Want me to bring you anything?"

"No, we're going to stop off and have some breakfast on the way home." At this point he could hear the baby fussing. "I'm going to feed Bella now. I just didn't want you to show up at the hospital and wonder where we were."

"Thanks," he said as he pulled on his clothes. "We were going to head out for some grub ourselves. We might see you at the Moose."

"I like Mel," she said suddenly. "I think she'll be good for your business. She has a very organized mind."

"Like you," he broke in.

She chuckled. "Yes, like me. She has some really great ideas. You should listen to them."

"Already done. We're having a meeting over breakfast." He remembered the kiss last night and glanced towards the door. Had it affected her as much as it had him?

"On a personal note, she's single," Dylan said.

"Don't be cheeky." He smiled.

"Me? Never." Dylan laughed. "As I said, I like her. I hope she sticks around."

He didn't say so, but he hoped so as well.

"If I don't see you, have a good day. I'll see you and Bella this weekend," he said.

"Okay. Oh, and Brent, I hope your truck survived," Dylan said, causing him to laugh.

"It did. After a few washes."

"Good. See you later." Dylan hung up.

He could hear Mel moving around in the other room, so he finished getting dressed before stepping out into the hallway. Mel was coming out of the bathroom, looking fresh in a white buttoned-up shirt and grey slacks. She looked ready to head to work, which he supposed she was.

He was determined not to make things weird between them. After all, it was just a kiss. A kiss that had rocked his entire body and touched his soul.

"You don't have to dress fancy," he said and quickly added, "Not that I mind, it's just... we aren't officially open yet."

"I don't mind either. It's nice to dress up again." She smiled as her eyes ran over him. "I take it this is your standard uniform?"

He glanced down at his worn jeans and black T-shirt and laughed. "This is dressed up for me." He motioned to his pants. "See, no holes." She laughed. "Are you ready for some breakfast?"

"I know I had three slices of pizza last night, three glasses of wine, and some ice cream, but yes. I'm starving." She smiled.

"I'm always hungry," he admitted as they headed down the stairs. "We can stop by and check up on your truck on the way back from the store," he suggested. "Larry might be done fixing you up by now."

"That would be great." She slid into the passenger seat of his truck.

His truck was spotless, with no sign of yesterday's events

anywhere. Still, he scanned the inside of the cab as he climbed in just to make sure.

The center of the town was a little over a mile away from the bar's location and consisted of the town hall, the Dancing Moose, the grocery store, Granger's Market, and the Wet Spot, the largest and most known strip club in town. There were a few other small girlie shops that he'd never been in and had never really paid any attention to.

The schools were further out on the edges of town, closer to Meadows Park subdivision, the hospital, and the library, the opposite end of town from his bar. Which was a good thing because there were rules and regulations on how close a bar could be to a school. He'd found that out when he'd applied for his liquor license.

The fact that his place sat close to Crooked Creek Mill played a huge part in his business plan. What little plan he had. The Mill was open twenty-four-seven, and he knew a lot of people coming off shift wanted food and drinks. The Mill was the second largest employer in town, second to McGowan Enterprises.

"This is the main part of this town?" Mel asked as he parked in front of the diner.

"Yes. It's a small town, just spread out in the valley." He parked and turned off his truck as he pointed to the mountain range surrounding Haven. "It's all around us."

She leaned forward and scanned the horizon. "It sure is. I guess it makes you feel safe."

"That or trapped." He looked at her. "Depending on what you think about the town."

"I suppose at one point you felt trapped here?" she asked.

"I did. That's why I got out," he answered easily.

"But not anymore?"

He shrugged. "Not yet, at any rate." He smiled as he jumped out of the truck.

She followed him into the diner, and they grabbed a table along the windows. For the first few moments, she sat and looked out over the snowy mountain range beyond the small town.

"Ever wonder what would have happened if your parents hadn't died?" she asked.

"All the time," he admitted. "Dylan was slated to go to a great college after graduation, possibly even Harvard."

"Wow." Mel shook her head. "That's a pretty big jump."

"Yeah," he admitted.

"What about you?"

"I was going to a local college." He shrugged. "I wasn't the smart one." He could tell she was still thinking about something and opened his mouth to ask her, just when the waitress stopped by their table.

"Morning, Brent," Joanna said cheerfully.

"Morning, Joanna. This is Mel. She's going to be helping me out at the Hard Way."

"Oh, nice to meet you." Joanna pasted on her welcome smile. Charm oozed from her, from the tips of her frosted pink hair to the bottom of the black pumps she always wore. It wasn't easy being one of the only goths in town, but most everyone in Haven accepted her for who she was—one of the nicest people in town.

"Morning," Mel said cheerfully.

"Would you like some coffee?" Joanna asked.

"Believe it or not, Mel doesn't like coffee." He rolled his eyes as he held out his mug. "Me, on the other hand..." He smiled when Joanna poured him a full cup.

"What'll you have?" Joanna asked Mel.

"Orange juice, please," Mel said, taking the menu Joanna offered her.

"What's good here?" Mel asked him when they were alone again.

"Everything," he answered truthfully. "Breakfast is an easy enough meal to make, but these guys have it down pat." He leaned back in his chair. He knew what he wanted to have without looking at the menu. Steak and eggs with a side of biscuits covered in gravy. His favorite.

Just after they ordered, he saw Trey's new SUV pull up outside.

"My sister's here." He motioned towards the door. "This'll be fun. I bet you anything they'll be swarmed before they even sit down."

"With the new baby, I don't doubt it," Mel said, smiling at the window. They watched as Trey stepped out of the car and then helped Dylan out before opening the back door and gently pulling out the car seat carrier.

"I assume that's Trey?" Mel asked, nodding to the blond man.

Brent looked over and saw the other McGowans getting out of their own vehicles.

The McGowans were all cut from the same mold—tall and built like quarterbacks. They looked the same but different. Trey was the only blond-haired one in the bunch.

"Yes, and here come his brothers. That's Tyler and his wife, Kristen, and their three kids—Tim, Clare, and that's Reagan, their youngest daughter." He smiled at the toddler in Kristen's arms. "And that's his other brother, Trent, and his wife, Addy, and their daughters, Hope and Grace." He motioned to the large group of people getting out of two other cars. "Oh, and their mother, Gail," he added, seeing the older woman with them.

He'd known the family for a few years now, and it still amazed him how close they were. Never had his family been that tight. Well, except him and Dylan.

"It's a good thing we ordered before they came in," Mel joked.

They both watched and, sure enough, the moment Dylan and Trey stepped inside with Bella, they were surrounded by townspeople. Until Trey spoke up.

"I don't want to over stimulate Dylan and little Bella on their first day out. We'll be hosting a party later to celebrate her birth, but until then, I think my wife would like some real food instead of the stuff they served her at the hospital."

Several people laughed and moved aside for the large group.

"You made it," Brent said to Dylan as they sat at the larger table across from theirs, which had quickly been pushed next to theirs.

"Yes," she sighed, "and I already want a nap." Dylan turned towards Mel. "Morning."

"Good morning and congratulations." Mel motioned towards Bella.

"Thanks. Trey, this is Mel, Mel, my husband Trey and the rest…" She waved her hand.

"I've already pointed out who is who," Brent added.

"Good. I'm too tired to at this point," Dylan said, leaning back.

"Are you okay?" Brent asked, concerned.

"Yes, just… I didn't know that getting dressed could take so much out of you." She smiled down at Bella. "Totally worth it, but still…"

"Too bad you can't have coffee," Trey pointed out as he sipped his cup.

"I will hurt you," Dylan added playfully. She sighed and held her hand over her mug to stop Joanna from pouring some coffee into her cup. "Tea," she told her. "No sugar."

Joanna went around and finished pouring everyone else's coffee.

"So, Mel," Tyler said, holding his four-year-old daughter

Clare in his lap, "Dylan tells us Brent hired you to get his bar up and running."

"Yes," Mel said, glancing at Brent quickly. He could see her squirm at the possibility of answering a bunch of questions.

CHAPTER 8

*M*el's heart rate spiked as she answered a few quick questions from the group of people. Most of them were just the basics—where she was from, if she had family, if she planned on staying around Haven for long.

But the longer she sat around the group of people, the more comfortable she became, especially once they stopped talking about her and asking questions.

She felt a little overwhelmed at all the good-looking people around them. The McGowan men were tall and dark haired, except for Trey, who had curly blond locks. Their wives varied in height, but all were just as good-looking as their husbands. Kristen's long dark hair and stylish clothing was perfectly in place. Their kids—Timothy, nine and Clare, four—were very well behaved and sat quietly coloring on the placemats, while Reagan clung to Kristen and played with the brightly colored toys Kristen had pulled out of her diaper bag.

Addy, Trent's wife, was a pretty brunette with an

extremely peaceful nature as she delt with her two adorable and energetic girls, Grace and Hope.

She could tell that Brent was easy around most of them. He'd told her a few stories about when he'd first come into town and how he'd gotten in a couple fights with Trey, so she was impressed at how well they all got along now.

Their food came out and, as they ate, the talk turned towards baby Bella. For her part, the baby stayed asleep tucked in her carrier the entire time.

Dylan on the other hand looked exhausted and excited at the same time. The more she ate, the more she leaned on her husband and yawned.

When they walked out with the large group, Mel was surprised Dylan was still able to keep her eyes open.

"I guess having a kid really takes it out of you," Dylan had joked.

"Go home, get some rest." Brent walked over and hugged his sister, then kissed the top of her head. "Take care of baby and let your husband take care of you."

"Will do." Dylan hugged him back and then lifted her hands to his face and said, "I'm really happy you're back."

"Good, because I was thinking..." Brent said, causing Dylan to groan.

"What?" she asked.

He smiled. "I'd like to throw a 'welcome to life, Bella' party at the Hard Way. I was thinking of using it as some sort of soft opening."

"That's a great idea." Dylan perked up. "Will you be ready?"

Brent glanced over at Mel, who shrugged. She didn't know how much more he had to do to prepare the place, other than hire employees. "We can do it. This Friday," Brent assured his sister.

"If, you're sure," Dylan said, glancing over at Mel, who shrugged again.

"He's the boss," she said with a smile.

"I'll make it work. For Bella." He smiled.

Dylan kissed him again on the cheek and turned to get into the waiting car.

They stood there in the parking lot while all the others drove away. She remained silent, understanding that Brent was having a moment and needed the quiet. Then he turned to her and smiled.

"That gives us five days to get everything in order. Ready to get to work?" he asked her.

"I am if you are."

Their first stop was to Granger's Market. The massive warehouse store had everything you could ever possibly want, from cowboy boots to staplers. Thankfully, it was all laid out in a very orderly fashion, and she ended up spending most of her time in the office supply section.

She'd set up the computer system she'd found sitting in a box in the office but had yet to turn it on. She knew he'd purchased a new cash register system for the bartender and the waitstaff. He'd installed one at the drink station and the other on the back wall of the bar, as well as a system in the kitchen for the staff to read the orders. She assumed the system he'd had boxed up in the office would tie into all of those.

Brent had disappeared in the store shortly after they'd walked in. He'd informed her that she should fill a cart with whatever she needed, and he'd meet her up front in half an hour.

Since she didn't know what his budget looked like yet, she kept her purchases small—paper, pens, notepads, a few markers and other things for making signs. It wasn't as if she needed a lot, just the basics.

She found him, along with a full cart of things, waiting for her at the front register.

"That's all you needed?" he asked her, looking at the few items she held in her hands.

"Yes, for now." She looked down at his full cart. "Did you get everything you need?"

"For now. I've got to find a supplier for the rest."

"I can call around." She noticed the liquor in his cart. "Buying this all wholesale would be cheaper," she suggested.

"This is for the party."

"Right, the party."

"For Bella," he said, his tone changing slightly. "That I agreed to throw, this weekend." The last part came out as a groan, causing her to chuckle.

"Right." She patted his shoulder. "We've got this. It's not as if you have to hire half a dozen employees, come up with a menu, stock an entire bar and kitchen, and finish making the building ready." She turned to his full cart and asked, "Think you have enough?"

"No." He shook his head. "The entire town will be there to celebrate." He stopped and looked at her. "You're invited too, you know. Not just as an employee, but as a guest. My sister texted me and made a point to threaten me if I didn't invite you."

She smiled. "I'd love to go. Do I need to bring a gift?"

"No," he said, shaking his head. "Trust me, there are going to be so many gifts, Bella's going to be swimming in them. Just yourself."

She sat back and watched as he chatted with the clerk and then turned back to her.

"This is Mel. She's going to be helping me out for a while. Put whatever she needs on my account," Brent said as he signed the receipt.

"Sure thing," the middle-aged woman said with a smile.

"Thanks, Kelly," Brent replied, and then he pushed the full cart and started walking out.

"Just like that?" she asked, catching up with him.

"What?" He glanced back at her.

"Just like that, you're going to trust me to make purchases?"

"Sure." He shrugged as if it wasn't a big deal.

"What if I decide to buy a new wardrobe, or..." She motioned towards the heavy equipment sitting outside of the store. "One of those."

He glanced over and then chuckled. "A tractor? I doubt Kelly would let you drive one of those away from here on my credit."

"Okay, so we have established there are limits," she said, getting into the truck when he opened the door for her.

"Sure." He set the bags of items down in the bed. "I have enough money set aside for the opening of the bar plus a little extra, but not enough for a twenty-thousand-dollar tractor."

"Twenty..." She glanced back at the tractor. Sure, it was an impressive piece of machinery, but that much money? "Okay, steering clear of purchasing any heavy machinery."

He chuckled again. "My bank account thanks you." He got into the truck. "Now, how about we head over and see if Larry has your truck fixed yet?"

"Sure." She nodded, feeling the knots in her stomach grow. "Speaking of money..."

He glanced over at her. "I figured you wouldn't have enough to pay for the repairs. So if you're agreeable, we'll think of it as an advance."

She didn't know what to say, so she remained quiet until he parked at the auto repair shop. She could see her truck inside, up on the lift with its insides lying out on the ground around it.

"Looks like she's not ready yet," Brent said, turning off his truck.

"Nope." She relaxed slightly. For some reason, she didn't want to owe him that much. Not yet. Not when she wasn't sure how long she was going to stick around town for. She wanted a couple more days to think things through completely.

Then Reggie told her that there was a whole lot more wrong with her truck than just her radiator and she knew that it would be weeks before she'd get her truck back.

"Sorry about your truck," Brent said as they drove back to the Hard Way.

"It was on its last leg, or tire, as it were," she admitted.

Reggie claimed that he could get it all fixed for her in a few weeks. He was waiting for a couple parts and, after that, she was looking at about a thousand dollars for the repairs.

A thousand dollars she didn't have. Yet. The way she figured it, she could work off her debt for Brent and shortly after the bar and grill's opening, she could hit the road again.

To where, she didn't know. Part of her wanted to stick around. After all, she had a job, a roof over her head. But part of her screamed that, in such a small town, she was an easy target.

They parked in the back of the Hard Way, and she helped him cart in all the supplies.

The more she looked around the place, the more she realized it was almost completely ready. He still had to pour the resin for the top of the bar, but she knew that he was going to put that off until after the party, so that guests could bring items to seal in with the wood.

The rest were just small items that would be completed along the way, after they started hiring help.

"First things first." She walked over and put the "help

wanted" sign that she'd purchased at the store out in the front window.

"Think it'll help?" he asked, stocking the beer fridge with the items he'd purchased.

"It should." She turned and glanced around. "Let me do that while you hang up the dartboard and chalkboard." She motioned to where both were leaning against the walls. "I'll stock the bathroom down here with the supplies and finish setting up the kitchen computer system. I suppose I'll need to learn it, since I may be lending a hand or training employees," she said, more to herself than to him.

"Good. After you learn it, you can teach me." He moved over to hang up the boards.

"You don't know it already?" she asked with a frown. "But you purchased the system."

"Dylan did all the research. I just purchased the one she suggested." He shrugged.

"Okay." She turned to the touch screen sitting behind the bar. "Maybe..." Just then there was a knock on the door. The pair of them looked at one another, then Brent walked over and unlocked the door while Mel's heart skipped a few beats in her chest. Her mind screamed that it was Ethan, come to take her back or to teach her another lesson, then she spotted a dark-haired woman standing in the doorway and the ringing in her ears gave way so she could hear Brent talking to her.

"Come on in." He motioned and smiled over the woman's head at Mel. "Mel, this is Jamie."

"Hi." Jamie appeared to be roughly her age, shorter than her own five six, with long straight purple and blue hair that reached to the middle of her back, and mocha skin that assured Mel of her American Indian heritage.

"Mel is my new manager," Brent said with a smile.

"Oh." The woman perked up. "Then I suppose I need to speak to you about the job?"

"That was fast," Brent said. He motioned for her to take over and then walked back to continue hanging up the boards.

"Come on in." She waved the woman towards the bar. "We have several positions we're hiring."

She'd only interviewed a couple people in the past, but talking with Jamie came easy. The woman jumped in and listed off her years of experience as a bartender.

Since Mel didn't know much about the position, she motioned to behind the bar and the computer system.

"Do you happen to know this system?" she asked.

Jamie walked over and then laughed. "Yes, I've used it at my last two jobs."

Then Mel thought of an idea. "Can you make me a dirty martini?"

Jamie smiled and set her purse down behind the bar and got to work. "You're missing a few key items back here. I can make a note of them if you want?"

"Yes, please," Mel said as she sat down at the bar.

"I like this kind of interview," Brent said, sitting beside Mel. "I'll take a…"—he tilted his head— "Moscow mule," he finished finally.

Jamie nodded and, after setting down her dirty martini, got to work on Brent's drink.

She took a sip and was happily surprised at how great the drink was. She'd had several bartenders make mediocre drinks before. This was one of the best.

"Not bad," Brent said after he took a sip of his drink.

"You're hired," Mel said to Jamie, "if you can start work by this weekend."

Jamie smiled. "I could start work now, if you were open. But this weekend will do."

"Actually, if you want, you can make up that list now so we can have everything ready for you by Friday's party," Mel said.

Jamie nodded. "I'll get right to work, boss."

"Less than half an hour after putting the sign up, you already have a bartender." Brent held up his drink. She lifted hers and tapped their glasses together. "Congrats."

"If you want, my younger sister is looking for work," Jamie told them. "She's a waitress. She's been working at the Wet Spot and hates it."

"Tell her to come on over," Brent said. "Mary, right?"

Jamie laughed. "Yes, Mary. Kimberly is too young. She's still in school."

"She's hired. I like your family," Brent said, then he glanced at Mel. "I mean, if it's okay with my new manager."

Mel smiled and shrugged. "You're the boss." Then she turned to Jamie. "You don't happen to know anyone looking for work in the kitchen? Say, a very skilled chef?"

"I might." Jamie frowned. "I can ask around."

"I'd heard that TK might be available?" Brent said.

"TK?" Jamie frowned and then turned to Mel. "TK's my cousin. I can ask. Last I heard, she was working in Helena."

Three hours later, when they took a break to eat the pizza Brent had ordered, they had four new employees all scheduled to start their training with Jamie, who had agreed to train everyone on the new computer system, since she knew it very well. TK, Jamie's second cousin once removed, or something like that, had rushed down for the interview. The thirty-something woman claimed she was tired of driving to Helena every day for work and jumped at the chance to run her own kitchen here in Haven.

Shortly after that interview, a young man named Ed, who was still in high school, stopped by and applied for a busboy job.

Mel figured that since they'd hired half the staff that they needed in the first couple hours of having the sign out, they would easily have the rest of the employees hired by that weekend.

"Not bad for the first day of hiring," Brent said.

She laughed. "One would think that there's a job shortage in town," Mel joked.

"It would appear that people are tired of working for the same businesses," Brent said. "I know that when I moved into town the first time, if I hadn't gotten a job at McGowan, I would have been limited to where I could work. And I wasn't any good at working a stripper pole."

Mel laughed and enjoyed the sexy smile Brent gave her.

"It's nice having a new place in town. It causes commotion," Brent added.

"It causes people to talk. Especially after the party this weekend. We will either impress or…" She dropped off.

"Or everyone will make up their minds not to come back," he agreed with a sigh.

"Right." She nodded.

"With TK in the kitchen, we're bound to impress. I've heard that she's won the blue ribbon three years in a row at the county fair for her chili, as well as her pies and jams."

"I was totally convinced after I sampled the fresh cookies she brought along to the interview," Mel added.

Brent laughed. "I'm just thankful we have a few more to enjoy after the pizza."

"How you can eat so much and look like you do is beyond me," she said, finishing her second slice of pie while he reached for his fourth.

There was only so much Brent could do to keep his mind from returning to the kiss last night. Watching the way Mel enjoyed those cookies had driven him completely nuts.

He'd allowed her to make the first move for a reason. He didn't want her to think for one moment that her job security was tied to what happened between them.

Maybe his actions last night, the way he'd pulled away from her, hadn't been a clear enough clue. Maybe he needed to say it out loud. Still, every fiber of his being wanted to run the other direction while also wanting to pull her into his lap.

"So are we going to talk about last night?" he asked when he was finished with his pizza.

Her eyes met his for a second. "There's nothing to talk about. I think you made it very clear that you're not interested. I'm sorry I—"

He pulled her into his lap and covered her mouth with his in a kiss that sent a zip throughout his entire body.

"This," he said against her lips, "is what I've been fighting to avoid doing since seeing you at the gas station the other night. This has nothing to do with your work here or with—"

This time it was Mel who pushed her lips against his. She took the kiss further, sliding her fingers into his hair, holding him close as his body tightened against her soft one.

He wanted to lock the doors, carry her upstairs, and enjoy the rest of the afternoon with her. But a soft knocking on the door outside had her pulling away and sliding off his lap.

"I think you'd better get that," she said.

He took a deep breath and nodded. "Yeah." He stood and walked over to the door and flung it open to see Tyler and Trent standing on the other side.

"What?" he asked, sounding a little annoyed.

"We're here to help," both men said at the same time.

"We figured you might need a hand around the place. You know, to get ready for this weekend," Tyler said as he stepped through the door past Brent. Then he stopped and looked around. "Wow, you're pretty much done in here."

"Yes." He held the door open, only to have Trent walk in.

"So where do you need us? What can we do to help?" Trent added.

"I'm good," he started to say, but Mel jumped in.

"Didn't you say you needed some help with the tables and chairs outside on the patio?" she asked.

He wanted to kick them out, to take Mel upstairs and to… "Yeah," he relented. "I'm hoping to have an outdoor section where people can hang out, maybe with their kids. You know, play games while they eat outside."

"A giant Jenga set, corn hole, and horseshoes, that sort of thing?" Tyler asked.

"Yeah." He walked to the side door and showed them the area. There was already an old deck off the back of the building. He planned on expanding it to the side door and getting one of those kite sun shades for overhead to give the area some shade. As he showed the brothers the spot, he talked about his plans. If Tyler and Trent could do most of the work outside, then he would be free to finish the rest of the work inside. He listed off everything that he hoped to accomplish. He showed them the stack of wood he'd purchased to accomplish everything that he'd dreamed of and opened up his tool shed. Then he left them to get to work while he headed back inside to Mel.

But when he stepped in, Mel was busy interviewing two other women in the kitchen, so he went to finish hanging up a couple of new neon signs he'd gotten for around the place.

He wasn't planning on the bar being a full-on kid friendly place, but he was going to serve food. Hence the grill part of the business name. He knew that a lot of couples wanted to sit down to dinner and drinks without being at one of the strip clubs in town or stuck at the brightly lit Dancing Moose diner.

There were also the customers that he expected to bring in from the Mill. Most of the workers lived in the newer subdivisions across town, and he was in the perfect location for lunches or meal breaks for the workers.

He heard Mel complete the interview with the women as he finished hanging the last sign. He watched as the two women left and walked back into the kitchen to find Mel talking on her phone.

In the few days she'd been there, he'd never seen her take a personal call. He figured to give her some privacy, until he saw the look in her eyes. The sadness and anger had him moving a step closer to her.

"I know," she said into the phone as she closed her eyes. "I'm sorry," she said after a moment. "I can't do that." She listened again, keeping her eyes closed, and he watched in horror as a tear slipped down her cheek. He wanted to gather her up, to hold her and toss her phone across the room.

Better yet, he wanted grab the phone from her and yell at whoever was on the other side making her cry. Instead, he stood there and watched and listened as she finished her conversation with a simple, "I'm not going to, and if you can't respect my—" She broke off and opened her eyes, locking them with his own. "There's nothing more to say then. Goodbye," she said quickly, and hung up. Instantly, her phone started ringing again.

Without saying a word, he walked over and turned her ringer off and set her phone down on the counter.

"You can always change your number," he said, wanting desperately to know who had called her but knowing it was up to her to tell him more.

She surprised him by laughing as she wiped the tears from her cheeks.

"I've changed it three times in the past four months," she said with a sigh. "I suppose I should have changed cell phone carriers or…" She shook her head. "Something. I'm not sure how they are getting it."

"They?" The question slipped out before he could stop himself.

She sighed again and rolled her eyes. "My parents."

He waited, watching as anger replaced the sadness behind her eyes.

Instead of telling him more, she walked over to the office and walked in, leaving her phone on the counter as it continued to vibrate.

He followed her and stood, leaning against the doorjamb.

"I've hired both Jennifer and Lisa as waitstaff. They have a few more friends that might be interested and will come in later tomorrow to apply," Mel said, sitting down behind the desk.

"Okay," he said slowly, getting the hint that she had told him as much as she was going to.

"It sounds like the McGowans are busy out there." She motioned to the window, through which they could hear a table saw and a drill.

"Yeah. I know them. They'll have it all done in a few hours." He watched her closely, still seeing the anger and hurt behind her eyes. How many times had he seen that same look in his own eyes?

"Are you okay?" he asked when she stopped and just looked at the computer screen.

Her eyes moved up to his and she nodded slowly. "I… can't talk about it right now."

"Okay," he said again. "Then we'll do something else." When she nodded, he shifted slightly. "Want to work out some of the anger? I could use some help." When he felt angry and hurt, he had to move, and there was plenty of busy work around there for them to do.

She followed him out to the main room, and he motioned to the stack of boxes.

"New glassware. Wine glasses will hang there." He motioned to the wood racks that he'd built and hung above the bar. "All others, stacked here." He tapped the counter behind the bar. "There are dishes in there as well, somewhere. Those will go in the kitchen."

"Shouldn't we wash everything first?" she asked, opening the first box.

He frowned slightly. "I guess. Shouldn't it all come clean?"

"Some of it might have been sitting in a warehouse for a while and be dirty."

"If you think… we can put it all through the machine." He picked up the box and carried it back into the kitchen. When he turned around, she had a box in her arms and was following him.

They worked in silence for a while, opening the boxes, unwrapping everything, and making sure it all fit in the large dishwasher he'd purchased and had installed in place of the old one that hadn't worked.

When they were done, he had worked up a sweat, something he'd never done doing dishes before. Turning to her, he could still see the frustration behind those amber eyes.

She surprised him by punching the stack of empty boxes. She glanced at him, and he smiled and motioned towards the other stack. She punched and kicked the boxes until they all lay in a heap, broken or smashed.

"It just…" She threw up her hands. "All of my life, I did what they wanted. I followed their rules. Whatever they said, I did, like a good daughter. Then I married Ethan and… They expected me to go to counseling. Like what was wrong with our relationship was my fault." She closed her eyes and wrapped her arms around herself.

Once again, he wanted to go to her, to hold her, to shield her from the pain, but instead he remained rooted to the spot and listened instead.

"The first time I went to them with my problems"—she started pacing as she continued— "they called their pastor and had him explain how it was a husband's right to control certain aspects of his wife's life." She turned suddenly and met his eyes. "I had just purchased a blender. A blender." She threw up her hands. "Ethan was pissed that I had spent his money. *His* money!" She started pacing again. "But he didn't like the color or…" She threw up her hands. "Whatever. The fight wasn't even the worst one we'd had up to that point." She stopped moving and looked down at her hands, then up at him and added softly. "It was the first time he hit me."

Brent's hands fisted. "Did you tell your parents?" he asked, between clenched teeth.

It wasn't as if he was a saint. Still, he'd never raised a hand to any woman. Nor did he tolerate men who did.

"Yes, that's when they called their pastor. I spent three

months in counseling sessions to learn what some man I didn't know thought it took for me to be a good wife." She rolled her eyes. "All while Ethan was taught that it was his place as the head of the household to keep me under control."

He said a couple choice words under his breath, which caused her to stop pacing and look at him.

"Exactly. Of course, I didn't understand that part until almost half a year later."

"What happened?" he asked.

She closed her eyes for a moment. "He threw me through a wall. It's not like it is in the movies at all." Her eyes opened and met his. "Wall studs stop you from going all the way through it."

"Tell me you left the bastard after that," he said in a low tone.

"Of course." She wrapped her arms around herself again. "I rushed into the arms of my parents. The first chance they could, they called Ethan over so we could attend more counseling." She turned and looked out the window. "I ran away and filed for a divorce instead."

"Is that when you jumped in your truck and drove out here?" he asked.

"No."

"What have you been doing since?" he asked as she moved over and sat down on a stool.

"For the first few weeks, I worked and moved into my own place." She looked weary and a little lost, and he felt his heart break at her silent anguish. "Then one night Ethan decided that he no longer wanted to play divorced and showed up at my apartment." She wrapped her hand around her left wrist as she looked down at it. "When things turned… dark, I called my parents."

"Not the cops?"

Her eyes moved up and locked with his. "Ethan *is* the

cops. He has almost eight years on the force. He knows everyone and has persuaded all of his coworkers that I'm… disturbed emotionally and to blame for all of his actions."

He felt his blood boil further. If he ever met the man… He didn't want to think about it.

"So, you left?" he asked.

"I moved across state. Three months later he found me again. It wasn't as if I was trying to hide, that first time. But my parents had led him directly to me. After that, I stopped telling my parents where I was. I even changed my phone number. The type of jobs I took were even different. Each time he found me, I'd lose a little more of my self-worth, of who I was." She looked down at her fingers. "He never broke any bones; he didn't have to."

"How many more times did he come after you?"

"Four," Mel answered, not looking up from her hands. "The last time, he broke into my place at night. I had just finished working a double shift as a server at a family restaurant." She glanced up and her eyes met his again. His eyebrows shot up, but she continued. "It was just like a scene out of an eighties horror movie. Unsuspecting girl comes home at night while the madman waits in the dark closet for her to climb into bed and drift off before he pounces." She visibly shivered. "I think he actually gets off on it. You know? Keeping me jumping at shadows."

He opened his mouth to respond but realized he didn't know what to say to her. Just then a loud crash sounded outside, and they both looked towards the windows.

He relaxed when he heard the McGowans laughing and turned back towards her.

"You'll get used to the McGowans. They tend to play jokes on one another." He rolled his eyes. "Still, they've treated Dylan and me like family."

Just then the dishwasher signaled that it was done with

the first load, and they moved over to start unloading the clean dishes.

As they worked, she changed the subject to employees and what else they would need before the party.

As they were finishing up, a couple more people walked in to inquire about jobs. Mel took them back to her office while he finished putting the rest of the glasses behind the bar.

His mind kept returning to what she'd told him about her parents. For years after his parents' death, he'd been angry at them. Had even blamed them for the accident and for how things had ended up afterwards.

In the twenty-one years he'd had the privilege of knowing his parents, not once had they been as abusive as Mel's. Thinking back to his childhood, they had always stood up for their kids. There had never been a doubt in his or Dylan's minds that they would go to bat for them in any way.

The fact that Mel's parents had taken her ex's side just plain pissed him off. A few things were obvious to him now. He never wanted to come across either her parents or her ex.

CHAPTER 10

Mel couldn't believe that she'd opened up to Brent as much as she had. With the truth of her past came embarrassment. She knew she shouldn't feel that way, but she just couldn't help it.

For the rest of the day, she avoided him as much as she could. It wasn't too hard. After the ladies she'd interviewed and hired had left, one of the McGowan brothers came in and asked for Brent's opinion, and he disappeared outside.

She spent the next few hours entering the new employees' information into the computer system and learning the point-of-sale system.

She'd worked at a few restaurants in the past year, but none of them had computer systems for orders. Mostly, they had been on a ticket system and an old cash register.

Still, by the time Brent walked in, she had the system figured out. TK had promised to show up early the next day and start going over menu options so they could get the orders in for supplies and have menus printed up and put in the computer system.

"How about we head to the Moose for some burgers?" he asked her.

She wanted to tell him that he didn't have to entertain her each meal, but then her stomach growled, and she realized that a burger sounded really good. "Sure," she agreed. She logged out of the computer.

"Want your phone?" he asked her as they passed through the kitchen.

She wanted to throw it away but, instead, she tucked it in her purse and followed Brent outside.

She was shocked at the amount of work the McGowan brothers had gotten done outside.

They'd finished the rest of the deck area and built four more large picnic tables, two benches, a huge Jenga game set, and even set up a brick firepit area.

"Wow." She stopped and admired all the work.

"Yeah." Brent smiled. "I told you. The McGowans are overachievers." He chuckled. "Besides, I think they're really going to enjoy having a place in town to hang out with their kids."

"Not bad." She got into his truck when he opened the door for her.

As they headed across town to the diner, she thought about opening up to him further about what they'd talked about earlier, but the embarrassment was almost too great.

"So." He glanced over at her. "We should talk."

She felt her heart skip a few beats before it sank into her gut. "Brent, my ex—"

"Not about that. About the kiss." He looked at her again.

"Oh," she said slowly. With everything that had gone on that day, she'd put the kiss that had rocked her to her core aside. "Okay." She shifted slightly.

"I didn't pull away because I'm not interested," he said, pulling into the diner's parking lot and shutting off the truck.

"I'm very interested. I just… I don't want you to think that it's because… That what's between us has anything to do with…" He took a deep breath.

"I'm the one who kissed you," she reminded him. "I didn't do so because you're my boss."

He relaxed slightly. "And I didn't kiss you because you work for me," he said with a smile.

"So, where does that leave us?" she asked, wanting—no, needing—to know his thoughts. She'd wondered why he'd pulled away the night before. Had even spent most of the night thinking about it.

In her mind there was no doubt that he'd been attracted to her. She'd felt the heat between them from the moment she'd locked eyes with him. Heat so scorching that even now her knees felt weak, and she was still sitting down.

As an answer, he unhooked her seatbelt, pulled her across the console, and cupped her face with his hands. When his lips covered hers, she sighed and relaxed into the kiss.

Then his tongue darted out, and she got a taste of him and the heat flooded back. Her toes actually curled as he slanted his mouth across hers. His hands gripped her hips, holding her, rocking her ever so slightly over him.

She wanted to ride him, to feel him buck under her. How long had it been since she'd taken pleasure? How long since she had enjoyed the feeling of someone good under or above her? To feel the arms of someone who wasn't out to hold her back or hold her down surround her.

This time, when he pulled away, it was slowly, and she understood that there was no question that he'd want to kiss her again.

"That was…" He took a deep breath. "I'm not going to lie." He smiled at her. "I want to turn around and drag you upstairs and have my way with you."

She smiled as she felt her entire body heat at the thought of letting him do just that.

"But," he started to say, and then he chuckled when his stomach growled loudly.

"Burgers?" she added.

He chuckled and nodded. "Burgers."

They walked into the diner together. He surprised her by reaching out and taking her hand in his as they stepped through the front doors. Then she followed him as he sat at a booth near the front, looking out the large windows that overlooked the town.

"I guess with this being the only real place to eat in town, it gets pretty boring," she said, glancing around to the nearly empty diner.

"Oh, it's not the only place," he said with a smile. "A couple of the strip clubs have lunch and dinner specials. Pretty damn good ones too."

"Who would want to eat in a strip club?" she asked, wondering just how often he went to said clubs himself.

"The Wet Spot has the best steaks in Montana. Dinner and a show." He smiled slightly. "Does it bother you?"

"No." It didn't. Not really. After all, she'd been desperate for work in the past and could only imagine, if she'd had a stripper body, just how far she would have gone herself.

"Of course a few of them have closed down since the last time I was here," he said, handing her a menu. "Others have stopped serving food. That's why Haven is so eager for the Hard Way to open its doors."

They ordered and this time she decided to try the French dip sandwich. They chatted about the plans for the bar and grill until their food arrived.

She'd never seen anyone so in shape eat so much in her life. She knew that he spent most of his time working hard and figured that was how he stayed in shape.

She couldn't stop herself from comparing Brent to Ethan. They were so different.

Ethan was tall and blond with blue eyes. He had an athletic build, not because it came naturally, but because he'd spent most of his free time in the gym. Brent was more naturally lean, the kind of body a man got from being very active. She'd watched Brent chopping wood the other night out her window. She'd been transfixed, watching the muscles in his back move with each swing.

"Is there a problem with your sandwich?" Brent asked her. She'd gotten caught up in dreaming about watching him and had totally forgotten to finish eating.

"No." She picked up her sandwich again and took a bite. "It's fine," she said after taking a drink of her tea.

"I can't wait to see what TK comes up with for our menu. I mean, really, I'm so excited to just have something new and different." Brent held up the last bite of his burger. "Not that this is bad. It is the best burger in town. I guess I miss being in a bigger city and having more options for meals."

"I could go for some occasional lo mein and pot stickers." She heard him groan.

"I miss Mexican food. Some enchiladas, quesadillas, and green chili," he added.

"Fonda La Catrinas out by the airport." She groaned. "I used to go there with my friends in high school."

She hadn't realized she'd made the mistake of mentioning the Mexican restaurant in Seattle until Brent's eyebrows shot up. She felt her face flush and she avoided his eyes. Or at least tried.

"What part of Seattle did you live in?" he asked after a moment.

Taking a deep breath, she relented. "Federal Way. You?" Her eyes met his.

"Auburn," he answered. "Born and raised until our parents died."

"I didn't mean to lie to you about where I was from. I spent a few months in L.A. when I was on the run from Ethan," she admitted.

He shrugged slightly. "I had figured it out a while ago anyway. It's the way you talk. Even though we don't have official accents, we can tell one of our own."

She looked deep into his eyes and could tell it was the truth.

"Why didn't you say anything to me?" she asked.

He shrugged again. "It's your secret. I had decided to put my faith in you. Besides, it didn't really matter." Then he stopped and looked at her, his eyes narrowing slightly. "The rest of what you told me is true?"

"Yes," she said with a sigh. "All of it. Unfortunately."

"And school?" he asked.

"Yes, it's where I met Ethan," she reminded him, feeling her gut twist.

"What college?" he asked.

"University of Washington."

"I was going to UW when my parents died," he said, his eyes running over her. "We could have run into one another on campus."

"What are the odds?" she said as she felt her heart skip for other reasons. What would life have been like if she'd met Brent instead of Ethan? If she could travel back in time, she could avoid the worst years of her life.

"Dessert?" he asked her, shaking her out of her dark thoughts.

"No, thank you," she said quietly.

"Well, I'm going to get some cookies to take back with us." He smiled. "I'm somewhat of a midnight snacker."

She smiled. "Somehow, I figured that about you."

She stood by while he paid for their meal and got a box of chocolate chunk cookies to go.

As they were walking out, they stopped just outside while Brent chatted with a couple of men roughly their age. She climbed into his truck while he talked, trying not to overhear their conversation, but the two guys were loudly reminding Brent about something to do with a kidnapping.

When he finally climbed into the truck, he had a funny look on his face.

"Problems?" she asked.

"No." He reached as if he was going to start the truck, but then he leaned back in the seat and sighed heavily. "I don't know. I mean…" He turned to her. "Have you ever run into someone from your past and wondered why the hell you were ever friends in the first place?"

She glanced over her shoulder at the diner where the two men had disappeared to moments ago. Hadn't she kicked herself every single day for being the idiot who fell for Ethan and his tricks?

"Yes," she admitted. "Hindsight is most definitely twenty-twenty."

He leaned his head back on the headrest and nodded slightly. "Believe it or not, a few years ago, when I lived in Haven before, I was a complete ass."

"Were?" she joked. "Your sister mentioned a couple times how much you'd changed," she said more seriously.

"I want to be clear." He turned slightly towards her. "I was never as big of an ass as your ex. I could never be. My parents may have been foolish in leaving us with nothing, but they didn't raise abusers."

She smiled and reached over to take his hand. "I didn't meet Ethan's family until after we were married. The moment I did, I understood why."

She felt her stomach flip at the memory of listening to

Ethan's father yell at his mother for spilling a glass of water at the restaurant table. How embarrassed she'd been for the older woman and how appalled at the older man's attitude. Not to mention how Ethan hadn't stuck up for his mother. Instead, he'd rolled his eyes and then told his mother how much she'd embarrassed him in front of her.

"Yeah, regret is real with those two." He leaned forward and started the truck. "Jake and Seth Williams are trouble," he said as they headed across town.

"I overheard something about a kidnapping?" she asked, no longer able to keep her curiosity at bay.

"Yeah. Seth was getting married, and Jake thought it was a good idea to go around town and kidnap everyone for a bachelor party." He pulled into the parking lot and turned off the truck. "They didn't know that I was living above the garage at our rental instead of the main house where Dylan was staying. At the time, she and Trey were dating. Anyway, they broke in and she was home alone. She ran down the street in her bare feet in the middle of the cold night."

"That must have been scary for her."

"Yeah. At the time, I thought it was funny." He turned slightly towards her. "Looking back at it, I realize just how dumb it was. She could have been hurt. Hell, if she'd had a gun, like she does now, she could have shot one of them."

She looked down at her purse where her own 9mm was and then back up at him. "I carry."

His eyes went up. "I think in these parts, it's a requirement."

"It's just—" she started, but he held up his hand.

"I get it," he assured her and then took her hand in his. "You don't have to explain anything to me."

She tilted her head as she realized just how different he was from any other man she'd ever been with.

Somehow, she'd always ended up with controlling men.

The kind who needed to know where she was, what she was doing. Ethan had been that times a hundred.

She had believed that it was all part of her attraction towards bad boys. Still, as she ran her eyes over Brent, she understood that he fit that mold as well, at least in some areas of his life.

Just hearing some of Dylan's stories the other day assured her that Brent had gone through some tough times after their parents' death. But seeing him with Dylan, while she'd been in labor, confirmed that he was no longer that way.

"Something tells me that you didn't invite the brothers to your opening party?" she asked.

He laughed. "Hell no. Seth's married now and has two kids, but word around town is that he and Jake are still up to their old ways."

"And you aren't?" she asked. She needed to know just how he thought of himself.

"No," he said, shaking his head. "I doubt I could keep up with them, nor would I want to. Just the thought of going to a strip club in town…" He shook his head again.

"Not your scene?"

"Not anymore."

"Says the man who's about to open his own bar." She motioned to the building.

"And grill," he pointed out, causing her to chuckle.

He couldn't explain to Mel how he felt now. So much had happened in his life that he no longer believed he was the same person he was almost eight years ago when his parents died. Hell, he didn't even think he was the same person he'd been last year or even a few months ago.

The truth was, even when he'd been working in North Dakota, he was still shooting off his mouth, spending too much time in bars, and hooking up with any woman who looked his way.

Still, some of that time had been just sitting in the back booth at his favorite dive and working on his laptop. He hadn't told anyone, not even Dylan, but he'd been attending online classes for the past year. It wasn't as if it had gone anywhere. He was an average B student. Dylan had obviously gotten the brains in the family.

Looking over at Mel, he could tell that she was a lot like his sister in that arena. The woman obviously had looks and a brain. Hell, she'd been helping him for only a couple days and already the place was more organized than anything he would have been able to do by himself.

There were still several items that they needed, and he planned on heading into Helena to shop the day before the party.

"What about you?" he asked suddenly. Her dark eyebrows arched up in question. "Something tells me you're not the same person you used to be either."

"No." She rested back. "I can't afford to be the same." She glanced down at her hands. "I've dyed my hair, gotten a few tattoos, changed the type of jobs I take, and even changed the way I dress."

He ran his eyes over her pants and shirt and wondered just how she used to dress.

"All to hide from your ex? There has to be more to the story."

She glanced over at him and, in the dark, she could see the fear in her eyes.

"There is, but I'm too tired right now to go into it. Besides…" She shrugged.

"You only met me a couple days ago," he finished for her.

She locked eyes with his and then shook her head. "That has nothing to do with it. Not really. It's funny, it's as if I know you more than I ever knew Ethan. Being around your sister the other day really helped." She smiled.

"Dylan has a way of saying too much." He held in a groan and enjoyed the sound of her laughter.

"Right up until her water broke," Mel added.

This time it was him smiling. "Bella is the spitting image of her. I can't remember the day my parents brought her home, but there were pictures." He frowned. "Somewhere."

She surprised him by reaching over and taking his hand. "I left everything behind. I don't even have any pictures of when I was a kid."

He shook his head. "We're a pair, aren't we?"

She smiled slightly. "It's not the past we look forward to."

He nodded. "Who said that?"

She laughed again. "Me, just now."

He felt his face heat. "I mean…" He shook his head. "Never mind." He reached for the door handle.

She stopped him by holding his hand again. "I know what you meant."

"I agree. But it is nice to look back at the ones you lost. Even if they're still technically alive," he added.

Seeing the look in her eyes, he knew that she understood him. There was still love for her parents in her eyes. It was hidden deep, but still there.

"Come on, let's enjoy these cookies on my new deck. One of the brothers hung up a couple hammocks. I'll grab us a couple beers, and we can watch the stars."

"I like hammocks, cookies, beers, and stars," she answered.

He parked in the back and handed her the box of cookies before heading inside to grab the beer. When he came out, she had turned on the gas firepit and was sitting close to it, enjoying the heat. It wasn't cold, but when the sun went down behind the mountains, most summer nights were still chilly enough to enjoy a firepit. Which is why he'd put one out on the deck to begin with.

He handed her a beer and sat down next to her. She handed him the box of cookies. He took one and held up his beer for a toast.

"To leaving the past behind us and to choosing who we want to call family." He waited a heartbeat.

"I'll drink to that." She tapped her beer bottle against his. "Are all summer nights like this?" she asked after taking a sip.

He glanced up at the perfect star-streaked sky. The full

moon was hovering just behind the hills, making it seem a million times bigger than normal.

"Yeah," he agreed, "most of them are."

She sighed heavily. "I could get used to this."

"It's not bad. It's one of the reasons I wanted to come back here."

"In California, the lights from the city were so bright that you couldn't see the stars." She was looking up at the sky while he watched her.

He knew it was a cliché move, but he slung one arm over her shoulder and pulled her a little closer. She sighed and leaned into his shoulder while they ate their cookies and drank their beers.

They talked about the good parts of their pasts—childhoods, school, and friends they'd had growing up. It was strange, there were so many times in both of their pasts where they could have run into one another but hadn't. A couple basketball games where they'd been in the same gymnasium. Even a school dance she'd attended at his high school with an old boyfriend. He'd been there, but he and his buddies had rented rooms in the same hotel, and he'd spent most of his night upstairs with Crissy Goldbloom, making out and trying to convince her to go all the way. Which, of course, he had.

"So, there are more than half a dozen times where we could have possibly run into one another," she said softly, something close to frustration in her tone. "I just think of how differently my life could have been if I'd chosen…"

He lifted her chin with his fingertips until she was looking into his eyes. "You and me both." He kissed her.

Feeling her melt against him, he took the kiss deeper, letting his fingers trail down her jawline, filling his hands with her soft hair and letting it wrap between his fingertips as her soft body pressed up against his.

If he wasn't careful, he'd fall hard and fast for her. The last time he'd felt so much for someone so quickly… Who was he kidding? He'd never felt this much for someone so quickly before.

"I'd like to go upstairs now," she said against his lips.

He smiled. "I think that's a great idea."

In one quick move, he lifted her up in his arms, tapped the kill switch on the firepit with his toe, and shifted to set the box of cookies in her hands. "We'll need those later," he promised, making her chuckle.

Getting through the back door was a little more difficult than he'd expected. Thankfully, she bent down and flipped the deadbolt for him.

He kept the lights off in the kitchen but maneuvered through it easily enough. However, when he tried to walk through the dining room, he bumped into a table that they'd moved around earlier.

"You can put me down," she said with a chuckle.

"I don't want to. I'll get through this minefield," he assured her. "See?" he said when he was at the base of the stairs. Then he took a moment or two to kiss her again until they were both breathing heavily.

"If you don't head upstairs, we may not make it," she warned.

"That's an idea," he added with a grin. The thought of taking her right there at the base of the stairs rushed through his mind, causing his dick to jump and harden even further in his jeans.

Her body slid down his until she stood on the bottom step. His hands nudged her shirt slowly up and over her head. He tossed it on the stair railing, then leaned back to appreciate the simple black bra she wore underneath. She had a small tattoo on her left upper arm. A thin silver vine twisted around her arm, filled with thorns and flowers with soft pink and white petals.

He ran a fingertip over it and smiled.

"This looks fairly new," he said.

She glanced down and nodded. "To remind myself that I have thorns under all the softness."

He smiled when she reached for his shirt and then ran her fingertips over his tattoos. There was the one he'd gotten after his parents' death, along with a couple more that he'd gotten since then.

"Later, I'll tell you all about their meanings." He leaned in to kiss her. Feeling her skin against his had him growing even harder.

His hands ran over her pants, and he drew her closer to him as his fingertips sank into her soft hips. She was rubbing herself all over him, and he was concerned now that he wouldn't be able to keep the pace slow enough that he could fully enjoy her.

"Mel." He said her name slowly, letting it roll off his tongue.

"Brent, take me upstairs. I need to feel all of you."

He hoisted her up in his arms, this time with her facing him and her legs wrapped around his waist. Her mouth was still fused to his. He was lucky he knew just how many stairs there were and reached the top safely.

He walked them into his room and leaned their bodies against the door, closing it as she ravaged his entire being. Her nails scraped his skin, her lips heated everywhere they touched him. It was as if she were surrounding him completely. Her thighs squeezed ever so lightly as they continued to wrap around his hips.

She filled his senses with everything she was. Her scent was sexier than anything he'd experienced in his entire life.

Her skin was softer than any he'd felt before. Her soft little moans had his body vibrating.

He slowly peeled her pants off, waiting as she quickly pulled off her shoes. He kicked off his own, as well. When they returned to one another's arms, the speed had his head spinning, and he was thankful for the wall that was keeping them from falling to the floor.

"Brent." She ran her teeth over his shoulder.

A low, primitive growl rumbled deep in his chest as she scraped her nails over his skin. He saw stars when he slid his fingers under the black elastic of her simple cotton panties and found her wet.

"Mel, I…" In one quick move, he tore the material blocking the rest of her from his view. He played his fingers over her silky flesh as she gripped his length with her hand and started stroking him. He froze in place, taking a moment to enjoy the feeling of her pleasing him.

"Please," she begged, her eyes locking with his. "I need this. I need you," she said softly.

He hoisted her up in his arms once again and carried her across the room. He gently laid her down on his king-sized bed, thankful that he'd taken a moment to make his bed that morning.

Reaching into his nightstand, he pulled out a condom and slid the protection on before settling over her. As he covered her softy body with his own, her legs wrapped around his hips.

When he slid into her, he was once more reminded of how much more wonderful she felt than any other before. It was as if he was finally home. His heart jumped several times in his chest before he finally started to move. Then it was all speed as their bodies took what they each wanted, what they needed.

"We do that extremely well," Mel said with a slight pant as they lay side by side a while later.

He smiled as his hand continued to roam slowly over her thigh.

"Yes, we do."

He felt her shift in the bed and then looked up to see her looking down at him.

"You do that very well." She smiled down at him.

"Is this your way of you asking me if I've ever done that before? Because you're about fifteen years too late."

She chuckled. "No, it's just..." He watched her bite her bottom lip. "It's been a while for me. I mean, Ethan and I..."

"How long?" he asked, understanding what she was saying.

She shrugged slightly. "Over a year. Almost two."

His eyebrows shot up as he let out a low whistle. "No wonder you jumped my bones," he joked.

She nudged his shoulder playfully.

"I did have some build up," she agreed. She relaxed back beside him, resting her head in her hand as she looked at him. "You?"

He thought about it for a moment and then sighed. "A little over six months. It hasn't been on my to-do list for a while. I guess I've been a little more... cautious after Darla."

"Right." She nodded. "The one who was poking holes in your condoms?"

He nodded and pulled her next to him again. He could already feel himself building up and wanting her again. After all, he had just admitted that it had been six months since he'd had sex. A very long six months since he'd enjoyed himself with someone.

He was just about to pull her up over him when she leaned up and climbed over him instead.

This time she took the lead, and he let her set the pace. It was as if the urgency they'd both felt before was replaced with a desire to make these moments last.

Never in his almost thirty years had he felt so close to someone as quickly as he had with Mel. Falling asleep with her body wrapped around his, he kept playing over how different she was than anyone else he'd been with.

Maybe it was because he knew her twisted past or because, like him, she felt as if she had no one else in the world she could trust. It wasn't really true that he didn't have anyone. After all, Dylan had been there all along and now he had Bella and the McGowans.

The more he thought about it, the more he realized just how much he had changed in the past few months. Responsibility hadn't been an easy thing for him to handle before. Now, however, he was looking forward to the Hard Way's opening and to pursuing a deeper relationship with Mel.

The following day, he woke up to an empty bed. He could hear the shower turning off and figured she wanted to get an early start. He knew she was meeting TK that morning. Rolling out of bed, he grabbed his clothes and headed out to the bathroom.

He stepped into the hallway just as she walked out of the bathroom, fully dressed and looking fresh.

Smiling, he pulled her into his arms and kissed her.

"Morning," he said, enjoying the way she melted against him.

"Good morning." She smiled back at him.

"Meeting with TK this morning?" he asked, searching her eyes for any hint of remorse.

"Yes," she said easily. "I'm looking forward to creating a menu with her. I have some ideas."

"Just as long as there are wings included," he said with a chuckle. "One thing I hated about living in Haven before was there wasn't a place in town to get really good wings."

She looked a little surprised but then nodded. "I'll make a point to add them to the list. We should probably go over a few more options with you, if you have time today?"

"I'll carve some time out for you." Just then a knock sounded on the door downstairs.

"That'll be TK, Mary, and Jamie," Mel said, dropping her arms from around him.

"All three of them?" he asked. "This early?"

She smiled and started to walk down the hallway. "It's half past nine."

"Like I said," he called after her, "this early?"

The sound of her laughter warmed him as he showered and dressed quickly.

When he finally made it downstairs, there were more than half a dozen people rushing around the place, unloading the rest of the supplies that had been delivered and moving all of the dishes and glassware in the kitchen. Two metal shelves had been set up against the back kitchen wall and were now filled with all of the items.

"No, that doesn't go there," TK said, stopping Ed from setting a stack of trays on the shelves. "Those go over there on the table."

He moved out of the way and decided to avoid the kitchen until things died down. Stepping into his office, he found Mel and Jamie looking at the computer screen.

"Morning," he said cheerfully.

"Good morning, boss." Jamie straightened up and smiled at him.

"I'm heading into town to grab some donuts at the bakery. Want anything?" he asked Mel.

She arched her eyebrows at him. "Do they have anything besides sugar?"

He laughed. "Yes, breakfast sandwiches. Bacon, eggs, the whole works."

"I'll take one of those please," she said.

"You?" he asked Jamie.

"Oh, no thanks. We all ate before sunrise."

"That's a sin." He shook his head. "No one should ever be up before sunrise," he said as he walked out of the room. Once again, he heard Mel's laughter following him out.

He was smiling and in a cheerful mood when he stepped onto the sidewalk, until he spotted the sexy blonde woman leaning against his truck, waiting for him. He felt his blood turn to ice as he met Darla's eyes.

CHAPTER 12

Mel had never really expected her career to take as many turns as it had. Back when she'd signed up for classes, she'd never expected to work so much in the service industry.

She really hadn't known what to expect, not really. She supposed she was very naïve back then. Still was, to a degree.

The more she worked with the Alaqua sisters and their cousin, TK, the more she realized her classes had prepared her well for such jobs. She enjoyed making sure the accounting software was up to date and that she had a system in the works for purchase orders and receiving.

TK and Jamie were easy to work with and both had experience in the field, so they knew most of the rules for both. They both knew of local food and liquor services, and she spent the first part of her day setting up accounts at more than a dozen businesses that would supply everything from eggs to their hard liquor.

Brent had come back from getting them breakfast in a different mood than he'd set out in. She wanted to ask him what was up but was far too occupied organizing and training employees to take a moment.

When she met with TK and Jamie about their menus, she requested Brent sit in on the discussion, but he mentioned that he was too busy trying to get the stand-up freezer door repaired and would leave it to her to decide the final details.

Since TK had wanted to familiarize herself with the kitchen and try out a few menu items on them, she sat in the dining area and let Jamie serve her a mojito while she ate the best grilled chicken taco salad she'd ever had.

When Brent walked in a few moments later with a basket of buffalo wings and a large smile on his face, she couldn't help but laugh at him.

"You look like a kid in a candy store," she said as he sat down across from her.

Jamie slid a cold beer in front of him and then disappeared.

"I feel like one," he admitted as he dug in. "Cold beer and wings." He sighed. "Do you know how long it's been since I had anything this good?"

"Six months?" she teased and watched as he almost choked on the sip of beer he'd just taken.

Jamie walked over and slapped him a few times on his back until he stopped.

"You okay, boss?" she asked with a laugh.

"Yes, just... enjoying the food and beer too much." He looked at her and lowered his voice. "You are in so much trouble."

She smiled. "Promise?"

"Something tells me I'm going to have a difficult time keeping up with you." He took another wing.

She smiled. She couldn't explain how much she enjoyed watching him heat for her. It was so easy to get desire to flood his green eyes. Each time it did, her body responded in kind.

She had played over just how wonderful he'd felt inside her last night. How, at first, he'd been almost out of control, taking her quickly and passionately. The following two times had been slower, more seduction than anything.

She'd enjoyed listening to him tell her what he wanted, what he liked, how much he was enjoying her.

No one had ever been so open with her before. She'd not only appreciated it but realized how much it turned her on hearing his words.

"If you keep looking at me like that, you're going to have to come up with an excuse for why we're both going to have to disappear for a while," he said in a low tone, getting her attention.

She smiled. "I'm sure we can figure something out."

He set his almost empty beer down and picked up the napkin to wipe his fingers with.

"Put it on one of those notes you have to add moist towelettes to the tables," he said, frowning down at his barbeque-covered digits.

She couldn't help but laughing at his predicament. There was sauce all over his fingers and even some on his cheek. Reaching over, she used her own napkin to try and remove the sauce from his face.

"Now isn't this a pretty picture," someone said, causing her to jump apart from him.

A man in his mid-thirties stood just inside the doorway, glaring at Brent and her. She felt Brent tense as he finished wiping off his fingers and walked over to stand before the man. Mel took that time to assess the other man. He appeared roughly the same age and build as Brent, only instead of dark brown hair, the man had curly blond hair cut very short, with an almost reddish colored beard that was almost as long as her hair.

"Mark," Brent said. "Can I help you?"

The other man laughed. "You can start by getting off my property."

Brent sighed. "It's not yours anymore."

"The hell it isn't," Mark barked out.

"You lost it to me almost three months ago," Brent said calmly. "When you signed the place over to me on a grant deed. I filed all the legal paperwork shortly after returning to town."

"The hell I did." Mark's face grew a deep shade of red. "You know that was just a joke, right?"

"No, afraid not. Don Hathaway has assured me that the grant deed you signed was all legal. The Hard Way is mine," Brent said.

Mel cried out as she watched almost in slow motion as the man's fist swiped out and connected with Brent's jaw. She didn't know what was more impressive, the fact that Brent barely moved or that he blocked the second blow and stepped around to hold the man's arms down, successfully stopping the fight.

"I'll give you the one hit, only because I didn't see it coming, but that's all you get." He shoved the man away from him.

She watched as he braced himself for any more outbursts. Instead, Mark stood there, his face now a deep shade of red as he looked around.

Six other people stood in the dining area, watching what would happen next.

"You cheated. Everyone there that night knew you cheat at cards. I'm going to fight you on this. Just wait and see," Mark said before storming out.

"Are you okay?" Mel asked Brent as she moved next to him.

"Yeah," he said, glancing down at her. "Mark Phillips." He motioned towards the closed door. "Previous owner of the Hardwood Way Inn."

"I gathered that," she said dryly. "What you said is true, right? You've ensured that it's all legal?"

"Yes." He turned to the room. "Mark signed over the deed and Don Hathaway, my lawyer," he said for her benefit, "filed the paperwork and transferred this place into my name. Months ago."

Everyone turned away and got back to work.

"Are you sure you're alright?" she asked a little more quietly.

"Yeah." He reached up and wiggled his jaw. "He hits like my sister." He gave her a smile. "I'm going to get back to work."

She nodded and watched him disappear into the back room.

"That was fun," Jamie said dryly as she helped Mel clear the table. "Mark has always been a hothead." She shook her head. "His family owned this place way back when it was still an inn. Some say it was his crazy grandmother that burned down the rooms in the back." She shook her head, sending her multicolored hair flowing around her face. She swiped it away and then tied it back with a band. "When they tried to get the insurance money, they were denied. The place has sat empty ever since. I doubt Mark even remembered he owned the place until right before he lost it to Brent."

"Does Mark have something against Brent?" she asked.

"Brent and half the people in Haven." Jamie rolled her eyes. "The man is bad news. My family and I steer clear of him for other reasons," she said with a shake of her head.

Mel narrowed her eyes. "Why is that?"

Jamie looked a little surprised. "Mark and his family don't like"—she used air quotes— "indigenous people."

"You've got to be…" Mel felt her anger peak.

"You're pissed." Jamie smiled.

"You're damn right I am." She was glaring at the doorway. "From now on, that man, and anyone in his family for that matter, are no longer welcome here."

"Damned if I don't like you even more." Jamie laughed and slapped Mel on her shoulder lightly. "Come on, you can work off that anger by helping me unload the wine that my cousin just picked up," Jamie said easily.

Unpackaging more than a dozen cases of wine did help a little. However, once she was done with that, she was still stewing. Not only had the man come in and punched Brent because he couldn't handle losing his family's building, but he'd accused Brent of cheating it out from under him.

She hadn't known Brent long, but she could tell at least this one thing about him. He wasn't a cheat and, more importantly, he wasn't racist.

She'd thoroughly enjoyed working side by side with Jamie, TK, and Mary. All three women were hard workers who knew their jobs without being told. They filled their time and easily busied themselves with tasks that she hadn't even thought of, such as moving two of the long benches the McGowan brothers had built out to the front so guests waiting in line had someplace to sit.

They also rearranged the tables in the dining area, which somehow made the space appear much larger than it was. Now instead of a dozen tables, there were sixteen tables inside, eight tables outside, and enough bar room for more than a dozen patrons. Brent still had to seal in the bar top, but he'd put the word out that he was looking for unique items to seal in with the resin, and she knew that he'd get to that after the party.

After she and TK and Jamie finished fine-tuning the menu, she printed a copy out from the computer, and Mary ran into town and had more than a hundred of them printed out for them to use until she could order laminated copies.

They had even come up with a logo for the Hard Way—big bold letters stacked on top of each other with the words bar and grill in smaller print underneath, all surrounded by a thick line in the same shape as the building outside.

When she'd shown Brent, he'd liked it enough to run with it. She figured it would work for now until she had time to come up with something better.

The following day, the waitstaff—Lisa, Jennifer, and Amy—were going to arrive for training. They had three days before the soft opening party and there was still enough to do that Mel wondered if they were going to be ready.

Most of the food orders were scheduled to arrive the day before the party. However, some of the supplies were being delivered in the morning.

Brent had given TK and Jamie copies of the keys to the back door so that they could open up and lock up when needed.

After everyone left for the evening, she sat out on the back deck alone and wondered where Brent was and what he was doing. He'd taken off in his truck an hour after Mark had left and had yet to return.

She made herself a sandwich and heated up a few of the leftover chicken wings then carried it outside with a beer and ate around the firepit while watching the sun go down.

She'd just finished the meal when his truck pulled into his parking spot.

"Nice," he said as he got out of the truck, motioning to the stringed lights one of the McGowan brothers had hung up around the deck area a few hours before.

"Yeah." She smiled. "They add to the ambience."

He took two large boxes from the back of his truck and set them down by the back door before moving over to sit next to her.

"I finished off the last of the chicken wings," she said, motioning to the empty container sitting beside her.

"It's okay. I had a meeting at the Moose and grabbed a burger."

"Meeting?" she asked, trying not to pry.

"Yeah." He sighed and wrapped his arm around her shoulders and pulled her closer. She rested her head on his shoulder and enjoyed the extra warmth radiating from him. She'd pulled on the thickest sweatshirt she had, but still enjoyed the warmth from the firepit. "I figured I'd better meet with Don Hathaway one last time and make sure that everything was on the up and up."

"And?" she asked, holding her breath slightly.

"And he assured me that everything is legal. Mark signed a grant deed that night and even got it notarized. Thank god there was a lawyer and a notary at the bar that night. Don claims that if there hadn't been, I'd be screwed."

"That's good news. So there's no chance of you losing the place?"

"None. The grant deed is solid, and the property was in Mark's name and not his father's or brother's names, so they can't claim ownership." He ran his hand over her shoulder.

"Do you think they'll cause problems?" she asked. "TK and the others think so."

"I don't know much about them. I only knew Mark Phillips when I lived here before. He followed me to North Dakota from Bozeman. We both worked for the McGowans for a while. I would have never considered him a friend, which is why I didn't have any issues taking this place from him when I won it. Honestly, I think he went there that night trying to unload the property in the first place. Who just carries around a grant deed of property they own? I'd over-heard him trying to get someone to front him a few thou-sand for the deed before he'd placed it on the table."

For some reason Mel thought back to the friends that she'd had in school. There were a handful of people she'd trusted in her youth. Most of them had disappeared shortly after she'd married Ethan or had left when Ethan had deemed their relationships unworthy.

She doubted any of them had thought of her in the past few years. At this point, she even doubted her parents were really looking for her or that they cared how she was doing. Did they still believe that Ethan should have ultimate power over her? That their daughter shouldn't have dreams and a career of her own? Or even believe her that Ethan had been controlling and abusive to her in the first place?

A sense of loneliness filled her, threatening once more to consume her completely. Now, however, she had something new to focus on. The thing keeping her rooted was the feeling of Brent's arms around her.

CHAPTER 13

He had felt the change in Mel. The tension had caused her to stiffen. He'd tightened his arms around her and felt her relax against him. He didn't know what had caused her tension earlier but figured it had something to do with Mark's visit.

"Look," she said, motioning with her hand as a shooting star streaked across the night sky.

"Make a wish," he said into her hair.

"I wouldn't even know where to begin," she said with a sigh.

"Too many wishes?"

"No, too many things that need fixing." She glanced up at him.

"I didn't mean to scare you earlier," he said, cupping her face with his hand.

"When?" she asked, her eyes searching his.

"When Mark showed up," he answered softly. "I don't often get attacked." He frowned. "Well, at least lately I haven't," he admitted with a soft chuckle.

"Men." She shook her head and sat up a little. "Why is it a macho thing for you to go around hitting each other?"

He smiled. "It's primordial. Sort of like enjoying watching the fights or sports and eating red meat."

She chuckled. "Want to drag me by my hair up to your cave?" she asked in a soft voice.

He reached up, dug his fingers into her hair, and softly pulled her close for a kiss. "I just might do that," he said against her lips. He felt her shiver next to him.

He couldn't explain how being with Mel made him feel. She brought out the best in him. For the next two days, he worked side by side with her and slept with her wrapped around his body at night.

She met his every need with her own needs and, the more he was around her, the more he realized just how empty his life had become. He'd never laughed or enjoyed himself more than when she was around.

When his sister showed up with his niece a few days later, he sat in a chair and gave as much attention to Bella as he did to Dylan while she talked to Mel about all of the plans for the party the following day.

When Mel disappeared into the kitchen to handle a question from TK, Dylan turned her eyes towards him.

"I like her," Dylan said easily.

Bella had fallen fast asleep in his arms and, he had to admit, he was afraid to move for fear of waking the baby. His fingers were going slightly numb from holding her, but he didn't mind.

"Yeah, she's been great so far. I think we should keep her," he admitted, looking down at Bella.

"I mean Mel." Dylan slapped him playfully on the shoulder.

"Oh, yeah, she's been great too," he said with a smile.

"There's something between you two," Dylan said softly.

"Is there?" He played dumb, causing his sister's eyes to narrow.

"Well, whatever it is, don't screw it up. For once, I actually like a woman you're seeing," Dylan replied.

"I thought you liked Tilly?" he asked.

"Tilly was dense. Extremely so," Dylan said, causing him to laugh.

"It wasn't her brain I was attracted to," he admitted.

"No, but Mel seems to have it all." Dylan glanced towards the kitchen doors. "There's a hidden pain behind those eyes." Her eyes turned back towards him. "Tread carefully. You don't want to hurt her any further."

He opened his mouth to tell his sister he wasn't about to hurt her, but then Mel stepped back into the room.

After his sister's family left, he helped Mel and TK unload the fresh produce and set up the walk-in refrigerator. TK was very organized and wanted everything in specific places.

He couldn't shake his sister's words and the more he thought about it, the more he realized that his past experience with women hadn't been as great as he'd believed.

Clear back from when he'd first started dating his first girlfriend in grade school, he had always ended up hurting them. Not that he'd ever cheated on anyone. That was a line he hadn't crossed nor ever would. Not after he'd caught Rose with one of his friends at a party in junior high.

Still, that hadn't stopped him from pushing them away all the same.

It's not as if he had set out to pull away from anyone, but he had some deep-rooted issues, thanks to his parents. Even though they'd had a great relationship between them, how they had treated their kids had been less conventional.

He remembered how much he and Dylan had to rely on each other growing up. His parents had never really attended any sports or school functions, leaving Brent to shuttle his sister to her after-school activities.

Honestly, up until their parents' death, Brent and Dylan had been pretty much left on their own. After their death, things had taken such a dark turn for him. He knew it was the added financial burden that had caused him to party and drink instead of fending for him and his sister. He'd just... shut off.

He was determined never to do that again. And no matter what happened between him and Mel, he was going to do everything in his power not to hurt her further.

The night before the party, his nerves were in full gear. He and the rest of his crew rushed around the place, making sure everything was in order.

By the time they climbed the stairs, it was past one in the morning and neither had the energy to do anything other than to fall into bed together.

She had moved some of her things into his room and, since that first night, she had spent every night in his bed. It was almost an unspoken thing between them. Nothing had to be said. He could tell she was enjoying herself and, the way he saw it, if anything changed, he'd just have to go with it.

The morning of the party, he woke again just in time to hear Mel shut off the shower. He'd gotten the hint that she was a very early riser, something he wasn't. Still, he didn't mind when he walked into the kitchen after his shower and she handed him a cup of hot coffee and had a plate of fresh fruit ready for him, along with an omelet with green peppers, onions, and tomatoes.

"No sugary donuts for us today," she said, sitting beside him.

He groaned. "I could use the extra push, but this will do." He took a bite of the eggs. "It's very good." He glanced around. "TK make these?"

"TK should be here in about an hour. I made these." She smiled. "I like to cook."

"You're good at it." He took another bite. "Very good."

She smiled. "I haven't been able to enjoy moving around in a kitchen for a while," she said with a slight sigh.

"You could always lend a hand if you want," he suggested.

She tilted her head and looked at him. "I may just do that. If I have time."

He didn't know why, but he asked her, "Are you happy here?"

She set her fork down and looked at him, meeting his eyes so he could see the truth there.

"I am. For the first time in a long time. I never thought I would be." She glanced around the quiet kitchen. "I would have never pegged me being happy in a place like this."

"Like this?" he asked. "A bar and grill or Montana?"

She smiled. "Both, I suppose. I always figured I'd be happiest in a city."

"You've been here less than a week. You may tire of country living." He felt his heart sink at the thought of losing her. He was enjoying being with her and wanted to do everything he could to continue doing so.

She picked up her fork and started eating again. "You might, as well. You did mention you tired of Haven before."

"True." He nodded. "Now, however, I have reason to stick around." He thought of Bella and smiled. "Having this place and my niece changes things."

He thought about his plans to eventually purchase a home somewhere in town and rent out the rooms upstairs for an added income, after a quick remodel. Not that he figured it would be anytime soon. He'd sunk all his savings into the bar. But if things went well, he knew he'd want a home and a place away from work.

"Are you excited about today?" she asked, breaking into his thoughts.

"Nervous. You?"

"Both. I know things are going to go smoothly but there is always a fear."

"Something is bound to go wrong. It happens. I just hope it's not something too crazy."

"Whatever it is, I'm pretty sure we can handle it," she said with a smile.

Two hours later, he stood in one of the bathrooms, his shirt soaking wet as he worked on the broken pipe under the sink. Thankfully, he'd caught it before the room had flooded too badly. After a quick trip to the hardware store, he had the pipe repaired and the mess cleaned up just as everyone started showing up.

He rushed upstairs to change into dry clothes and was surprised to see Darla standing just inside the doorway at the base of the stairs when he came back down.

He'd been slightly shocked to see her the other day since he'd heard that she'd moved to the city shortly after he'd taken off himself. Rumors were going around that she'd been in rehab, but rumors had also swirled around that she'd married an eighty-year-old millionaire and had taken all his money and was living in the south of France.

He had to admit that she was looking a lot better than the last time he'd seen her. She'd stopped dying her hair the washed-out bleached blonde and had let it grow out to just below her shoulders. Now it was a more natural sandy blonde color.

She looked healthier than before too. She'd put a little weight onto her previously almost anorexic build. The biggest shocker was how modestly dressed she was in jeans and a blouse.

They hadn't left things on a good note. When she'd tried

to talk to him, he'd done everything he could to avoid her since he hadn't wanted to fall for her traps again. Looking back at their relationship, he knew that being with her had contributed to a lot of his own crazy attitude in the past.

Taking her arm, he pulled her out the door in hopes that she hadn't already caused any issues.

"What are you doing here?" he asked, glancing around.

"I was hoping we could talk." She followed him out front.

"I'm kind of busy today," he said, dropping his hand from her arm.

She took a deep breath and nodded. "I can see that. I'll just head inside…"

"No." He stopped her. "This is a private party."

Her eyes narrowed slightly. "I know, and I was invited."

He couldn't hide his surprise. "By?"

Darla smiled. "Your sister."

"Like hell you were." He remembered how Dylan had felt about Darla when they'd been dating. The last thing his sister would want is his crazy ex-girlfriend around for her daughter's first party.

"We bumped into one another at the grocery store the other day," Darla said easily. "She mentioned that you were throwing the party and invited me." She started towards the door again. "If you don't want me here, I suggest you take it up with Dylan."

She walked back inside, and he wondered just how bad things were going to go with her around.

CHAPTER 14

*M*el watched from inside as Brent talked to the pretty blonde woman out front. She tried not to let her jealousy spike, but the truth was, it stung seeing the spark of something between them.

But people were shuffling into the place quickly, and she didn't have much time to dwell on it. The blonde came in some moments later and sat at the bar, while Brent went to talk to Dylan, who was sitting with Bella at the center table.

She disappeared into the back room and helped out back there until Brent came and found her almost an hour later.

"Got a moment?" he asked her.

"Sure." She dusted off her hands and followed him into the office.

"First off, I wanted you to know that Darla is here," he said, his voice going low.

"Okay." She thought back to the blonde and felt her heart kick twice in her chest. She'd been jealous before, but knowing that the woman was Brent's ex hit her even harder.

His arms wrapped around her, then he bent his head and kissed her.

"You have nothing to worry about," he said against her lips.

"Yeah." She relaxed. "I wasn't worried," she lied.

He chuckled and then kissed her again. "How are things going back here?"

"Smooth. TK and her crew are on it. I've just been standing around watching them work."

"You should come out and enjoy the party," he suggested. "Dylan's been asking after you."

She didn't want to tell him that she felt strange being around his family and friends. Especially now that she knew who Darla was.

"I think…" She started to make an excuse as to why she shouldn't go out front, but he stopped her by kissing her.

"Just come out front for a few moments. It would please my sister."

"Alright," she agreed. "For a few moments."

When she stepped out front, she was thankful that it appeared that Darla had already left. Mel scanned the room twice just to make sure.

Brent pulled out a chair near his sister's seat for her to sit down on.

"Want some food?" he asked her.

Since she hadn't stopped for lunch yet, she nodded as he sat next to her. Brent waved Jennifer over, and she took their orders.

"How are you enjoying your party?" Mel asked Dylan.

"It's the best." Dylan smiled over at her. Bella was fast asleep in Trey's arms while he talked to his mother, Gail, and Kristen's mother, Trisha. The two women seemed extremely friendly and spent most of their time laughing and playing with their grandkids.

For the next hour, she lost herself in conversation and

even had a chance to hold Bella after the baby woke up and ate.

Mel realized it was the first time in her life that she'd held a baby so young and small. How many times in her life had she believed that, by her age, she'd have a family of her own?

She hadn't realized her eyes had watered until a teardrop fell on Bella's head. Embarrassed, she quickly wiped her eyes and glanced around to see Dylan and Brent watching her. Feeling foolish, she handed the baby over to Dylan and excused herself. She headed upstairs to wash her face.

When she walked back out of the bathroom, Brent was there waiting for her.

"Everything okay?" he asked, concern in his voice and eyes.

"Yes, just needed a break," she said, trying to sound light-hearted.

He reached up and took her shoulders. "You don't have to hide from me," he said softly.

"I'm not hiding."

"No?" His eyes searched her own.

She shook her head. "Not really. I'm just…" She sighed and figured she'd open a little more to him. "That was the first time I've held a newborn. It just got to me." She shook her head.

His eyebrows shot up. "The first?"

She nodded. "Yeah, I don't know many people who have kids."

"Well, then you need to get back downstairs. There's a bunch of the little rug rats running around," he said with a smile. "I was about to take them out on the back porch and help them make s'mores. Want to lend a hand?" He stilled. "You do like kids, right?"

"Yes." She smiled. "I do."

His smile matched hers. "Good." He reached down and

took her hand. "Then help me out. I'm seriously outnumbered."

For the next hour, she helped Brent outside with all the kids and ended up holding Clare McGowan, Tyler and Kristen's oldest daughter, on her lap while the little girl made a mess with chocolate and marshmallows. The almost-five-year-old's favorite words were *how come* and *why*, which Clare replied to everything Mel said. Still, she enjoyed her time with the kids and when the party was growing to an end, she realized she was more exhausted than she'd been in years.

Once all the guests were gone, they helped the crew clean up and were closed up shortly past nine o'clock.

During the party, so many people had dropped off small mementos to place in the bar top.

She helped Brent set aside the best of the items and then arrange all of the pieces in the bar. Then he mixed the resin to pour over everything.

She'd never seen the process before and sat back and watched with interest.

"So that's it?" she asked almost two hours later as he finished pouring the last small bucket of resin.

"After I smooth this out. Yes." He was holding a small spatula tool. "I'll run this over everything a few times and make sure all the air bubbles are out and then it will dry overnight. It may take a day or two to harden completely, but we'll put the fans on it overnight." He motioned to the two large fans he'd brought in from the back room.

"It looks amazing so far," she said, seeing how nice and shiny the wood looked now. Even the items he'd placed in with the wood gleamed. There were a few military metals from locals and an old Haven police badge that a local cop by the name of Dale Alaqua had put in. He claimed it had belonged to his great-great-grandfather, one of the first cops in Haven back when it had been a mining town. The man had also brought a few of his great-great-grandfather's arrowheads to represent the American Indian side of his family.

It wasn't until she'd overheard TK talking that she realized the man was her younger brother. She wondered just how big the Alaqua family was.

She'd always wanted a brother or sister. Watching the McGowan brothers with their extended families had her realizing just how lonely her own childhood had been. Sure, she'd had a handful of friends throughout the years, but no one who had stuck. Throughout college, she'd been so focused on her and Ethan's relationship, she hadn't realized all of her own friends had faded into the background.

It wasn't until after the divorce that she'd looked around and realized she had lost track of everyone close to her. And knowing her parents didn't really care where she was or how she was doing left her even more depressed. All they cared about was that she returned home and fulfilled her wifely duties.

She'd tried to put those thoughts in the back of her mind over the past few months, but there were times they crept in and made her want to bury her head. That or eat an entire bucket of rocky road ice cream.

"There, that should do it," Brent said a few moments later. "How about we have some ice cream to celebrate?"

She glanced over at him and smiled. "You read my mind."

She followed him back into the kitchen and waited as he pulled out a large tub of ice cream. "There are three pieces of pie left over," he said with a grin. "Makes me wonder what you're going to have."

She laughed and grabbed two plates and silverware for them.

"Let's take this outside," he suggested after giving them each a scoop of ice cream on top of their slices of pie.

Sitting under the stars once more with the fire crackling, she realized she could very well become accustomed to spending her nights like this, with Brent.

"Today was okay?" he said, making it more of a question.

"It was," she agreed. "I think everyone enjoyed themselves. I overheard several people mentioning coming back after opening day."

"Yeah." He nodded. "I did too."

"When do you think that will be?"

He glanced at her. "I thought you were making that decision?"

She laughed. "Is tomorrow too soon?"

He shrugged. "No."

"Good, because I might have mentioned to the crew and to a few guests that we'd be open tomorrow."

He laughed. "So, we're open then?"

She nodded. "Looks like you are."

"We," he corrected, taking her hand in his own. "I couldn't have done it without you."

"Sure you could have," she said, feeling a little heated. "All I did was—"

"Hire all the employees, create the menus, place a ton of orders, organize the entire office system and cash register system—"

"POS," she broke in.

"POS?"

"Point-of-sale system," she answered with a smile.

"Right, the POS, not to mention training all of the employees."

"Okay, you couldn't have done it without me," she admitted with a laugh, setting down her empty plate. He'd finished moments ago and was sipping a cold beer. He set it down and pulled her close and kissed her.

"Do you think you have the energy to head upstairs?" he asked against her lips.

"No," she admitted, "but since it's so nice here, under the stars…" She pulled him down onto the soft cushions of the deck chair. "I've never had sex under the stars."

"Never?" he asked, pulling back slightly to look down at her.

She shook her head and smiled up at him. "Never."

His lips moved down her neck as his hands pushed up her shirt and cupped her breasts. She moaned as she arched towards his touch, enjoying the way he took his time.

She felt her entire body heat when one of his hands moved lower and slid her pants down her hips. He cupped her through her panties. When he began rubbing her through the silk of her panties, her entire body bucked under his.

Her nails dug into his shoulders as he slid a finger slowly into her pussy. Then he was kissing her, and she realized she was no longer in control of her body, let alone anything else in her life.

She hadn't expected to feel so much so quickly with Brent. Being around him every day and sleeping wrapped around his body at night made her realize just how out of control her life was now. She was no longer able to deny that she was falling hard and fast for him.

For the first time in a long time, she had something stable to cling to.

Closing her eyes, she tried to deny those feelings and just enjoy the best sex she'd ever had. She helped him pull his jeans off his hips, and the moment she had her hands on him, she realized this wasn't just sex. Then he slid into her and she stopped thinking altogether.

She woke a while later and realized that she'd gotten chilled.

"You're cold," he said, his face still buried in her hair.

"No." She denied it even as her body shook.

Chuckling, he got up from the lounge chair, pulled her up into his arms, and carried her inside, still naked.

"Our clothes," she said, stopping him at the doorway.

"They'll be here in the morning," he said, but she stopped him again.

"We won't have a chance to get them before someone sees them," she warned.

He walked over, shifted her in his arms, and dumped everything into her arms before heading back inside.

"Just so we're clear, I'm not opposed to letting everyone know what we're doing," he said as he locked the door.

"It's not very professional," she warned.

"Who cares. It's my own business," he said as he climbed the stairs, her and their clothes still in his arms. "We know what's between us is separate from work."

"Right," she agreed.

"So, let them think whatever they want. I think my sister already knows. Which means a lot of other people know," he said as he stepped into his room.

She tensed slightly, realizing he was probably right. She'd heard that in small towns it was difficult to keep secrets.

"Okay, so next time we'll leave our clothes strewed all over the place," she said with a smile before dumping the pile of clothes all over the floor in his room.

He laughed and kissed her, warming her entire body up quickly.

CHAPTER 15

The following morning, he stepped out onto the back porch and smiled at the strip of black silk that hung over the lounge chair. Part of him wanted to let it stay there, but the more practical part of him picked it up and tucked it into his pocket before heading to the hardware store.

He had to get some more light bulbs to replace the ones in the stairwell that had gone out yesterday. He also wanted to get a few more of those lounge chairs and maybe an outdoor sofa. If people were going to spend a lot of time outside, he wanted to make sure it was comfortable for them.

The doors to the Hard Way were officially opening later that day. Mel and TK had come up with their hours of operations—eleven to ten, Monday through Saturday.

Since they had the day off tomorrow, he figured he would do something special with Mel, maybe take her into the city or into the hills on a hike. Did she even like hiking?

The more he thought about it, the more he realized he didn't know a lot about what Mel liked and disliked. He knew a little about her past and what she liked sexually, but, otherwise, she was an enigma.

That was something he was determined to fix over the next few days. Once again, he bumped into people he knew or had worked with at the hardware store. Normally, it wasn't an issue, but this time when he spotted Mark, he quickly darted down a different aisle and tried to avoid the man.

After his meeting with his lawyer, he'd been assured that everything was on the up and up, but he'd heard through the small town's grapevine that Mark had filed an injunction to get his property back from Brent.

Don had assured him that there was nothing Mark could do at this point and had filed a counter injunction to reverse Mark's injunction so that he could keep the Hard Way's doors open during the legal battle.

But that didn't keep Mark from running his mouth all over town, claiming that Brent had somehow stolen the land out from under him.

The way Brent figured it, the longer he avoided the man, the better. Someday soon, Mark was going to get the news that there wasn't anything he could do to get his land back.

As far as Brent knew, Mark had known what he was doing that night. It wasn't as if he'd been so drunk that he'd hadn't been sound enough to get the papers notarized. Brent wouldn't have known that he'd needed anything notarized, having never purchased property himself before.

The more he thought about it, the more the realization that he was a property owner hit him. Smiling, he walked up to the counter to pay for his items.

He was halfway across the parking lot, shuffling his three bags of items out to his truck, when he was blindsided by a blow to the back of his head. Two of his bags flew out of his hands. The next attack came from a completely different angle, causing the last bag to go flying and making him see stars.

Before he could turn around and defend himself, the attack continued from two different sides. His guess was that his attackers were two very large men. The only thing he had time to do was shield his head from the worst of it as he was shoved to the ground and kicked repeatedly.

Luckily, he never lost consciousness as the men continued to kick and hit him. He recalled the words *thief* and *cheater* being thrown around before someone yelled loudly to call the police and the hitting and kicking stopped.

"Are you okay?" someone asked him.

He glanced up through swollen eyes and saw Martha Brown, the mayor of Haven, standing over him.

He started to get up, but she held him still.

"Don't move. The ambulance is on its way," she said.

"I don't need…" She gave him a look, and he shut his mouth. He figured it wouldn't hurt to be looked at. His ribs ached so bad that he was having a difficult time breathing.

He sat up and waited on the ground, surrounded by his purchased items, for the ambulance and the police to arrive.

Dale arrived a few moments before the ambulance did. Thankfully, the man agreed with him that there wasn't anything the clinic could do short of giving him an ice pack and an X-ray of his ribs.

When Dale asked him if he knew who had jumped him, Martha jumped in.

"It was Everett and Matthew Phillips," Martha said firmly. "If I hadn't been coming out of the store at that moment, I wouldn't have believed it myself. Two of Haven's long-standing residents beating up a person in broad daylight." She shook her head. "First we had an explosion, then a drug ring busted up, now thugs." She closed her eyes. "What is this town coming to? I'm going to have to get tougher on people around here." She turned towards Dale. "Correction, you're going to have to do that. You can bet we'll be discussing this at our next city council meeting."

At this point Dale turned towards him and groaned lightly. "I'll go bring them in. Do you think this has to do with the Hard Way?"

"Most likely," he said with a twinge when one of the EMTs poked him in the ribs.

"You might need an X-ray," the kid said.

"Yeah, I might, but for now, I'm heading home to put some ice on it." He stood up slowly. When he didn't pass out, he considered it a win. Martha and Dale had gathered his purchased items and had set them in the bed of his truck.

"I'll be around later to fill you in on what I find out from the Phillipses," Dale said to him.

"Thanks." He shook the man's hand and then climbed into his truck and drove back to his place. His entire body was aching, but no more than it did after a long day's work, with the exception of his ribs, which stung each time he took a deep breath.

Someone must have called Mel because she was waiting for him in the parking lot. Before he could put the truck in park, she was opening the door.

"Martha called TK, who told me what happened." She ran her eyes over him. "My god." She reached up and cupped his face. "You're bleeding."

"Again?" He groaned, wiping his nose, but then she touched the side of his left eye, and he winced, feeling the split skin there.

Mel helped him out of the truck and wrapped her arms around his waist as they walked towards the back door.

"Here," TK said. She handed him a raw steak as they walked through the kitchen. "For your eye."

"Thanks," he groaned and placed the steak over his left eye as he followed Mel upstairs.

When she nudged him down onto the bed, he fell willingly. Even though he hadn't even had a chance to raise a fist, he was completely exhausted.

He sat there, motionless, as she peeled off his boots and pants and removed his shirt carefully.

When she hissed at the sight of him, he glanced down and noticed the deep red marks all over his body.

"They kicked me," he said. He leaned back as she placed the raw steak over his left eye again.

He closed his eyes and jumped slightly when a cold washcloth landed on his chin.

"Sorry, I'm just cleaning the blood," she said softly.

He kept his eyes closed. They were aching and, at this point, his vision was a little blurry. While she gently cleaned up his face, he thought about his plans for the following day and held in a groan.

"Sorry," she said again, making him realize he hadn't held it in as well as he'd thought.

"It's not you." He cracked one eye open. "I had plans for us tomorrow and now I doubt I'll be able to even crawl out of bed, let alone climb up a mountain."

She stilled, her eyes meeting his. "You wanted me to climb a mountain?"

"It's more like a steep hill," he supplied. "Do you like hiking?" He frowned a little, which had the split in his lip cracking open. She reached up and wiped it with the cloth.

"I do. It's just..." She paused.

"What?" He took her hand so that she'd stop wiping his lip.

Her eyes met his again. "I didn't think... I thought this was more of a casual..." She motioned between them with her free hand.

He felt his heart take a dive in his chest.

"It is if that's what you want," he said quickly, feeling stupid. Of course she wouldn't want more with him. He'd been foolish to think so.

"No, I mean, I..." She shrugged. "At this point, I'm not really sure what I want." She pulled her hand free from his and stood up to walk into the bathroom and clean the cloth. Then she was back with a fresh one and started dabbing at his hair. "You have dried blood in it."

"Leave it," he said, taking her hand again. "Mel, I like spending time with you. In and out of the bedroom and outside of work. If you want to keep what we have between us in just those two zones, let me know now."

She sucked in her bottom lip and bit it gently, a move he knew meant that she was thinking.

"I can't promise anything. My ex left me pretty messed up," she said after a moment. "My parents' betrayal cut so deep. I don't think I could take being jerked about emotionally like that again."

"I get it," he said, wanting to take the sadness from her eyes. "Then again, I can't promise you won't fall in love with me." He smiled. Her instant smile made his smile grow, but it was worth splitting his lip open again. "But I will make you a promise right now." He took both of her hands in his and pulled her down to hover just above his lips. "I won't hurt you. If we tire of one another, we'll make it a mutual separation that has nothing to do with our friendship or our work arrangement. We'll promise to be honest with each other at all times. Deal?"

She sighed lightly and then nodded in agreement.

He nudged her until her lips laid gently over his.

"Why don't you get some rest. I'll bring you up some lunch in a while. I need to go open the doors," she said, leaning back a little.

"I could use some aspirin," he said as she stood up. "It's in the bathroom cupboard."

She got him the pills and a glass of water before heading downstairs.

He wanted to be there for the first official day of being open, but he just couldn't keep his eyes open and his ribs ached so bad, he doubted he would be able to make it down the stairs by himself.

He woke sometime later when Mel sat on the edge of the bed.

"How are you feeling?" she asked, her eyes running over him.

He'd slept like the dead and felt like he'd been hit by a train.

"Better," he lied, and her eyes narrowed.

"I thought we agreed to be honest with one another," she said.

He smiled. "Okay, I feel like death," he admitted. "But I'm hoping whatever that is will help." He motioned to a platter of food that was covered with a cloth as he sat up slowly. He winced when the pain shot through his ribs as he moved.

"Need help?" she asked, moving closer.

"I've got it." He leaned against his headboard.

She grabbed the tray and set it on his thighs, then removed the lid to expose a plate with beef tips, rice, and gravy.

"Today's special," Mel said with a smile. "It's really good."

"Did you eat already?" he asked, taking a bite and letting the meat melt in his mouth.

"Yes, I had a quick lunch a while ago. It's crazy busy down there." She glanced out the window. "The back patio is full, as is the dining room." She smiled. "There was a line out the door a while back. I need to head back down there." She glanced towards the door.

"Go, I'll be okay." He already felt better now that the food was hitting his stomach. "I may be down in a while."

She turned back to him and winced. "You might want to shower and take a look at the mirror before you do. You could end up scaring some of the families away."

"That bad?"

She nodded slightly.

"Ouch," he said.

She shrugged. "We are going to be honest with one another, right?"

He chuckled. "Go, get back to work. I'll stay up here and hide my ugly mug."

She stood up, then leaned over him and brushed a kiss across his forehead. "If you need anything…"

"I'll text you," he replied, then he watched her go before finishing off his meal. Setting the tray aside, he slowly got up and walked down the hallway to the bathroom.

Taking a look at himself in the mirror, he winced. He'd known his clothes had been torn, since Mel had removed them before helping him into bed. Now, standing in front of the mirror, he could see one large bruise forming over his left ribs where he'd been kicked repeatedly. His left eye was swollen almost all the way shut where he'd taken one of the first fists. There was a large scrape on his chin, most likely where he'd hit the pavement.

He ran his hands over his ribs and hissed at the pain. After assessing it, though, he figured he was just bruised and nothing was broken, as the pain wasn't terrible.

He turned on the water and stood under the hot spray until it turned cold. Climbing out, he figured he felt at least eighty percent better than he'd felt earlier. Still, after pulling on a clean pair of jeans and a shirt, he figured Mel was right. That puffy black eye and the scrape along his jawline weren't too appealing.

It had been almost three months since he'd taken a day off. He almost didn't know what to do with himself. Almost. Making his way to the sitting room, he turned on the television and lost himself in reruns of a hockey game.

He must have fallen asleep again, since he woke when Mel sat beside him on the sofa.

"I wondered if you ever used this room," she said, running her eyes over him. "You look better." She reached up and touched his eye. "Your black eye isn't as swollen."

"The steak helped." He pulled her closer to him. "Are you going to take a nap with me?" he asked as he pulled her down onto the sofa next to him.

"I wish I could." She smiled up at him as she wrapped her arms around his shoulders. "But my boss is playing hooky today and someone's got to do some work."

He smiled. "I don't think your boss will mind if you take a few moments…" He bent down and kissed her, letting his lips linger over hers while he slid his hands up and cupped her breasts.

She arched into them and moaned softly. He took that moment to dip his tongue in and taste her, enjoying the way she melted underneath him.

"I'm sure TK and the crew can handle things down there for a while," he said, nudging her shirt up until her crisp white bra was exposed to him. Dipping his head down, he ran his mouth over her silky skin, pulling the material away until he could take her nipple into his mouth.

Her fingers sank into his hair, holding him to her breasts.

"Brent," she sighed as she wrapped her legs around his hips.

"I want you," he said against her skin. "Don't make me beg."

"No," she said softly, "I'm the one begging."

He doubted there would be any returning to normalcy

after he'd had a taste of her. The more he was with her, the more he wanted to be with her. Not just like this, with her panting underneath him, but in every aspect of life.

He knew that if he wasn't careful, he was bound to hurt her, even though he'd promised he wouldn't. His entire life he'd been a screw up. He just wasn't built for happiness. It wasn't in his cards. At least he hadn't thought so.

But now that Mel was here... He looked down into her hazel eyes and watched desire flood them as she reached up for him. He knew without a doubt that she was his one shot at happiness. He just needed to make sure that he didn't fuck it up.

CHAPTER 16

Mel couldn't stop herself from wanting Brent. She'd come upstairs for a quick break. Her back was hurting her from being on her feet all day, but more importantly, she had wanted to check up on him.

She'd been slightly surprised to see Brent fast asleep on the sofa in the television room when she'd come upstairs. She'd spent a few moments just looking down at him.

His dark hair fell over his forehead, and somehow he looked even more handsome with the black eye and scratched chin. Maybe it was because she knew he'd been a little vulnerable or maybe because she knew that he'd chosen not to fight back. That was something Ethan would have never done.

The stupid thing was, she'd fallen for Ethan since he'd been the strong controlling type. Man, had she been such a fool. She'd believed that he would take care of her, watch out for her. Never in her wildest imagination had she believed that he'd turn and control her instead.

Everything she'd said or done, he'd been there, hovering

over her, criticizing, accusing, and yelling at her for the choices she made.

She hadn't known Brent all that long, but there was no doubt in her mind that he wasn't that kind of man. Not after the conversations she'd had with his sister and everyone else that knew him.

Dylan had been honest with her about her brother's past struggles, none of which Mel could judge too harshly, since she'd had a few of her own struggles.

But when she was around him or when he started kissing her, she melted against him and everything was forgotten except for the way he made her feel.

It was as if her body had a mind of its own. The more he touched her, the more she opened for him. Her legs wrapped around his hips, pulling him closer, needing to feel his hardness against her.

It had been a long time since she'd felt this much about anything or anyone. Her hands shook when she reached for the snap of his jeans. She'd already gently removed his shirt and quickly assessed the bruising over his ribs. He was blue and purple, but she noticed that he wasn't hissing with pain when he moved like before.

When they were finally skin to skin, she doubted that she could wait much longer to feel him inside her. The anticipation of being with him was almost more than she could bear.

He hovered over her, but instead of gliding into her, he held there, looking down at her.

"Mel," he frowned, "what does that stand for? Melony?"

She tensed and her instinct to pull away, to run, flashed quickly in her mind.

"You don't have to tell me if you don't want to," he said, leaning in and kissing her until she relaxed again.

"Soon you'll trust me enough to let me in. I want to know who I'm making love to," he said between kisses.

"Brent." She nudged him until he slid into her. Part of her wanted to tell him her name, tell him everything else she'd kept from him, but the fear kept her from speaking.

Instead, she held on to him and enjoyed the moments she had, knowing that someday they too would come to an end like the rest of the good days she'd had.

After she'd dressed again, she left Brent upstairs and headed back downstairs to help with the after-dinner cleanup. She hadn't been stretching the truth when she'd told him there had been a line out front earlier.

Even now, there were a handful of people standing out front, waiting for tables. When she stepped out the back hallway door, the patio area was full as well.

She made a mental note to talk to Brent about the possibility of making a designated smoking section, as several people had suggested it or complained about the smoke.

There were also a handful of other suggestions she wanted to talk to him about, but she figured they could wait until he was feeling better.

Just before closing, she glanced towards the front door and froze. Seeing the man in uniform walk in the door had her pulse jumping. She couldn't stop the panic from almost consuming her, even though the man looked nothing like Ethan. Ethan had been fair skinned with curly blond hair and a lean but athletic build. Dale Alaqua was taller and had jet-black hair and darker skin that showed his heritage. His arms were the size of tree trunks. Yet when she'd spoken to him at the party the other day, he'd been kind and funny. But he hadn't been wearing his uniform then, and she hadn't been intimidated by him like she was now, as he walked up to the bar and talked to his cousin.

It was the uniform more than the man himself that had her shaking. Since Ethan, she'd never been able to look at a police officer without fear.

She had to take several deep breaths before she could walk over and talk to him.

"Evening," she said, trying to sound casual.

Dale turned to her and smiled. "Good evening. Mel, right?" he asked her, and she could have sworn that her heart stopped beating.

"Yes," she said, trying not to hold her breath. "Did you get the guys who attacked Brent?" she asked, hoping he would relay the information quickly and leave.

Instead, the man leaned against the counter and took the soda Jamie had set in front of him.

"Sort of," he said after a sip. "How's he doing?" the man asked, running his eyes over her.

"He's resting. He has a black eye, bruised ribs, and his chin looks like it went through a shredder," she supplied.

"Well, Everett and Matthew Phillips, father and brother to Mark, previous owner of this building, are sitting down in my jail cell at the moment. But by the time I'm done drinking this Coke, chances are that they'll be out on bond." He shook his head. "I'll want to get Brent's official statement, for the records and all."

"Right, I can—"

He stopped her by raising his hand. "No rush." He glanced around. "It looks like you guys have been busy," he said, changing the subject.

"Yes." She felt her nerves almost exploding.

His eyes narrowed and he leaned closer.

"Is it the uniform? Most women find it an added bonus." His smile almost doubled. "But you seem downright jumpy around me right now. We had a nice conversation a day ago when I was in civilian clothing, so I have to figure it's the uniform."

She swallowed and figured a hint at the truth was good enough.

"My ex is a cop," she said.

Dale winced. "That bad, huh?"

Nodding, she motioned for Jamie to get her a water.

"Well, I won't keep you from your work. Tell Brent I'll be around tomorrow to get his statement. I'm going to head back to the kitchen and see what I can beg off my sister," he said with a chuckle. Then he leaned closer and lowered his voice. "Not all cops are asses, like I assume your ex is." Without waiting for a reply, he walked back into the kitchen.

She kept herself busy until the last customer walked out the front door. Then she locked the door and turned around to cheers.

A glass of wine was put in her hands by Jamie.

"What's this for?" she asked, smiling.

"To a successful first day. Even without the boss man," TK said. "We did it." TK held up her glass and everyone cheered. She laughed and then took a sip of the wine.

She hadn't expected everyone to hang out after they finished cleaning up, but they did, and the more she hung around them, the more it became apparent that everyone already knew one another.

"If this keeps up, we'll beat out the Moose as the most popular place to eat in town," Jamie said.

"Eventually, the newness will wear off. Trust me," TK added. "People are just excited about some new options."

"Especially the wings." Everyone glanced over as Brent walked into the room.

"Ouch," TK said. "You look like…"

"I got jumped in the parking lot by two men twice my size?" Brent offered.

"Yeah." Jamie sighed. "How are you feeling?"

"Like I got jumped in the parking lot by two men twice my size," Brent said with a shrug. "I could use a beer."

Jamie stepped behind the bar and grabbed a beer, opened it, and slid it down the slick countertop.

"You did a fine job with this beauty," she said, wiping the bar top with a rag.

"Thanks," Brent said after a sip.

Mel noticed that, after Brent showed up, some of the employees had shuffled back to the kitchen. She thought they'd left, but a few moments later, they returned with a tray full of food.

To her surprise, everyone sat around the tables and shared leftovers while they talked about the day.

It surprised her, seeing how everyone acted. Like one big family. They laughed, joked, and even hassled one another. She had to admit that it was nice.

She brought up the few changes she'd thought of to Brent as they ate, such as hanging a few flat-screen televisions behind the bar for patrons to watch sports on.

She also mentioned a few issues she'd come across, like the lack of trash cans behind the bar. There was one, but it wasn't big enough to hold all the trash created during a shift, and she'd watched Jamie empty it more than half a dozen times during the lunch rush.

She lost track of how long everyone sat around talking about improvements that could be made around the place. Brent considered each and every idea and even suggested an immediate change.

When people started leaving, she overheard Jamie saying to her sister that she appreciated a boss who actually listened to them for once.

"You made an impression," she told Brent once they were finally alone.

His dark eyebrows shot up. "How so?"

"I think everyone appreciated that you listened to their ideas."

"Why wouldn't I? I want to keep them and the customers happy." He glanced around. "Besides, they had some really great ideas." He motioned to the bar. "I don't know why I didn't think of hanging a few televisions up back there myself," he said with a slight sigh. She could see that he was tired. His eyes were dull. Well, at least his right eye was. His left one was still almost completely shut.

"Dale stopped by earlier," she blurted out.

"Oh?" He glanced at her. "What did he have to say?"

"That Everett and Matthew Phillips were probably going to be out on bail tonight."

He nodded. "I figured as much. I was never in for long myself," he said with a half smile.

She gave him a surprised look. "Have a lot of experience with being arrested?"

His smile slipped slightly. "A few times in my past. I used to get in trouble a lot. Nothing serious, but..." He smiled again. "Dylan was always there to bail me out." His eyes met hers. "I can't believe how lucky I've been to have her all this time."

She felt her heart jump in her chest and her knees turn to jelly at his admission of love towards his sister. How was it that she had come to trust this man so quickly? What they had between them wasn't anything like what she'd had with Ethan.

The more she looked back on their relationship, the more she realized Ethan had pursued her and had hidden everything from her. Brent was anything but guarded. Every aspect of his past and his life was right there in front of her.

Just looking into his eyes she could see how far he would go to safeguard against the destructive behavior Ethan had engaged in. She doubted that Brent would even raise his voice towards her.

He stood up suddenly and walked over to dump his

empty beer bottle in the trash can. Then he turned to her. "Since I probably won't be up to a hike tomorrow, what do you say we head into Helena and do some shopping. It appears I'll need some new trash cans and a few television sets."

She thought about the few items she'd like to get, now that she had a paycheck, and nodded. "What are the chances of me getting an advance?" she asked him.

He smiled. "I think after today, you proved your worth." His eyes narrowed suddenly. "Did we ever decide on just how much I was paying you?"

She laughed as she shook her head. "I think we were both too desperate."

He laughed as he walked over to her and helped her stand up. "I'll agree with that." He kissed her lightly. "But I'll have to be honest with you. When it comes to being with you, I'm still very desperate."

CHAPTER 17

By the time they climbed the stairs after locking up downstairs, he was exhausted. He'd thought that heading downstairs after closing time would allow him to release the burst of energy he'd felt after being with Mel. He'd had no idea it would drain him completely instead.

Then again, the wings and the beer probably had helped.

"You look tired," Mel said in the hallway.

"I am," he admitted, then he turned to her. He noticed her eyes darting to her own bedroom and suddenly a flash of fear raced through him. Was she trying to pull away so soon? What would he do if she decided she wanted to revert back to being just friends and coworkers?

"I… I'd like a shower or a hot bath to soak in," she said, looking a little embarrassed. He relaxed instantly and pulled her into his arms.

"You deserve to relax," he said after brushing his lips across hers. "If you want to crawl in my bed after, I won't kick you out," he said, trying to keep things light between them.

The smile she returned assured him his words had done the trick.

He turned to go into his room as she disappeared into her own. Tugging off his clothes, he fell face-first into bed and didn't wake again until the sunlight hit his eyelids, turning everything pink and red.

"We get to sleep in today, remember?" Mel's soft voice said after he shifted to get up. Hearing it, he rolled over to pull her into his arms instead.

"Morning," he said into her hair. She smelled like his shampoo and her hair was still a little damp. The rest of her was plastered against him, soft and feeling so damned sexy that parts of his body instantly woke.

"Good morning," she said with a slight purr.

Just as he was leaning in for a kiss, he heard his phone buzz and realized the vibration from it had been the thing that had woken him up in the first place.

"Sorry," he said, reaching over to answer it. Seeing his sister's number he answered it quickly. "Morning."

"Brent?" Dylan's voice was off, and he sat up, instantly worried.

"What's wrong?" he asked, concerned.

"Bella was acting funny," Dylan said. "We're down at the clinic. She didn't look right. They're running tests." His sister sniffled.

"We'll be down there in five," he said. He quickly pulled on the clothes he'd tossed off last night.

Mel seemed to guess something was wrong and rushed out of bed into the other room to get dressed.

She met him at the base of the stairs less than two minutes later.

"Bella?" she asked.

"Yeah, she was acting funny and looked off," he said as they rushed towards the door together.

Fifteen minutes later, they walked into the clinic. They talked with Gail briefly while they waited for the doctor to come out and tell them something. The rest of the McGowans were either already there or just showing up and asking questions.

Gail had quickly told them that Trey had said Bella had started fussing in the middle of the night and had a slight fever. Shortly after eating breakfast, she had puked up everything and then gone limp in Dylan's arms.

"That's when they rushed her down here," Gail said. "Trey and Dylan are back there with Bella. I came out to fill everyone in on what's happening. I should probably get back there," Gail added, looking tired and worried. "To see if they know anything more."

Everyone stood around the small waiting area without saying anything. It was if everyone was holding their breath until they heard how Bella was doing.

He couldn't imagine life without his little niece in it. She was less than a week old and had already pierced his heart.

He hated the thought of anything bad happening to her and knew that, if it did, Dylan and Trey would be crushed. The entire McGowan family would be.

Just then, Trey came out, his eyes red from worry. Brent felt his heart jump in his chest.

"She's okay," Trey said with a slight smile. "They've gotten the fever down and they're telling us that it's jaundice." He looked relieved as he hugged his brothers. "They want to keep us overnight but they're pretty sure she's okay."

He shook Trey's hands and then stood there while the man hugged him, like he'd hugged his own brothers.

"Dylan wants you to go back for a quick visit," Trey said. "Room one-eleven."

Brent glanced over at Mel.

"Go, I'll be here. You drove, remember?" she said with a smile.

"Right." He nodded and turned to walk down the hallway.

When he stepped into the private room, Gail stood up and touched Dylan's shoulder. "We'll run and grab you some breakfast and be back soon," she said to Dylan and then she left.

He walked over and looked down at his niece, fast asleep in a hospital crib. Dylan sat close to the crib, looking down at her child.

"How's she doing?" he asked quietly.

"She's finally sleeping," she said with a slight sigh. "They gave her some intravenous fluids that had her screaming." Dylan reached up and wiped a tear from her face. "I couldn't stand hearing her cry in pain." His sister's eyes searched his. "It about broke me."

He pulled his sister up into his arms and held her while she cried quietly. "I don't know what I'd do if anything happened to her."

"I know," he said as he brushed his sister's hair with his fingers, a move he'd done all of his life. "She's going to make it through this."

"I know," she said with a sigh. "She has the best of us and the McGowans." She smiled slightly, looking up at him. "Besides, she takes after her uncle."

"Smart? Good-looking?" he said quickly.

Dylan chuckled as he wiped the tears from her face. "She's stubborn. Like you are." She reached up and touched his face gently. "Hard to put down."

"We're both strong," he agreed.

"This isn't your first black eye, but it is the first one you didn't do anything to deserve," she said.

"Yeah."

"I wanted to go down and punch the Phillipses myself when I heard what they'd done to you," Dylan said.

He smiled. "I bet you could've taken them both."

She chuckled then sighed. "Keep a lookout for them. I doubt this will stop them from sniffing around."

"Yeah," he agreed. "I was going to head into the city and buy some more cameras for the place. I wouldn't put it past them to try and burn the place down."

"If they can't have it…" Dylan shook her head. "Yeah, I can see that."

Bella made a soft sound and they both turned to look down at her.

"They want to keep us overnight," Dylan said.

"I heard. Do you need anything?"

"No, Gail and Trisha are going to go grab us some stuff. Along with some food." She turned to him. "It's your first day off." Her eyes narrowed. "With Mel."

He smiled. "Yeah."

"Go." She nudged his shoulder, and he winced. "Sorry. Go have fun. She'll probably sleep all day."

He bent down and placed a soft kiss on his sister's forehead, then did the same to his niece.

"Let me know if anything changes," he said.

"We will. Thanks for coming."

He nodded and then turned and left just as Trey was coming back into the room.

"How are they doing?" Mel asked when he stepped back into the waiting area.

"Good. Bella is sleeping and Dylan…" He shrugged. "She's worried but happy that they figured out that it wasn't anything too serious."

"That's good," Mel said.

"What do you say we head out and grab some food, then

head into town to do our shopping? Dylan said she'd call or text if anything changes."

"Are you sure?"

"Yeah." He took her hand in his and started towards the door but stopped to talk to both Tyler and Trent before finally leaving.

"It must be nice," Mel said once they were in the truck, "being part of a family that actually cares."

He glanced over at her. In his youth, he'd been lucky to have his parents. Not that they had been perfect, but they had never shown him or Dylan anything but love and kindness. Even though they'd left them to their own devices for the most part, they'd always been there when they were needed. Sure, they'd fucked up royally in planning for their children's futures, but until then, they had given them a wonderful life.

From what Mel had told him about her childhood, she hadn't had any of that. Not really.

He reached over and took her hand in his. "They've been great and have adopted Dylan into their fold."

"And you as well," Mel pointed out.

He thought about it and then nodded. "Yeah, I guess so."

He headed towards the donut shop, figuring he'd need the sugar boost for the day.

When they parked out front, he spotted Darla sitting at a table just inside the large windows. He thought of turning around and leaving, but then Mel said, "Is that Darla?"

He held in a sigh of frustration and nodded. "We can go somewhere else," he suggested.

"No, it's a small town. You can't always run away when you see your ex. Besides, it might be a good thing for her to see that you've moved on," she suggested. He glanced at Mel and saw her chin rise slightly.

"I'm game if you are." He took her hand and brought it up to his lips to brush a kiss across her knuckles. "Let's do this."

He jumped out and rushed around to open her door, something he had never done for Darla or anyone else he'd dated before.

When they walked into the bakery, hand in hand, he avoided glancing over to where Darla was sitting. Instead, he focused on placing their orders and paying.

Then they found a seat at the countertop while they waited.

"I bet it's killing her," Mel said quietly.

"I think she's long over me," he admitted. "It's been two years or…" He shrugged. "About that long."

Mel glanced around like she was looking at the place, then looked back at him. "She's not looking over here. I'd wager she's moved on as well."

He thought about how Darla kept showing up everywhere he was and realized that what Mel had said was true. It was a small town. How had he expected not to run into her all the time? Now he felt like a fool for thinking that bumping into her was anything but a coincidence. After all, when he'd broken things off with her, it wasn't as if she'd come back begging for his attention.

She'd been working at the strip club back then and had quickly moved on to dating… Well, he didn't know whom she'd dated, since he'd left town shortly after. Still, there had been rumors. Lots of rumors regarding Darla. Most of them had her moving to Helena into a rehab center there. Others had her heading to Vegas to dance on the big stage or gamble her life's savings away or to marry a millionaire and take all his money.

Whatever the case, he figured it was better for him to steer clear of her since they had been a pretty toxic mix when they'd been together.

They were just finishing up their breakfast when Darla stepped over to the counter and got his attention.

"Hi, I know this is a bad time, but I was hoping to talk to you," Darla said.

"Darla, I don't think…" he started, but she held up a hand.

"Sorry." She stopped him. "Not you, Brent. I was talking to Mel." Her eyes turned to Mel. "I hear you're still short a few hands and wanted to turn in my resume. I've worked behind the bar a few times before and am looking for something… different than what I did last time I was in town."

"I don't think…" he started again, but this time Mel stopped him by putting a hand on his arm.

"Why don't you stop by sometime tomorrow?" Mel suggested. "Maybe just before we open? I'll be around and we can talk then."

Darla smiled and nodded. "Thanks," she said, and then her eyes turned to him. "I… need to talk to you sometime too. About private matters."

It was then that he noticed the fear in her eyes, a look that had never been there before. Before he knew what he was doing, he nodded in agreement.

"Thanks." Darla touched his arm and then nodded to Mel. "I'll see you tomorrow. Thank you," she said again and then left.

"That was…" Mel started.

"Strange," he finished. "So unlike Darla."

"Everyone's allowed to change," she said softly. It made him want to ask her questions, but she stood up and dusted off her pants. "We'd better head out if we're going to getting everything that we need in one trip."

CHAPTER 18

The drive into the city didn't take as long as she'd expected. Maybe it was because the conversation with Brent was light and enjoyable. They talked about everything from their childhoods to other changes they wanted to make around the bar and grill.

Their first stop in the city was at an electronics store, where she helped him pick out two large flat-screen televisions to go behind the bar. The second stop was to a huge hardware store, where they purchased large garbage cans as well as some smaller items that had been on everyone's lists.

At this point, Brent suggested lunch and she almost laughed, until she realized she was hungry as well. Since he knew the town better than she did, she let him pick a family Mexican restaurant and had some of the best enchiladas that she'd had in years, as well as a margarita.

"What about themed nights?" she suggested as they were finishing up.

"Themed?"

"You know, a variety of foods like this." She motioned to her empty plate. "Mexican, Italian, American and so on."

"Not bad. TK definitely has a wide range of cooking skills. We can bring it up tomorrow. Although, I think the wings are the biggest hit by far."

She smiled. "They are indeed. I think everyone in town really likes the entire atmosphere of the place. The outdoor patio is a huge hit."

"For now." He chuckled. "Come winter we'll have to shut it down."

"With the firepits you built, there will still be some people strong enough to brave the elements," she added. "Especially if we offer hot drinks—hot chocolate, hot rum toddies, and such. Along with some hot appetizers."

"Everything is hot." He laughed.

"I mean spicy." She smiled. "Spicy wings, jalapeno poppers, those sorts of things."

"I like it."

In her mind, she could already see people enjoying the area. "Of course, we'll need to make sure they don't get snowed on."

"I've been thinking of adding an awning or some sort of overhang to keep the sun off the deck. We can build it strong enough to hold the snow load," Brent said.

"One of the old restaurants I used to go to in the city had those tent-like walls they put up in the winter to keep the heat in."

"Not a bad idea." He nodded. "Then again, we could always build on to the main dining area. There is enough land. Actually, I have about a dozen acres behind the main building."

"What are you planning to do with the land?" she asked, curious as to what he saw in his future.

"I'm not really sure. I guess eventually I'll build a home. Maybe on the back of the land?" He tilted his head as if he was thinking about it. "I think my land actually butts up against the tree line. It would be a pretty choice spot to have my own place back there."

She thought about the beautiful field that separated the bar and grill from the trees along the hillside and nodded. She could just imagine a very masculine log cabin home nestled amongst the trees, much like the places she'd seen all over Haven.

How many times in the past few days had she caught herself dreaming about living in such a place? Settling down and putting down roots finally.

If only. The more she dreamed about it, the more she realized that there was no way she could chance staying still for that long.

Sooner or later, she'd slip and hint to her parents where she was or, worse, do something to call attention to herself. And then Ethan would be looking for her again, stalking her, most likely in the night and under the cover of his badge and the law.

"You turned quiet," Brent said as they walked out towards his truck.

"Just… thinking," she admitted.

"About?"

"My future." She tried to sound casual. "For the past few years, I've never been really free to think any farther than a few months ahead."

"And now?"

She leaned her head back against the seat and thought about it. "Now I'm too afraid to make waves. To try anything new for fear that I'll get his attention again."

"It was that bad?" he asked.

She turned and looked at him, wishing she could tell him everything. They'd promised to be truthful with one another, but that didn't mean she'd open up and tell him all the raw bits.

"I'm not looking to attend any family reunions," she admitted dryly. "Or any holidays."

"Then, what? Just avoid your family for the rest of your life?"

"That's the plan," she answered as he started to drive. "Where to now?" she asked, hoping to change the subject.

"Now," he said, thinking about it for a moment, "we head wherever you want to go." He turned towards her. "I'm pretty sure we got everything off my list. It's your turn to do some shopping."

She felt her heart melt slightly. When was the last time she'd gone shopping for anything for herself? How long had it been? Years. Since before her marriage to Ethan. When she'd had her own money. Well, her parents' money that they had graciously given her just as long as she obeyed their rules and lived the way they wanted her to. Which had all ended the moment she'd divorced Ethan.

"Where to?" Brent asked.

She thought about the things she'd wanted over the past few years and, somehow, she no longer cared about any of it. Instead, she thought about getting some pretty underthings to wear for Brent as well as a few necessities she'd needed for a while.

"How about a Target?" she asked, knowing she wanted to try and save most of the money Brent had advanced her to pay for her truck's repairs.

"Target it is." He pulled out of the parking lot.

They walked inside the big store, and he grabbed a cart and followed her around. It was the first time in her entire life that she'd ever felt normal shopping with a man.

Ethan had never allowed her to shop for anything, let alone have a good time with her in a store. Instead, she'd followed him around and cringed at the items he'd thrown in their cart.

Since Ethan had only allowed her to pick items such as toothbrushes and hair combs, she hadn't gotten to just pick things for herself until after the divorce. Even now, it felt foreign to her. She kept expecting Ethan to walk around the corner and yell at her for picking items that were stupid or not up to his standards, something he'd said often when he didn't like whatever she'd picked out.

Instead, Brent joked with her and even threw in a couple items of his own—a package of boxer briefs, some socks. When she went to the shampoo aisle, he disappeared and came back with a box of condoms. He gave her a sly sexy look that had her smiling when he tossed them into the cart.

After checking out, they started the drive back to Haven. She couldn't believe how tired she was and felt herself nodding off several times. It was nice being with someone and not feeling the pressure to talk all of the time.

She allowed herself to drift off to sleep and woke only when the truck turned off. Blinking a few times, she turned and saw Brent looking off into the field behind the bar and grill.

"I'll have to meet with the lawyer to see just how far the land stretches, but I think all that is mine." He glanced at her. "Plenty of room to grow."

She stretched slightly and asked. "What would you do with the rooms?" She glanced behind them at the main building.

"Like I said, rent them out." He shrugged. "Or revamp the entire building and somehow turn them into more space for the dining room." He turned and looked behind them. "Someone who knows more about construction could possibly figure out how to do that."

She glanced over at him and noticed that his swollen eye was almost completely back to normal, except for the color. He'd gotten a couple looks in the store when they'd been walking around together, and when she suggested he put on some sunglasses, he'd shrugged and told her that it didn't really matter.

It was another example of how different Brent was from her ex. Ethan had cared so much what others thought that he had gone out of his way to not argue in public.

He'd found plenty of other ways of controlling her in and out of the public's eye. The main one had been the hand squeeze, which had usually meant that, when they were finally alone, she would have to sit through at least an hour of listening to him explain just how she'd embarrassed him.

Having him tear her down until she was raw emotionally and mentally was somehow worse in her opinion than the times that he'd physically hurt her. The physical pain disappeared more quickly. It was the emotional pain that clung to her and was much harder to get over.

"You've disappeared again," Brent said softly as he took her hand in his. "I notice you do that a lot. Part of me wants to ask you why, but I know better than to ask until you're ready to tell me more."

"There isn't much more to tell," she said, feeling too drained to go into any further details at the moment.

His eyes scanned hers, and she knew he could see through the lie.

"How about we take all this inside and see what we can scrounge up for dinner?" he suggested.

She helped him carry in all their purchases. While she carried the few bags of their personal items upstairs, he put the televisions in the office until he could hang them up behind the bar. Then they decided on a spot for the trash cans behind the bar together. It was nice having a man listen to her opinions. They found a large pan of lasagna in the fridge and heated up a couple plates to take outside under the stars.

They sat at one of the tables with candlelight and hanging lights overhead and ate dinner and drank some really good red wine while he talked about the possibility of doing something more with his land.

She doubted that she could think of a better day than what she'd just spent with Brent. She'd felt so carefree. But the real joy of it was just knowing that he had enjoyed being with her in return.

The more she thought about how wonderful her time with Brent was, the more she wanted to be around him. But the truth was, she'd felt that way about Ethan at first as well.

Just reminding herself of that kept her from exposing too much of her heart, which she was finding more and more difficult as the days rolled by.

"You're quiet again," he said as they sat by the firepit after finishing their dinner.

"It's a quiet sort of spot," she replied as his arm wrapped around her shoulder and pulled her closer.

"That it is," he said with a sigh. "My sister called when you were upstairs. Bella is back to one hundred percent. They actually let them go home already."

"That's good news." She glanced up at him. "I know you were worried all day."

He nodded. "Dylan and I were texting one another more today than normal."

"It must be nice, being so close."

"It is now." He brushed a hand up her arm until he cupped her face. "Thank you for today."

She smiled and melted against his chest. "I should be the one thanking you. You've done so much for me since I came into town. I'm lucky you came along when you did. I would have hated to have to hurt that old man."

"Jimmy," he supplied. "In case I haven't mentioned it, that move you did on him was sexy as hell."

"Jiujitsu," she said with a slight shrug.

"No kidding?" He sat up slightly. "Did you take classes?"

"Yes." She smiled. "Krav Maga too."

"Hell." He ran his green eyes over her, and she watched something close to pride flood the green pools. "You could always show me some of your moves," he offered.

"Think you can take me?" she teased, and he laughed.

"Hell no, but it would be fun trying." His smile was back as he reached to pull her close.

She easily dodged his hands, pinning them above his head as she climbed onto his lap, holding him back against the bench.

"Like I said, sexy as hell," he said in a soft whisper. "What are you going to do with me now?" His eyes darted down to her lips. The smile was instant on her lips as she felt her entire body heat against his.

She started rubbing her jean clad body against the hardness of him that pressed against her core.

Then her eyes met his, and she lessened her hold on him.

"I haven't decided yet," she admitted just before she kissed him.

CHAPTER 19

*D*ays turned into weeks. The only major thing that changed was the fact that Mel had hired Darla to wait tables and help Jamie behind the bar. Since he wanted to trust her opinions, he stayed out of the way and tried to avoid Darla as much as he could.

Which wasn't as hard as he'd thought. Actually, it wasn't until her second week working there that he'd realized the big change in her. For one, she didn't smoke or drink anymore.

She was actually friendly and showed up to work on time and stayed until after closing time to help clean up. Mel had commented on several occasions how well Darla was doing and even hinted that he should have that sit-down talk with her that she'd asked him for.

Still, he continued to avoid it, wondering if it was all a ruse. He didn't doubt that people could change, but Darla? He would need more proof than this.

Mel had a little more freedom since they'd gone and picked up her truck from the shop. She often ran on supply runs and was more confident now that her truck was, according to her, purring like a kitten.

This freed his time up, and he used it to start building the awnings over the decking area. Since he didn't want to interrupt the customers enjoying their meals, he was stuck having to work early in the mornings.

The best part of the last few weeks had been that the joint seemed to always be packed. From the time they opened the doors to the time they locked them again, people packed in and enjoyed TK's cooking or drank beers while watching sports on the new TV sets he'd hung.

Game days were always fun, and, since he wasn't really needed to run the place, he spent most of it behind the bar, helping Jamie. He, of course, left the fancy drink orders to her while he stuck to opening bottles of beer or pouring drafts. Mel often helped out with delivering meals or clearing tables.

The day after Bella had been released from the hospital, he'd gone to visit her and Dylan. He must have sat for more than an hour, holding his sleeping niece. Never had he expected to fall in love with her so quickly. She was so tiny, so perfect. He knew there wasn't anything he wouldn't do to protect her or Dylan.

He made his visits more frequent over time and ended up having a lunch with them at least twice a week.

Since Mel and TK had taken over the running of the Hard Way, he figured the less he was in their hair the better.

Nights, after everyone left and the place sat dark, were his favorite times. He and Mel usually sat out around the firepit and watched the stars. He'd purchased more patio furniture, including a large sofa where they spent most of their time.

He honestly couldn't believe he'd gotten so lucky as to have her in his life. He doubted he would have enjoyed sticking in Haven as much if it wasn't for her.

She still struggled opening up to him and, as time passed, he could tell she was hiding something deeper from him. But every time he tried to bring up her past, she would shut down completely and, for hours after, she'd sulk around the place. So he avoided bringing up the subject.

The only time he'd gotten a hint at what she'd been through was the day she'd opened up to him about her ex in the kitchen. Still, she'd confessed enough that he understood the hell she'd gone through.

He wanted to do some research on her ex and her parents but was beginning to doubt that she'd given him her real name. The biggest sign of that fact was that she requested he pay her in cash. When he suggested she open a checking account at the local bank, she had paled slightly. He'd agreed to pay her however she wanted, but told her that, to keep the books on the up and up, he'd have to keep track of the payments for tax purposes.

He'd talked to Don, his lawyer, about expanding the bar and grill or building his own home on the back of the land. The man had immediately had his land surveyed. He had just gotten back from the lawyer's small office on the other side of town and had the survey in his hands. He parked beside Mel's truck.

She was out on the patio, clearing a table, when he walked over to her. She'd gained a soft glow to her skin from the sun from working outside, and he'd noticed that she'd stopped jumping at shadows. At this point, she probably knew more people's names in town than he did.

"So?" she asked, shielding her eyes from the sun. He stepped around her so that she didn't have to squint. "What did he say?"

"Our counter injunction against the Phillips's initial injunction has won out. The judge ruled out any ownership the Phillipses had on this place," he answered with a smile.

"So, it's yours once again?" she asked with a smile.

"It is."

"Did you get the survey then?"

"Yes." He held up the folder and motioned with his head. "I thought you'd want to take a break and walk around my land with me."

She set the tray of dirty dishes down and wiped her hands. "Let's do it. Ed can finish this."

They stepped off the porch, and he pulled out the survey and tilted his head as he tried to figure out which way it went. In the lawyer's office, he'd stopped himself from looking at it. He wanted Mel to be there with him when he did.

"Here is the road." Mel pointed to the map. "Let's start there." She pointed to the corner of the lot.

They walked towards the front of the property and he frowned down at the map when he realized part of the parking area wasn't on his land.

"Looks like we'll need to move some of the parking area," he said.

"No, see." Mel took the map from him. "We aren't even at the corner yet." She started walking towards a fence line that was half fallen down. He'd believed the fence had been his property line, which is why he'd kept the parking area inside it. When Mel climbed over the wood fence and kept going, he followed her. "This is it," she said, stopping by a small orange flag on the end of a wood stick. "See, the survey crew left the stakes here to show the corners of your land." She held up her hands and shielded her eyes. "There's the other one." She motioned across the parking area along the road. Sure enough, on the far end of his building sat another stake. "This is the front northeastern corner. That's the southeast one, and we'll find the western markers out along the tree line." She pointed towards the field.

"It's wider than I thought." He looked between the two front markers. "We could expand the parking area. People won't have to park on the grass."

She smiled. "You could even put up a free-standing sign. Something to draw people in," she suggested.

"Let's check the back markers," he suggested, and they started walking together through the field. "The old hotel rooms used to be in the shape of a U," he said as they walked along.

"The foundations are still here." She stepped over the old cement. "Wiring, plumbing. It all probably needs to be updated, but if you wanted to rebuild…" She dropped off and stopped as they stood in the middle of the U shape. "You could do a nice B&B or…" She shrugged and tilted her head. "Maybe an RV park. You know, like the campsite kind. Put a swimming pool in the middle, some swing sets for the kids. People are starting to love camping again."

"That's not a bad idea," he admitted, and in his mind, he already saw the idea clearly. "When I was eight, my parents bought a travel trailer. You know, the old silver kind that looks like something out of an old family movie."

"Airstream?"

"Yeah, that's the kind. Anyway, we spent a whole summer going from state park to state park." He smiled, remembering the fun they'd had.

"What happened?"

"Dad grew bored. After he found out that he had to pay several hundred dollars to store the thing, since we couldn't park it in our driveway, he sold it," he said with a sigh.

"The state park isn't far from here," she said, looking towards the hills. He'd taken her hiking there on their last day off. They'd spent an entire day walking the trails and enjoying a picnic TK had made for them while they looked out over the town from above.

"The campgrounds are always full this time of year. I bet we could have this place packed out quickly. We'd just need to have some minimal work done. Electric, plumbing." He started thinking about what would need to be done to the place. "A pool would be a nice touch," he admitted. "Maybe a hot tub?"

"Ah, I haven't sat in a hot tub in years." She rolled her shoulders. "I bet most people coming back from a full day's hike would love to soak in a hot tub."

"Okay, you've sold me on the idea," he said, taking her hand. "Now, let's finish seeing just how much land we have."

He hadn't realized his slip, until he felt her tense next to him. Glancing over, he replayed his words and held in a wince. Trying to be casual about it, he tugged her until they started walking again.

"If there's enough, I'd still like to build a place back here," he said, chatting on about how he'd like a home away from work. As they continued to walk, he felt her relax more and figured she'd forgotten about his slip. He hadn't meant anything by it, but whenever he thought of this place, he thought of it as theirs. After all, she'd done just about as much work to make it happen as he had.

Actually, now that the doors were open, she was probably doing more work than he was. Sure, he pulled out his hammer and repaired things or made whatever they needed, but she was the one doing all of the ordering, bill paying, and dealing with employees while he just did stupid manual labor.

"It's bigger than you thought," Mel said, breaking into his thoughts.

"Hm?" he asked, returning to the now in his mind. They had walked to the edge of the trees, and she was frowning down at the survey. "See the markers?" She motioned to the trees. "They're on the other side of the hill."

He glanced through the trees and saw the orange flags through the thick brush about halfway up the hillside.

They were standing on the edge of the tree line. There was a small dip that rolled down towards a creek that separated them from the other side of a larger hill. The side of the hill that held his markers.

"You probably have enough land on the other side of the creek to build yourself a place over there," she suggested.

He glanced down at her work clothes and his good jeans and knew that they couldn't cross the creek dressed like this.

"We could go change and take a look at it now?" she offered.

"No, we'll do it later. For now, we know there's more land over there. Besides, I skipped lunch." He took her hand again, and they started walking back. "We can start coming up with a plan for the RV park."

"Sure, I can come up with a budget. We'll need to get some quotes for electric and plumbing," she said and continued to talk about what would have to be done as they walked back.

They took a lunch break together, sitting out on the crowded patio while eating chicken sandwiches. He enjoyed the way Mel made lists of items that would have to be looked into to make their next project come true.

Since he figured his sister knew about permits and dealing with the town's regulations more than he did, he sent her a text message and asked her to look into that portion of the business.

He shot a text message to Don and asked him which part of the land was still zoned for commercial use. He'd forgotten to ask the man if the back portion could be used for a private residence, and asked him in the text message now, after Mel reminded him to.

"I don't know what I would do if you weren't around," he

admitted when they were done eating. "I mean, I would have obviously had to hire someone to do what you do around here, but I doubt Haven has anyone as capable as you."

He had meant his statement to be a compliment but when a worried look crossed her eyes, he reached out and touched her hand.

"That was meant as a compliment," he said softly.

"I know." She sighed. "It's just…" She glanced away from him. "I've been thinking."

He felt his heart sink to the bottom of his gut as fear of her leaving surfaced.

Just then his phone chimed with his lawyer's response.

"Go on, read it." Mel motioned to his phone. "I should get back to work anyway." She stood up and started to clear their table.

He stopped her by taking her hand. "Later?"

She nodded and then left. He sat there for almost a full minute before he finally looked down at the message.

"Yes, the front part of the land is zoned commercial, the back five acres are residential. You could very well open an RV park on the land behind the bar and grill. There are some codes you'll want to watch out for. We can go over them the next time we meet."

He set his phone down and glanced out at the field behind the place. The view alone was worth a lot to him, and he knew that if he set aside some of the land for an RV park, people would probably pay to stay there just for the same view.

It would be an added bonus that they had a place where families could sit down and eat meals. If he added a swimming pool and hot tub, it would make it even more highly desirable. He could build a small gift shop and playgrounds for added draw. Maybe put some of those small portable cabins near the back of the property for people who didn't have RVs. Make it a cross between a B&B and an RV park.

He sat there for another few moments, dreaming about it, until his phone chimed one more time, breaking him from his dreams.

"You think this is over?" the text message read. "Screw you, McCaw. I'm coming for you and yours."

He punched Dale's number into his phone.

"Think you can swing by before you clock out?" he asked the man.

"Sure, what's up?" Dale asked.

"Just got a nice threatening text message I'd like to officially report," Brent said casually.

"From?" Dale asked.

"Who else. He didn't even try to hide who it was from." He chuckled.

"I thought his dad and brother were dumb," Dale said with a sigh. "I'll be there in half an hour."

"Thanks," Brent said and hung up.

Just then Darla stepped out onto the back patio and locked eyes with him, then set her empty tray down and moved towards him. Shit. The day had just gotten worse.

CHAPTER 20

*E*ven though she trusted Brent completely, it still caused her some concern when she saw him sitting outside talking to Darla.

Over the past three weeks, Darla had been nothing but a perfect employee. It wasn't until after she'd hired her that she had overheard some of the horrors the woman had inflicted on the townspeople. But, for the most part, everyone seemed to deal with her just fine.

Actually, she was one of their better employees at this point. Besides the Alaqua family members. She'd gotten along great with the woman and, after several conversations with her, she knew just how much the woman had gone through. She figured she was the last person who should judge.

Still, it weighed heavily on her to know that someone could change so much. She wondered if it was possible for Ethan to change. After all, it had been over a year since she'd seen him last.

Had her parents changed? Could they? Did they even

want to? She doubted they even had an idea that they needed to. After all, the entire time she was growing up, not once had they apologized for forcing their beliefs on her or for how they had treated her.

There had been a time in her youth when she'd actually fallen for some of the stuff her father had preached at her, some of his stronger beliefs about how women and girls shouldn't get too many ideas. How they were destined to fit into certain roles in life. Even with his power, he'd believed other men's lies over the word of his family.

"Trouble?" Jamie asked, taking a moment to stop and look out the back window, where Mel had been watching Darla talk to Brent.

"No," she answered quickly and turned away, but Jamie stood there watching the pair for a moment.

"You know, there's nothing there," Jamie said, friendly bumping her hip against Mel's.

"Yeah, I know." She started wiping the bar top.

"I mean it," Jamie said, moving closer to her. "There was, at one point. The entire town stood back and watched that train wreck happening. We all held our breaths, expecting the explosion that never came. Instead, Brent scurried out of town, and Darla moved out shortly after and disappeared until recently."

"And now she's back a changed woman," Mel said firmly.

"Yes," Jamie agreed. "For now," she added as she walked away.

Just then Mel turned towards the door as Dale walked in. She still tensed each time she saw the uniform, but she relaxed just knowing it was Dale. The man was not only the nicest cop she'd ever met, he was the most trustworthy and honest man that she knew in town, besides Brent.

"Afternoon," she said, smiling at Dale. "Can I get you

something to drink?" she asked, knowing that he'd ask for an iced tea.

"I'll take my usual." He leaned against the bar and glanced around. "Your man around?"

She arched her brows. "*My* man?"

Dale smiled. "Unless you don't want him. I hear there's a line forming…"

She chuckled. "He's out back talking to Darla." She waved towards the doorway and watched Dale's eyes narrow. The man's entire attitude changed in a heartbeat, so she took that moment to turn around to grab him his iced tea.

Whatever Darla had done to Dale in the past, she figured it had nothing to do with her.

She handed him the tea and went back to work as he headed out back to talk to Brent.

She wanted to know what happened, but she was stuck helping deliver a tray of food to a large family in the dining room instead, taking away her chance to spy on them through the window.

Actually, for the rest of the afternoon, she was too busy to hunt Brent down and ask him anything. She'd passed him as he'd headed up the stairs just before the dinner rush and didn't see him again until just before closing time.

He helped the crew do the final clean and close up and then grabbed a couple plates of TK's chicken cacciatore. Since the weather had grown chilly and she'd overheard several people mention there was rain in the forecast, they sat at the bar and had dinner.

"I had a nice text message from Mark today," Brent said.

"Nice?" she asked.

He chuckled. "Nice enough that I had to show it to Dale."

She nodded. "That's why he stopped by."

"Yeah, that and to argue with Darla, apparently." Brent rolled his eyes.

"Oh? I thought he acted strange when I mentioned that you were talking to her."

"Dale and Darla go way back. Their rivalry started long before he became a cop, and she became…"

"A stripper?" Mel supplied. She'd heard all the rumors and stories. She didn't care. Darla was nice to all the customers and kept things clean. If she didn't, Mel wouldn't have any problem tossing her out of the place.

"Yeah." Brent nodded. "She has a dark past."

"Sounds like you've forgiven her for poking holes in your condoms?" Mel said, running her eyes over him.

She could tell that whatever had been said between him and Darla, it was going to stay between them. Not that she was a prying sort. She understood the need to keep your past to yourself.

"No, but that doesn't mean I can't move past it like she has. Like you said, everyone deserves a second chance, if they're willing to take it themselves first."

"So, what happened?" she asked.

"Dale took my report and then asked for a moment alone with Darla." He shrugged. "I left them alone and headed up to start this." He pulled out a piece of paper from his back pocket.

She opened it and started reading the long list of things that would have to be done to start the RV park plans.

"What's this?" she asked, pointing to a few items on a side list.

"I figured we could have some of those small portable wood cabins. You know, the tiny home kind. We could rent them out for people without RVs." He shrugged. "After my parents sold ours, we would have loved to still take family trips and stay in places like this is going to be."

"Not a bad idea," she admitted. She still grew tense every

time he talked about their future. He used the words *we, ours,* and *us* a lot, and even though she didn't tense as much as she had at first, it still caused her stomach to knot each time.

"So, you've decided for sure then?" she asked.

"Yeah, I think so. It's a solid idea. No one else has anything like it for about a hundred miles. I checked," he said with a smile.

"What will you need to start the ball rolling?" she asked, pulling a pen from her pocket and flipping the piece of paper over to start jotting down some notes of her own.

She was happy to use some of her knowledge to help Brent come up with a business plan. Actually, in the past two months, she'd really enjoyed her work. It was a lot different than just having a job where she showed up, worked, and then left after.

For the first time in her life, she felt invested in something and it felt wonderful. Really wonderful.

Every time she thought of leaving Haven and the Hard Way, she felt her insides twist. Yet part of her knew that sooner or later she would have to go. If not for her sake, then for Brent and everyone else in Haven.

Ethan Melbourne would not be ignored or give up that easily. There was no doubt that he was out there, searching for her. His anger building. His calculated mind plotting his revenge.

She just hoped that when he found her, no one else would get hurt because of her.

The next day, the weather took a turn, and they spent most of the day in bed. They spent some time working on his laptop, looking at RV parks and trying to create a list of items they wanted or needed.

They retreated to the television room and watched an old movie after lunch, then made love and fell asleep in each other's arms. When she woke, Brent was nowhere to be found. He'd laid a blanket over her and, after dressing, she made her way downstairs and heard him banging on something.

When she walked into the kitchen, he was just taking a pan off the stove.

"Dinner will be ready in five," he called over his shoulder.

It had become their standard Sunday evening date. Brent would make some sort of dinner, which they would enjoy out on the patio.

"How about some coffee?" she asked, knowing that he often drank a cup in the evening. She walked to the large coffee station. Frowning, she turned back to him. "It's raining."

"Yeah," he said with a sigh. "I know. We'll have to eat inside tonight."

"I didn't even hear it," she said, keeping her eyes fixed outside. She was still a little groggy from her afternoon nap. When she spotted a dark figure standing just on the other side of the tree line, she tensed. Her entire body went on guard as the figure moved slightly towards the building.

She didn't remember screaming or dropping the coffee mug, but suddenly Brent was lifting her up in his arms and carrying her until she sat on the countertop.

"You've cut your foot," he said softly, and she watched, still in shock, as he dabbed at a large gash on the top of her foot. She hadn't even felt the sting of the cut. Hadn't even noticed it. Instead, her mind was locked on the figure moving closer to her, to them.

"He's here," she said, her vision turning grey around the edges.

"Who?" She felt Brent tense.

"Ethan, I saw…" She motioned towards the window.

Brent rushed over to the window and looked out. "Where?" he asked her.

"By the tress." She closed her eyes. "I saw… someone." She took several deep breaths and tried to slow her heartrate down.

"There's no one there now," he said, coming back to her. "I'll go out and—"

"No!" She grabbed for his hands. "Stay here with me."

"Okay," Brent said after a moment. "I'll call Dale."

Mel relaxed slightly. She doubted that Ethan would harm one of his own. He was many things, but he was a patriot through and through.

She sat there breathing through the fear as Brent called Dale and asked him to swing by and check out someone on his land.

It wasn't until she heard him mention the Phillipses that she calmed down. Of course. She was such a fool. It wasn't Ethan coming after her, it was one of the Phillips men sneaking onto the land to cause problems.

Jumping down from the counter, she winced when the sting of the cut became obvious to her for the first time. Walking over, she dabbled it with a paper towel until Brent got off the phone.

"Here, sit down." He helped her into a chair. "I'll go get the first aid kit."

She sat down and waited until he returned with the kit. Then she held still while he cleaned the cut and dabbled ointment on it before carefully putting a bandage over it.

"There, that should hold you over." He leaned up and kissed her. "Feel better?"

"Yes." She smiled. "I'm sorry I freaked. I wasn't thinking about it being one of the Phillips men."

"I didn't either until Dale brought it up," Brent admitted

as he wrapped his arms around her. "I'm sure it was just one of them checking on how they can cause problems."

"Think they can?" she asked, already feeling better.

"No. If they get too close to the place, they will be seen by my new security system." He smiles.

"Right." She'd helped him install the new cameras a few weeks back. "So, what now?"

"Now, we eat our dinner and enjoy the rest of our day off as planned and let Dale and the rest of Haven's finest do their jobs," Brent said easily.

She helped him carry the steak, rice, and steamed broccoli into the other room then waited as he returned to get them each a glass of wine.

"No coffee for you today?" she asked.

"No, I think I've had enough excitement for one day. This'll do." He held up his glass.

"Thank you for the dinner," she said. "I think it's my favorite so far." He'd brought a bottle of barbeque sauce with him that was so good, she'd had to check the bottle just to see the brand name of it.

"It's a local company," he said when he noticed her reading the label.

"If we had that gift shop, you could sell all sorts of local items," she suggested. "Have you thought about offering breakfast? I mean, I think we have lunch and dinners covered."

"Yes and no. I like opening later for now, but yeah, I get the need for being open earlier. Of course that would mean I'd have to hire another chef and crew to work the extra hours."

"Maybe TK has another family member that needs work?" she said with a chuckle.

He smiled. "The Alaqua family is very extended, for sure.

I think they have more cousins than any other family in town."

"I think they easily rival the McGowans," she added with a chuckle.

"True." He relaxed back. "I always wanted a big family. You know, cousins, grandparents. The whole works."

"Same here. At least you have Dylan," she said with a sigh and felt the same pain over her heart she always got when she thought about her empty childhood.

Suddenly, he jumped up from his spot.

"I forgot." He turned and started walking away, but then stopped again and held up a hand. "I have a surprise. Stay right there." He disappeared into the back room. She heard a few things bang around and then he cursed loudly. She chuckled. A few moments later, he rolled out a large object covered in one of the tablecloths, a large silly grin on his face.

When he removed the cloth with a flourish, she gasped and jumped up from her spot.

"You got it?" She rushed over to the classic jukebox that she'd been eyeing at an antique store he'd taken her to on their last day off.

"Yes," he said, bending down to plug it in. "What do you say we try this thing out?" He motioned for her to pick a tune.

It took her a few moments, but finally, she settled on the first song, "At Last" by Etta James.

She stood there and watched the old forty-five-inch record being loaded.

She laughed when Brent took her hand and whirled her around and started moving with her towards the small dance floor.

The laughter died in her throat when the music started, and they began to sway slowly together under the soft lights.

She'd attended a lot of school dances before, but it had

been years since she'd danced with a man. Never in her life had she felt so… connected to someone before.

Resting her head on his chest, she listened to his heart-beat and felt her own beat settle to match. She felt her entire body moving along with his and wondered how she was ever going to let him go.

For now, she was determined to enjoy as much of Brent as she could.

CHAPTER 21

*B*rent had felt the change in Mel over the last few days. She'd slowly tried pulling away from him, which only made him try harder to keep the smile on her face.

He'd even worked out a deal with the antique shop owner to get the expensive jukebox that she'd liked. For the next year, Betty and George Kincaid were getting free meals at the Hard Way.

He liked the older couple and could vaguely remember them from his time in Haven. They seemed to remember him, which is why they hadn't agreed to the deal at first.

He knew that the jukebox was a good investment. After all, he couldn't afford to hire a band every weekend and, this way, people could enjoy listening to something other than the games on the televisions.

Besides, the thing would practically pay for itself since people had to pay a dollar for four songs.

The other benefit was currently in his arms, swaying to one of the most romantic songs ever written. The thought of being able to enjoy lazy days like they'd just had and nights like this, dancing with Mel as the rain continued outside, made him really appreciate his decision.

Especially since her body felt so wonderful pressed tight up against his own. Her hands were slowly roaming over his shoulders while his own lowered to wrap around her hips. He felt his body reacting to their closeness.

When she brushed her lips over his neck, he realized he'd stopped moving completely.

Dipping his head down, he claimed her lips and felt the urgency rush through him to have her. In the almost two months since she'd come into town, the urgency he felt to be with her hadn't once wavered.

When he felt her respond to him, he hoisted her up and walked her until her hips rested on the edge of the bar top as they took the kiss deeper.

"Brent," she said as she ran her fingers through his hair. "I need…" She arched back when he hoisted her shirt up and over her head and brushed his mouth over her exposed breasts. "Please," she said on a sigh.

He felt his body responding to her and knew that there was no way he would be able to carry her up those stairs. Instead, he tugged those sexy grey yoga pants off her hips. They slipped from her legs easily and landed in a pile on the floor.

When she wrapped her legs around his hips and reached for the clasp of his jeans, he smiled.

"I've always wanted to do it in a bar," he joked.

"Now's your big chance," she teased as she tugged his jeans off his hips and reached into his back pocket for the condom that she knew he kept there. He held still while she rolled the protection on him. Their eyes locked and the need continued to grow.

When he slid into her, it was as if he was coming home. He'd never felt so involved before. Had never cared as much as he did with her. This mattered more than it had before.

A sudden wave of tenderness took over him as he leaned in and covered her mouth with his in a kiss that reflected his inner mood. Their movements slowed as the next song started to play on the jukebox. This time the Drifters sang about the magic moment, and he realized just how magical it was.

No matter what happened, he would remember his time with Mel for the rest of his life and the exact moment when he'd lost his heart.

They had just pulled their clothes back on when a knock on the front door sounded.

"Brent? It's Dale," he heard over the sound of thunder.

The storm had grown progressively worse as the night had grown later.

He glanced over at Mel and waited until she'd slipped on her tennis shoes before walking over to let Dale inside.

"Evening," Dale said to Mel. Brent watched the man's eyes move around to the candlelight and the empty dishes sitting on the table. "Sorry, I didn't mean to interrupt your evening."

"It's okay," Brent said. "Did you find anything?"

"No, but the field is too muddy to see any footprints. I had my partner stop by the Phillips's place." He sighed. "All family members were present, and agitated that we'd bothered them."

"Right," Brent said with a nod. "Thanks for checking."

"No problem." Dale turned to go, then stopped. "Let us know if you see anyone else sniffing around. You know that the Phillips' place isn't far from here, less than half a mile."

"Right." He hadn't. Actually, he was surprised he didn't know where any of them lived. Did the sons still live with the parents? The more he thought about it, the more he realized he hadn't cared until now.

"I wouldn't put it past them to do something, but I just can't see any of them coming out on such a terrible night." Dale shook his head. "One word everyone in Haven would easily use for the Phillips men is lazy."

"Right," he agreed. "Thanks again." He shook the man's hand and let him out before locking the door.

"If it wasn't them…" Mel said, and he turned around to see that the soft pink color in her cheeks from their love-making had drained, and she was now too pale. She'd wrapped her arms around herself, so he walked over and pulled her into a hug.

"It was probably them," he said into her hair. "Let's head upstairs. I could use some sleep." He turned and unplugged the jukebox and the music stopped.

"The dishes." Mel pulled on his arm.

"Can wait until the morning," he assured her. "We need sleep." He took her hand and walked with her upstairs into their room.

Before lying down, he glanced out the back window one last time and thought about installing motion sensor flood-lights, ones that would light up the entire field if need be, just as long as it made Mel feel safer.

She laid against him, and he listened to her breathing settle as she fell asleep. It took him a little longer to finally settle down. His mind kept playing over everything Mel had told him about her past.

The fact was, he still couldn't get a lot of details from her. She'd mentioned what school she'd gone to, and he knew that it would take just a quick online search to find out more about her.

But something kept holding him back. Maybe it was the respect he had for her privacy? Maybe it was the fact that he wanted her to tell him herself?

The next morning, he met with TK and talked to her

about the possibility of turning the place into a RV park. Her reaction surprised him.

"How much money do you need to start this venture?" the woman had asked him.

"Um, money?" He shrugged. "We haven't really—"

"I'm in," TK said. "I've got some savings."

He held in a chuckle. "I wasn't planning…" he started but then he thought about it. He'd sunk everything he had into the bar and grill. He hadn't once thought about how he was going to pay for the updates needed to make the next phase a possibility.

"What are you thinking?" he asked her.

She tilted her head. "Well, since you've got ownership, how about a loan with interest?"

He thought about heading down to a bank and frowned. His credit score wasn't good. Hell, it might even be in the negative, if that was a thing. Which is why he'd paid cash for everything and had saved every penny he could in the past few years.

"We might be able to work something out," he said. "Let me talk it over with Mel."

TK nodded. "Let me know. You'll probably want to offer breakfast. Maybe some picnic options." She leaned against the counter and crossed her arms over her chest. "You could host events as well. Maybe turn a little portion of the land into a romantic setting? Build a gazebo? Host weddings, birthday parties?"

"That's… a great idea." He smiled and nodded. "Know of anyone who would want to lend a hand in the kitchen?"

TK smiled. "I've got a few connections."

Just then Jamie walked in. "Connections for what?"

By the time Mel walked in, every single one of the Alaqua employees had all chimed in with ideas about possibilities for his land.

They spent the next half hour replaying some of the highlights for Mel while the kitchen crew started lunch.

After, he and Mel disappeared into the office and worked on a budget. He made several calls and got quotes for electric, plumbing, and even cement slabs for the trailers to sit on.

A knock on the office door had them both looking up. Jamie stood there, a slight frown on her lips.

"There's a reporter out here," Jamie said, her eyes turning to Mel.

"A reporter?" he asked.

On opening day, he'd been interviewed by the local paper and even a paper from the next town over had come and taken pictures of the place. He had copies of both papers hanging up on the wall behind the bar.

"I'll be out—"

"No, she's looking for..." Jamie nodded towards Mel. "You." Jamie's eyes flashed to his, and he understood something was off.

Standing, he laid a hand on Mel's shoulder.

"We'll be right out," he said.

"It might be better... You might want to show her back here?" Jamie suggested. "It's just... we have a full dining room."

He nodded. "Okay, we'll wait here."

He sat back down and turned to Mel as Jamie disappeared. Mel's face was pale again, and she had yet to move or say anything.

"Are you okay?" he asked her.

Her eyes moved to his. "I..." Whatever she was going to say fell away as a thin woman with dark hair and thick glasses and dressed in a stylish skirt and jacket suit stepped into the room.

"Melinda Hawk," the woman said slowly. "I thought that

was you. I saw you in the dining room earlier." Brent watched as the woman's smile turned wicked as she lifted her camera and snapped a few pictures of them before Brent could stand up and block Mel behind him.

"Can I help you?" he asked.

The woman spared him a glance. "Sure." She fumbled and pulled out a phone and flipped it on. "Mind if I record this?" she asked and, without waiting for an answer, asked, "Do you know you are harboring one of the most wanted women in America?"

Brent's entire body tensed. "Out." He motioned towards the door.

The reporter looked shocked and then actually laughed at him.

"You don't, do you?" She shook her head. "Melinda Hawk, daughter of Roy and Belinda Hawk, ex-wife to Ethan Melbourne, is wanted for extortion, intellectual theft, and—"

"Out!" He practically shouted it. The longer the woman had talked, the paler Mel had become.

"I'm just–" the woman started, but he walked over and held open the already opened door to his office. "I won't ask you a second time," he said softly. "You're not welcome back on this property. If I see you, I'll call the police."

The woman's smile grew. "Maybe we should call the police?" She turned towards Mel, who was holding onto the desk. Her knuckles had turned white.

Brent reached up and took the woman's arm, just as Dale rushed through the door.

"I heard there was—" Dale started, and upon seeing Brent trying to get the woman out of his office, stopped talking. "Do we have a problem here?" Dale asked calmly.

"Yes. This reporter was just leaving my premises, where she is no longer welcome," Brent said before the woman could say anything.

Dale, taking the hint, motioned to the open doorway. "I'll be happy to walk her out."

The reporter narrowed her eyes at Mel and then said in the sweetest voice, "This isn't over." Then she turned and strolled out in front of Dale, as if he was her personal protection.

Brent shut the office door and flipped the old blinds shut. Instead of saying anything, he walked over and pulled Mel up into his arms and held her as she shook and cried.

He didn't have any doubt that Mel was Melinda Hawk instead of Mel Hawthorn. What he did doubt was that she was responsible for extorting anyone, let alone intellectual theft. He'd seen how little money she had when she'd arrived and how grateful she'd been when he'd given her her first paycheck and taken her shopping. She'd acted like a woman who hadn't gone shopping for herself in years.

Someone guilty of those crimes wouldn't be driving a beat-up secondhand pickup truck and be so excited to shop at Target.

"Are you okay?" he asked when she settled down.

"I… I'll leave," she said against his chest.

As a gut reaction, his arms tightened around her.

"No," he said quickly, "you won't." He placed a kiss on top of her head. "Not because of this. Whatever is in your past, we'll deal with it, together."

Just then there was a knock on the door and TK walked in.

"Mel?" she asked, worry in the woman's eyes. "Are you okay?"

Mel leaned back and wiped her eyes as she nodded. "Yes," she said, her voice low.

Instead of leaving, TK stepped into the room and shut the door. "What are we dealing with?" TK asked.

Brent felt Mel tense beside him but waved the woman

further inside. Mel sat back down, her palms lying flat on the desk.

"After I divorced Ethan, my parents' transferred money into an account with my name on it. I never touched the money." Her eyes searched his, and he could see that she was telling the truth. Not that he doubted her in the first place.

"What happened?" he asked.

"The night that Ethan showed up at my new apartment, he took the checks and probably cleared out that account." She closed her eyes. "Since I left shortly after, I didn't know what happened...." She looked over at TK. "Ethan was a cop and the son of the chief of police. I'd heard that he'd persuaded my parents to file charges against me if I wouldn't come back to him. I left town. I guess they made their choice."

"That bastard," TK said under her breath.

"I agree," Brent added.

Just then the door burst opened, and Dale stepped in. His eyes went between all three of them.

TK stood up and laid a hand on his chest. "Not now, brother."

He glanced over TK's head and asked.

"Is your name Melinda Hawk?" he asked Mel.

Brent watched her chin rise as she stood. "It is." She took a deep breath.

"Shit." Dale sagged slightly. "I hate to..."

"Don't you dare," TK said calmly. "Not until you hear the whole story."

"That's not my job. Not my decision," Dale said calmly.

"He's right," Mel said softly as she moved around the desk. She turned to Brent. "I'm sorry." Then she walked over to Dale. "Let's go."

He stood there, helpless, while Dale followed Mel out of his office and out the back door.

CHAPTER 22

*B*eing booked in the Haven police station was the lowest she'd gotten in her life. Being finger-printed, photographed, and taken back to a holding cell was the most humiliating time. However, her one saving grace was that Dale stuck with her from the very first moment until she was sitting in the small cell alone.

When she was asked if she wanted to make her one phone call, she declined, knowing that everyone she would have called already knew where she was.

She must have only sat in the cell for an hour before Dale was unlocking the door again.

"You've made bail," he said with a smile.

"I have?" She frowned. She hadn't even known bail had been set for her yet.

"They're waiting for you," Dale said, motioning down the hallway. "For what it's worth, I'm sorry."

She touched his arm. "You were just doing your job."

He nodded. "As I said before, not all of us are asshats."

She smiled. "Thanks."

When she walked out to the small waiting area, she was slightly shocked to see Dylan standing by Brent's side, waiting for her.

Dylan rushed forward and wrapped her arms around her. "Are you okay?"

"Yes," she said, trying to hold in her tears. She convinced herself to cry later, when she was alone.

"Brent told me…" Dylan leaned back. "We're going to fight this."

Instead of answering, she nodded as Brent walked over and took her hand.

"Let's go home," he said softly. "Don's going to meet us there."

Again, she nodded and let him lead her out of the building. She sat in Brent's truck, silently watching the small town go by outside the window. She was going to miss this place.

She'd hoped to be around to see what it looked like in the fall or after the first snowfall, but now… She knew she no longer had a choice. She had to either run or return home and face the music. Either way, Haven, Montana, and Brent McCaw would be in her past.

Tears stung her eyes as he pulled into the parking lot of the Hard Way. When he parked, she realized that the parking lot was empty.

"We closed down for the rest of the day," he said as he shut off the truck.

"You shouldn't have," she said, letting her shoulders sink.

"You're part of a new family," he said, turning towards her. "One that doesn't take too kindly to bullies." He motioned towards the door, where TK stood, her arms wrapped around Jamie and Mary. "They wanted to wait and make sure you were okay." He smiled. "They put together your bond money."

That did it. Tears burst from her eyes, blinding her from

everything. Brent must have rushed around and opened her door because he was there, his arms wrapped around her as she cried.

"We're here," she heard TK and Jamie say at the same time.

She blindly stumbled into the building, guided by her friends, the only people in the world who had shown her true kindness and love. The people she'd just convinced herself to leave behind.

She was nudged into a chair and a glass was set in front of her.

"Drink," Jamie said softly.

When she did, she coughed and choked on the bite of the whiskey.

Several people chuckled, causing her to smile.

"Jesus, Jamie, warn a girl first," she joked, and then she downed the entire shot.

"If you want milk or water, go to the Dancing Moose," Jamie said with a chuckle. "Here at the Hard Way, we do things…"

"Hard," three other people cheered at the same time.

"Damn straight," Mel said with a sigh as she looked down at her hands and the empty shot glass. "I've made a mess of things."

"No," Brent said, sitting next to her, "we have."

"We should have shown you that you can trust us. We're here for you now," TK said. "No one messes with family and you're family." She laid a hand on Mel's shoulder. Mel reached up and laid a hand over TK's.

"Thanks," she said, looking around the room. "But I'm afraid it's not as simple as a court battle."

"We've been through worse," Jamie said, looking between her sister and TK. "Trust us."

Mel wished she could believe that but knowing the power that Ethan had, she doubted it.

"Ethan won't stop at the law," she said, looking to Brent.

"Good, and when he crosses that line," Dale said stepping into the room, "I'll be here to catch him." He wrapped an arm around TK. His eyes moved around the room and landed on Darla.

Mel hadn't even realized Dale or Darla were there, along with all of the other employees she'd hired over the past few months. Her heart ached and her eyes teared up once more.

"Thank you," she said softly. "All of you. I don't know how I'm going to pay you all back,"

"This time off is payment in itself," someone said, causing everyone to chuckle.

"Drinks," someone else said.

"Chicken wings," someone else added.

Mel laughed. "I suppose since we're officially closed down for dinner, a round of wings and beer is on me," she said and everyone cheered.

By the time Don Hathaway, Brent's lawyer, walked through the front doors, most of the employees, her family, were all enjoying wings and beer while listening to the jukebox and watching a game.

Brent, Dale, and Mel sat at a table discussing her case.

Her parents had not only filed extortion and intellectual theft cases against her, they had actually filed a corporate espionage suit against her as well.

Corporate espionage. As if she would be even capable of such a thing.

"Who are your parents?" Dale asked.

"Roy and Belinda Hawk," she answered. Only after seeing Dale's and Brent's blank stares did she realize that the men didn't know who her parents were. Sighing, she closed her eyes briefly. "Regal Intellectual Corporation," she said and met Brent's gaze.

"RIC?" Dale's eyes grew wide. "The company that created the big brother system that protects and watches everyone's bank accounts and credit scores. Holy… mother of…" He stopped himself, then gasped. "You're an heiress."

She felt her entire body sag. "I'm… me," she said, feeling suddenly tired. "Penniless. The manager of this place." She met Brent's eyes and could see the worry there. The one thing she didn't see was anger or, as she would have with so many other men in her past, dollar signs. She'd missed that in Ethan's eyes before marrying him.

"Where does this leave us?" Brent asked Dale.

Dale was quiet for a moment before taking a deep breath. "Seriously? That kind of screws us. Sorry," he said to her. "Your parents are what? In the top ten richest people in the States?"

"Fourth," she said, dryly. "They are. I'm not," she tried to assure Brent.

"I don't care if you're the queen's niece," he said, taking her hand. "Family doesn't define us." She remembered he'd said that to her before.

"They do when these are your family members," Dale added as the group behind them cheered when a team made a goal. "Nutjobs, each and every last one."

Mel smiled. "I'll take these nutjobs over the two-faced people who raised me any day."

Brent squeezed her hand. "Whatever it takes, we're with you."

"And your ex?" Dale asked. "I'm going to head into the station and see what I can come up with on Ethan Melbourne."

"His father is the chief of police in Auburn," she said, avoiding Brent's eyes. "He works for the department as well."

Dale nodded. "Haven's a little out of his jurisdiction," he said with a smile just as Don moved over to sit in the chair Dale had vacated. "Besides, if the man steps foot in town, we've got ourselves a nice new chief of police ourselves. One that doesn't take too kindly to people coming into town and messing with our own."

"Brian Laster," Brent said with a shake of his head. "Never thought the man would amount to anything."

Dale smiled. "He's turned out to be a first-rate chief."

For the next hour, the three of them talked legal options. Since Mel had been unaware of the charges filed against her when she'd left Washington State, he believed he could get the charges of eluding felony charges dropped. Especially since she'd never been convicted. Her other saving grace was that she had proof that she didn't have the funds her parents claimed she'd taken off with.

Honestly, she was pretty sure that if her parents had known that she hadn't taken the money, they never would have pressed those charges in the first place. Still, she doubted they would press charges against Ethan even if they had proof that he was the one who had taken the money. After all, according to her father, Ethan was the head of the house and therefore responsible for all financial decisions.

What had Ethan done with two hundred thousand dollars? How had he hidden it from her parents? Was he even still in the Seattle area?

Shortly after nine, everyone left and they locked up. Feeling slightly better after the talk with the lawyer and her friends, Mel headed upstairs with Brent.

"How about you head in, take a bath or shower," he said to her. "I know how being locked in the slammer makes one feel dirty." He smiled.

She did feel dirty. She had ever since the reporter had stepped into the office and spilled her secrets. But the kind of dirty she felt couldn't be washed off with soap and water. Still, she nodded and gathered a pair of her pajamas to change into after the long hot shower she planned on taking.

From the moment she stepped under the hot spray, she allowed the rest of her emotions to flow out of her. She sat on the cold tile floor, hugging her knees to her chest as the water flowed over her, washing away her tears and the day's weariness from her muscles until she was nothing more than a pile of jelly.

When the water turned cold, she turned it off and took a few moments to compose herself as she slipped back under her careful protective shield.

Then she walked into the bedroom she'd shared with Brent for the past two months and stepped into a wonder world filled with soft candlelight and music. He'd somehow gone and gotten soft pink roses, a dozen of them, which he held out in front of him as she stepped into the room.

"I'm sorry," he said, his eyes running over her face. "I couldn't protect you against your past. But I'm hoping that you'll take this promise from me now that, no matter what happens, I will be here for you in the future."

"Damn," she said, reaching up to wipe another tear that had escaped her eyes. "I told myself I was done crying," she said softly as she stepped into his arms.

Her head ached from all the tears, but when he kissed her, everything, the entire day of horrors, fell away.

With Brent's arms wrapped around her, she felt she could stand up against anything. Even her parents and her ex.

Then he kissed her, and she knew that whatever her future held, she would never let go of this feeling. The feeling of being loved. Even if they hadn't said the words yet, she knew that she'd lost her heart to him long ago.

She knew how he felt. Every single time he touched her or kissed her, he showed her. He told her how he felt about her in his daily actions too—the way he would go out of his way to do the little things for her that most would overlook. Holding the door open for her. Stopping and picking a purple flower in the field and handing it to her. Saving the last slice of pie for her. And sipping tea with her when she knew he wanted coffee instead.

So many times he'd sacrificed little things on her behalf. Ethan never had and never would do that for her. Not even her parents had sacrificed as much.

As she slept with his arms wrapped around her, she thought about the possibility of leaving now. Could she make it on her own again? The Haven police had the make, model, and registration information for her truck, which meant she'd have to find other means of travel. Where could she go? Her plans to head to Helena were out, since several people around her knew she'd been heading there in the first place.

Was there anywhere she could go now?

What if Ethan came here? What if someone she had grown to care for got hurt? What if Ethan came after Brent? Or Dylan and baby Bella?

That thought had her almost jumping out of bed. If it wasn't for Brent's arms resting over her stomach, anchoring her to the spot, she would have left.

TK's and Jamie's words played over in her mind. They were so trusting, all of them. And they had stuck their necks and their hard-earned money out for her. Not one of her friends from school would have done that.

She doubted that even her parents would do that at this point. They probably still thought that she had taken their money and run. No wonder they'd demanded she return home every time she'd talked to them. Even though they had given her the checking account in the first place.

She frowned. How was it possible for them to file charges

if they were the ones who had opened the account in her name?

She'd been too dazed from the day to really ask the lawyer any questions or give him any vital information. She vowed to have another meeting with the man the following day and then forced herself to shut everything down. She fell asleep counting Brent's breaths as her head rose and fell with his chest.

CHAPTER 23

Three days after Mel had been taken in, they were sitting out on the patio having dinner when a shiny black Rolls-Royce drove into the parking lot.

"And it begins," Mel said under her breath.

In the past few days, they'd discussed the possibility of her parents or Ethan showing up. They had decided how to handle any situation and had Don and or Dale waiting on standby for either scenario.

"Parents first," he agreed and took her hand. "Together."

"Together." She nodded and stood up and moved to the edge of the parking lot along with him.

He felt her tense when her parents stepped out of the car.

Since the other day, he'd done a little research into Roy and Belinda Hawk. Still, the couple looked younger than he'd expected. Not that he'd been expecting old people, but the stylish clothes they were wearing took years off their lives.

Mel looked so much like her mother that he would have known they were mother and daughter from across the room.

"Mom, Dad," Mel said in a calm voice.

If he hadn't known her, he would have believed she was the essence of quietude. The fact that her hand still clung to his was the only outward sign that she needed his strength.

Her parents ran their eyes over him, over the building behind them.

"Melinda, we think it's high time you came home," her father said in a strict tone.

Mel took a heartbeat before chuckling. "Go to hell," she replied. He smiled and gave her hand a slight squeeze. "I didn't take your money."

"Didn't you?" Her mother spoke for the first time.

Mel turned towards her and, instead of answering, she tilted her head slightly.

"Mr. and Mrs. Hawk, why don't you come inside? We can discuss…" he started, only to have her father jerk his eyes towards him.

"Keep your dog on a leash," he barked.

Brent's eyebrows shot up. "That was your one chance," he said calmly. "I'll ask you to leave my property."

Mel's mother chuckled and looked down her nose at him. "Really, Melinda, you left Ethan for this." She motioned around them. "You're in the middle of nowhere. Shacked up with this… mountain man?"

"I'm home," Mel said, her chin raising slightly. "Where people treat me with respect and love. Something the two of you never managed."

Her father's eyes narrowed.

"This is your last chance," he said in a low tone.

"Have you asked Ethan about the money?" Brent heard her voice rise slightly.

"You're disturbed," her mother said softly, looking pained. "You need help."

"The only thing I needed help with was to escape an abusive husband. The man who threw me through a wall for purchasing the wrong kind of milk. The man who, after I divorced him, used his connection to you to hunt me down, then broke into my apartment and shoved a gun in my mouth until I gave him the checks to the account that you'd given me." Brent jerked at hearing this piece of news. The desire to kick Ethan's ass went up a few more notches. "Then I was forced to work several jobs just to save up enough to escape him once more. I had to hide who I was and keep that knowledge from the two of you for fear that you'd lead him to me once again. Because next time, I didn't think he'd stop at just threats, something neither of you could ever understand. Because all that time, while I was jumping at shadows and hiding in fear, you took his side." Mel's eyes narrowed, and she took a deep breath. "Go. There's nothing in Haven for you. I'm no longer your daughter. I don't want a thing from either of you." Mel's voice had risen slightly.

Her parents' eyes moved past her, and when Brent glanced over his shoulder, he noticed TK, Jamie, Mary, and Darla standing in the doorway of the Hard Way, watching and backing Mel up.

"I have a family here," she finished up. She jumped slightly when everyone behind her erupted in applause. Mel smiled at them and then turned on her parents again. "Just go," she said, and then she took his hand again and pulled him back towards everyone waiting for them.

When they approached, they were both engulfed in hugs.

To his surprise, when he looked back, her parents were still standing there, talking to one another. Her father got on the phone as they walked inside.

He stood and watched her parents from the windows, while Mel was surrounded by their friends. It appeared as if her father was yelling at someone on the phone, then he hung up and said something to his wife, who immediately broke down and rushed into her husband's arms.

"Mel?" he said, getting her attention. "Something's up." He motioned to the windows.

Mel moved over to stand next to him and, after a moment, sighed. "They are not my problem anymore." She turned to go, but he stopped her.

"I think…" he said softly. "That they are hearing the truth for the first time." He pulled her into his arms. "Look at them." He motioned again.

This time, she took a longer look, as her parents stood in the parking lot, holding onto one another. Both of their eyes were wet with tears.

He felt her shoulders sag slightly. Then she pulled out of his hold and stepped outside. He wanted to follow her but held back. He overheard her ask them, "Do you want to come inside? We can head upstairs to talk?" Mel stood back as her parents walked inside.

"Want me to come?" he asked her as she walked by him. When she nodded, he followed her and her parents upstairs.

Since he figured this was her second chance with her parents, he stood back and listened as they talked.

"We had no idea," her mother said before sitting down in the television room upstairs.

"I called the bank and confirmed that it was Ethan who cleared out that account," her father said. "He told us that you took off with it and the only way to get you to come back out of hiding was for him to take care of it."

"He put a warrant out for my arrest," Mel said. "You signed the charges against me for extortion, intellectual theft, and corporate espionage."

"The hell we did." Her father's voice rose slightly. Brent stepped forward and put a gentle hand on Mel's shoulder. She reached up and covered it with her own hand.

"That's what this says." She shoved the folder Don had

given them a few days back towards them. "Those are your signatures?" she asked calmly.

Her father opened the folder and ran his eyes over the papers and then shoved them back.

"Is this some sort of joke?" he asked, his eyes going to Brent's.

"No. Mel spent a couple hours in lockup three days ago," he supplied. "Her court date is next week." He motioned to the paperwork. "You can call our lawyer if you want. His card is there."

Her father opened the folder again and took a few moments to read everything carefully.

Then, without a word, he stood up and pulled out his phone. Everyone in the room remained silent while he called someone.

"Jim, it's Roy. Can you check on a few things for me? I know it's late, but this is important. Yeah, it's a legal case. Number…" He read off Mel's court case number and then gave the man Don's name and number. "I'll be waiting," he said before hanging up. Then he turned back to Mel. "We'll get to the bottom of this," he assured her. "It's growing late. I don't suppose there's a hotel in this town?"

He glanced over at Mel and nodded when she gave him a questioning look.

"You don't need a hotel. We have an extra room just across the hallway," she said.

Her mother opened her mouth, as if she was ready to turn Mel down, but her father laid a hand on her arm.

"That would be great." He turned to Brent. "We drove straight through and whatever that smell is coming from downstairs, it smells wonderful."

Brent smiled. "You're in luck. We have the best wings in town." He smiled and motioned for them to follow him back downstairs.

The four of them sat at a corner table. Since their own dinner had been interrupted, they ordered more food along with her parents. Even though the silence was awkward at first, after he started asking her parents questions, it dissipated quickly enough. He kept the conversation light, talking about sports, the weather, their drive from Helena.

Then he mentioned he was from the Seattle area and finally spiked some real interest for the first time. They asked after his family and where he'd lived. To his amusement, they were surprised at the neighborhood he'd grown up in.

His parents, when they'd been alive, hadn't spared any expense. And since his father had been in banking, he'd known just how much he could spend each year without going bankrupt.

"You grew up just down the street, basically," her mother said.

"Yeah," he said, holding Mel's hand under the table. "We figured that out."

"What brought you to… here?" her father asked.

"Fate," he said, winking at Mel before telling the quick story of how their parents had died and how he and Dylan had ended up in Haven. How Dylan had married and had a daughter now.

He was just finishing up his story when Tyler and Kristen and their kids walked into the room. Spotting them, the family made their way towards their table.

"Looks like we showed up just in time," Tyler said, easily shaking Brent's hand.

Clare, their four-year-old daughter, climbed up into Brent's lap, stuffed dolly and all. He held onto her, making sure to bounce slightly like the little girl liked.

"Pull up a few chairs," Brent said and motioned to the table next to them. Tyler and Timothy quickly pushed the tables together as Kristen held onto their youngest daughter.

"Mr. and Mrs. Hawk, this is Tyler and Kristen McGowan. Their son, Timothy, their daughters Clare and Reagan. These are Mel's parents," he added.

Tyler reached out and shook Mel's father's hand, then paused. "Hawk?" Tyler's eyes grew big. "Well, shoot, if I'd known we'd be having dinner with the head of RIC, I would have..." He glanced down and then smiled. "Good, I am wearing my good shirt."

Kristen chuckled and slapped her husband playfully on the shoulder.

"McGowan?" Roy frowned. "Tyler McGowan? McGowan Enterprises?"

"The very same," Tyler said.

"Uncle Brent, fix my dolly's dress," Clare said, getting his attention. For the next few moments, he helped the little girl dress her doll while Tyler and Roy compared bank accounts. Or whatever it was rich business tycoons did when talking to one another. Mel and her mother talked with Kristen about how well Timothy was doing in sports. Really, he'd gotten the long straw, entertaining a four-year-old.

When their food arrived, the McGowans ordered their food. Before Darla had finished taking their order, Trent, Addy, Hope, and Grace came in the front door as well. Without waiting for an invitation, the family pulled another table up to theirs. More introductions were made and, suddenly, three girls were vying for his attention and dolly-dressing skills.

He was just beginning to wonder how the little dollies ended up naked all the time when Trey and Dylan walked in. He excused himself from the three girls and went to grab his niece from her carrier.

He didn't know how they had lucked out, getting all the McGowans there for dinner to help support and impress her parents, but it seemed to be doing the trick. Not only were her parents more relaxed with the McGowans around, but they stopped looking at him as if he was the most foul-smelling thing in the room.

When he took his niece back to the kitchen to show her off to TK and the rest of the kitchen crew, TK answered that question for him.

"You have Darla to thank for getting the McGowans in here tonight," TK said, gently rocking Bella in her arms.

"Darla?"

"Sure. When she noticed Mel's parents snubbing you, she figured you might need backup." TK smiled when the little girl reached up and wrapped a hand around her fingers. "She even made sure the tables around you were free."

He glanced towards the front and watched as Darla laughed at something Addy said.

"She's changed," he said under his breath.

"You have no idea," TK said, handing Bella back to him. "Now, as much as I'd like to spend the rest of the night playing with this beauty, I have orders to fill," TK said with a smile.

When he walked back out and sat next to Mel, she looked a little overwhelmed. He handed her Bella and took over the conversation for a while.

When Darla stopped by to clear the table, he made a point to pull her aside and thank her for calling in reinforcements.

"I figured that since they were talking down their noses at you, you should be able to rub their noses in your connections," Darla said with a shrug. "It was the least I could do for all the hell I put you through."

"It wasn't hell," he assured her.

She smiled. "Mutual hell then."

He chuckled and nodded. "Okay, mutual hell. Thanks, anyway."

"Thank you for not firing me after Mel gave me a chance when no one else in town would," Darla said.

"No one would?" He frowned.

Darla shrugged and then turned to grab her next orders. "Water under the bridge," she said and disappeared.

"Who was that?" he asked Mary when she walked by. Mary chuckled.

"We've been asking that question for a few weeks now," Mary said as she ducked back out front.

When he stepped out of the kitchen, Mel was standing and talking to his sister, who was rocking Bella back and forth while strapped in her carrier.

"She's fussy," Dylan told him. "The car ride home will calm her down." She reached up on her toes and laid a kiss on his cheek. "I think we impressed them," she whispered in her ear. "The rest is up to you. Night," she called out, and then she followed the rest of the McGowan families out the door.

Yes, he thought, the rest was up to him. Now, he just had to impress some of the richest and meanest people in the world so they would stop trying to put their daughter in jail and take her away from him.

CHAPTER 24

There was nothing more nerve-wracking than having dinner with the man you loved and your parents who wanted to lock you up and send you back to your abusive ex-husband.

Having the McGowans there through the rest of dinner relaxed things. Especially with all the kids running around, playing with Brent.

When he'd been holding Bella, her mother had leaned over and whispered to her, "At least he's good with kids."

What did that even mean? Was her mother trying to tell her that she approved of Brent? What about trying to ship her back to Ethan?

Sure, they had sat upstairs and listened to her side of the story. Her father had even called his lawyer, Jim Parker, to look into her legal issues. Did they really not know what they had signed? That they were basically turning on their daughter and having her hunted down by the police? As the reporter had put it, she was one of the most wanted women in the States because of them. Still, she figured she'd play along with their game, just as long as Brent and the rest of the gang were standing by her side.

Besides, the way she figured it, the longer her parents hung around, the less likely it was that Ethan would do anything crazy.

The entire time they'd been together, he'd gone out of his way to impress them, lying and hiding everything he'd done to Mel.

It had stung that her parents had so easily taken his side. Then again, her entire childhood had been them buying her off one way or another. They thought money solved all of their family issues, including absolving them from the need to show love.

Growing up, she hadn't minded. She hadn't wanted or needed love. Not when they had given her a credit card without any limits, new cars that rivaled those driven by movie stars, clothes from only the best designers, and anything else she'd asked for. She could look back now and realize just how spoiled she'd been.

She'd been ripe for the picking by the time Ethan came around, giving her something she'd never had before. There was no doubt why she'd fallen hard and fast for him.

She kept telling herself that she would never fall for anyone like that again, and as she lay wrapped in Brent's arms that night with her parents across the hallway, she knew she hadn't. Brent was nothing like Ethan. Nothing.

No matter what happened, she couldn't imagine Brent losing his temper or hitting anyone. But every man had his limits.

"I can hear you thinking," Brent said, breaking into her thoughts.

"Sorry." She smiled and looked down at him. "I thought you were sleeping."

"I was. Those gears up there"—he tapped the side of her

head lightly—"woke me." He leaned up and kissed her. "What's up?"

She sighed before speaking. "It's weird, right? My parents."

Even in the dark, she could see his eyebrows arching upward. "If you mean how much you look like your mother, then yes."

She sighed again. Her entire life she'd tried to avoid looking like her mother. Now, however, she no longer cared. She was what she was.

"I mean them sticking around here. I've never known them to stay in a place with fewer than five stars and two butlers." She shifted slightly so she could relax against his chest.

"If they expect me to butler around after them, they'd better get used to disappointment," he said, making her chuckle.

"I doubt it. My mother was impressed with your skill to tame the girls tonight," she added, unsure of why she was bringing it up.

"I do have a way with the ladies," he said easily as his arms tightened around her. "Maybe they'll leave in the morning?"

"One can hope," she said with a sigh.

"Do you think they'll call off the law?"

She'd been wondering the same thing but hadn't wanted to voice it for fear she would get her hopes up.

"I'm hoping," she admitted. "Daddy looked shocked after hearing what Ethan had tricked him into signing. It's strange —my father has always been a very shrewd businessman. But where Ethan was concerned, it was as if he was suddenly a blind man being led by the devil himself."

Brent was quiet for a moment. "I won't be so easily fooled."

"No." She leaned up and looked down at him again. "You wouldn't be." She placed a soft kiss on his lips.

The next morning, since it was a Sunday, Brent woke early and headed downstairs to make their usually Sunday morning meal. She showered earlier than normal, since she knew that her parents were late risers, and headed downstairs to help Brent cook.

By the time her parents came downstairs, they were sitting out on the back patio, her sipping her tea and Brent on his second cup of coffee. The scrambled eggs, bacon, and toast they had made sat in the warmer waiting for them to come downstairs. She had cut up some fresh fruit for her mother and had put out some yogurt since she understood her mother had been on a diet her entire life.

Not that she'd needed it, since she and her mother weighed the same.

"This is nice," her mother said, stepping out on to the back porch, "having the entire place to ourselves for the morning."

"We're closed on Sundays," she supplied.

"We've made breakfast," Brent mentioned. "Coffee?"

"Oh no, I don't touch the stuff. If you have tea…" her mother said.

"I'll get it." Brent stood up and offered her mother his chair next to the firepit. The morning was a little chilly, even though she knew the late-summer heat would hit mid-morning. "Do you like honey? Sugar?"

"Milk," her mother said. "Half and half, if you have it."

"Roy?" Brent asked.

"Coffee, black," her father replied, taking a seat across from her.

When Brent stepped inside to get their drinks, her dad turned to her.

"I just got off the phone with Jim. He's assured me that by

the end of today, all the charges against you will be dropped and any history of your arrest will be cleaned up as well." Just hearing her father's words allowed her to release some emotions that had kept her wound as tight as a spring for months.

She actually started seeing stars and had to take a few deep breaths as she looked out over the countryside to get back in control of herself.

"Thank you," she said finally.

"I've also pulled a few strings to find out about your ex." Her ex? The fact that her father hadn't called him Ethan or her husband told her that the bromance was officially over between her father and Ethan.

When her father had been under Ethan's spell, the pair would hang out and watch sports and go on excursions together. The kinds of things that her father had never done with her.

"And?" she asked after a moment.

Her dad took a deep breath. "It appears that after he withdrew the five hundred thousand—"

"Five?" She sat up. "You mean two hundred thousand."

Her father frowned at her. "No, there was five hundred in that account."

She shook her head. "What?" She swallowed. Just then Brent stepped out holding a tray of hot drinks over his shoulder, much like a waiter would have done. The reality that he was in fact butlering for her parents had her holding in a chuckle and forgetting all about her ex stealing half a million dollars from her and her parents.

Smiling, she watched Brent pass out the drinks.

"Will you press charges?" she asked her father after he took a sip of his coffee.

"I'm having Jim hunt the man down," her father said when Brent sat next to her on the sofa. "Apparently, after he cleaned out the account, he took an extended leave from his job for a few months. He came back shortly after you went MIA, then took off again about a month ago. Rumors are that he has a place in Mexico somewhere."

"Ethan hates Mexico." She frowned. "Well, foreigners at any rate." The more she thought about it, the more she realized that Ethan would probably hate American Indians as well. Anyone with dark skin had been a target for him.

She glanced over at Brent and relaxed into his arms. If she wanted proof that the two men were nothing alike, all she had to do was look at the people they kept close.

"At any rate, his father says that he's due back in the office this next week. We'll get some answers from him one way or another," her father finished.

"So, you're planning on returning to Seattle?" she asked.

"Yes, our flight leaves this evening," her mother said. "We were hoping we could convince you to tag along, at least for a while?"

"No," she automatically answered, then she glanced over at Brent. "I'm needed here. I have a job and..." She turned back to her parents. "I don't want to leave just now."

Her mother nodded. "We thought so. Anytime you want to come back, for a visit," she added quickly, "you're welcome." Then her mother turned her eyes to Brent. "You as well, Brent. We can't thank you enough for taking our Melinda in when she needed someone."

"I'm the lucky one," Brent answered, wrapping his arm around her shoulder and pulling her closer.

"Now, did I hear someone mention bacon?" Her father stood up.

They all sat on the porch under the new awning, which Brent had finished a few days previous, and ate breakfast.

Less than an hour later, they walked her parents out to

their rental. She stood stiffly when her mother hugged her and said her goodbyes.

"I like your new man," her mother had softly. "He has a nice family."

Mel understood and translated her mother's words easily to mean that she'd been impressed with Brent's connections to the McGowans.

When her father approached her, a very stern look upon his face, she stiffened even more. She was shocked when he wrapped his arms around her and whispered.

"I'm sorry." Nothing more. Then his arms fell away as quickly as they had grabbed her.

In all her years, she'd never once heard her father apologize for anything.

She stood with Brent's arms wrapped around her as her parents disappeared down the road in their rental car.

"Well, that went better than expected," Brent said as they started walking back inside.

"My father apologized," she blurted out.

"Good." He turned her in his arms.

"They're dropping the charges and expunging my arrest." She turned back to look at the empty road. The dust from the dirt lane was still settling.

He smiled. "Think they can do that with my records?" he joked, causing her to smile.

"I never thought…" She shook her head and felt tears stinging her eyes.

"Don't do that," he said softly, cupping her face.

"I can't help it." She smiled as the tears rolled down her cheeks. "For almost a full year, I feared I'd end up in some cell waiting for Ethan to come get me."

"He's not going to get close to you. Not ever again," Brent promised her, and she believed him.

Then he leaned down and kissed her. "Let's go on a hike.

It's a nice day and we have nothing to do now that we got rid of your folks."

She smiled. "I'd like that. Maybe we can cross the creek? See your land? Plot out where you want to build that log cabin."

He took her hand and lifted it to his lips. "That is an amazing idea."

They headed back upstairs and changed into their hiking clothes, which consisted for her of her worn jeans, an old T-shirt, and a sweatshirt, along with the waterproof hiking boots that she'd purchased on her last trip to Helena.

Brent's attire was basically the same with the addition of the small backpack that he wore, which carried their refillable water bottles and some snacks for later.

They crossed the field, taking their time to stop and talk about where they would put each of the thirty-five RV spots, the firepits, the swimming pool, and the general facilities, which would include laundry rooms, bathrooms with showers, and a large outdoor dining area attached to the pool area. They also talked about where they planned to build the gazebo for those special events TK had suggested.

When they entered the trees, she was surprised at just how far the creek was beyond the tree line. The thicket had gotten denser, and the orange flags were no longer visible through the underbrush.

"Wow, I guess things have really grown up since the last time we were out here," Brent said. "It's amazing what a few weeks can do."

"It's been almost two months," she said, turning to him. "How can it be only two months?" She shook her head as he pulled her closer.

"The best two months of my life." He kissed her, then took her hand. "Now comes the fun part."

By the time they reached the other side of the small creek,

they were both soaking wet and covered in fresh mud. Still, they were laughing and enjoying every minute of their journey.

It took them a while to find the markers on both property corners.

"There's about two acres over on this side of the water." He looked around as they stood on the side of the hill.

"Is that enough for a home?" she asked.

"Yes, plenty, if we plan it right. You haven't been up to the McGowan's homes, have you?" he asked, and she shook her head. "Trey and Dylan's place hangs out over a creek sort of like this. Of course their land is a little flatter, but I bet something like what they have would work, with a long wide deck, two stories, the main floor on the top, so we could overlook the field." He turned her shoulders slightly, making her look out over the field and his property. The view was simply breathtaking.

The entire time she'd been there, she'd only enjoyed the view behind the Hard Way. Now, as she looked out through the trees and over the field, she could see the Hard Way's building in the distance. Then she noticed the high peaks on the other side of the valley behind everything. Snow covered the high mountain peaks, which jutted up into the blue sky while an occasional white puffy cloud floated slowly by. She had never seen anything more beautiful.

"Best view in town," he said softly, then he turned her back towards him. "I can't think of a better place to tell you that I love you."

She tensed, then smiled. "It's perfect." She wrapped her arms around his shoulders. "You're perfect. I love you too."

He bent his head down and kissed her. "I want you to stay here. With me." She was about to agree, but then he motioned around them. "Here. Build this home with me. Stay here with me. It's only been a few months, but I spent a lifetime to get to this moment. To get to you. I guess you can say I did everything the hard way, and I'd gladly do it again, just as long as I could be assured that I'd end up here, with you. Right now. At this moment."

He surprised her by dropping down into the soft dirt and pulling a small black box out of his pocket.

"It's the only thing my parents owned that I didn't pawn. It was my great-grandmother's, but if you don't like it…" He opened the box and she looked down and saw the most perfect vintage platinum ring. Two perfectly cut diamonds sat nestled on the top, making it appear as if they were one large diamond. Several diamonds sat on either side and wrapped around the entire band.

With shaky hands, she reached for the box, but just then he pulled it back slightly with a chuckle.

"I think I deserve an answer first," he joked.

"Yes," she said quickly. "Yes," she said again, this time a little louder.

Smiling, he pulled the ring from the box and slid it onto her finger smoothly.

"If it's a little small or too large…" he started, but she stopped him.

"It fits perfectly." She pulled him up to stand next to her and kissed him.

CHAPTER 25

For the next week, Brent had his head in the clouds. He told anyone that he crossed paths with about his and Mel's engagement. By the end of the first day, he'd told so many people that Jamie had written the message on the chalkboard that he'd hung up by the dartboard. She claimed it was so he could save his voice, and she'd even drawn little hearts and flowers around the engagement notice.

Dylan was so excited for them that she insisted on throwing them a huge engagement party, which they had all agreed to having at the Hard Way to accommodate all the people they wanted to invite.

He'd met with some local contractors and had received bids for the work for the RV park. So far, he'd been impressed at how little really needed to be done. Since some of the foundations were already in place and were pretty much perfect for the first twenty RV spots, the conversion would be simple enough.

They discussed modeling the next fifteen spots after the first ones, spacing them out in the same pattern and direction and making them the same size as the small buildings that used to be there.

They would have to add cable television connections, but the water and electric for those first twenty spots were there and usable.

For the main structure for the pool, laundry room, and bathrooms, they chose a location near the front, so the utilities didn't have far to travel. The view from the pool and gazebo areas was important to him, so he and Mel took the time to make sure those spots were situated just perfectly.

One of the contractors suggested they had enough land to host about fifty spots, but for now, he figured the thirty-five spots were a perfect start.

The most difficult part would be convincing the city and the mayor to give him a chance and allow him the permits for the park.

To grease the wheels, they had decided to simply call it Haven RV Park and Event Center. He figured by tagging the name of the town onto it, they could boast a boost in tourism as a benefit for allowing them the necessary paperwork.

He and Mel were scheduled to have a few minutes at tonight's town hall meeting. He'd never attended a town meeting before, and he had to admit that he was pretty nervous.

How had he gone from the town's screwup to a respectable business owner? Even most of the people who had tried to avoid him when he'd lived there before now walked up to him and chatted as if they were old friends.

Not that he minded, but it was starting to feel like he was in some sort of *Twilight Zone* episode. Any minute now, the bottom would drop out from under his feet.

Just as long as he didn't lose anyone he'd grown to care for, he was fine with taking the wild ride.

Mel had locked herself in the office shortly after lunch to

prepare for the town meeting. The way he figured it, all he had to do was wear his good clothes and a dress-up shirt.

He wasn't quite sure what she was doing in there, but every time he passed by, he heard her typing on the computer or printing something out and figured it was best to stay out of her way.

He spent the rest of the day hanging up more string lights, setting up another firepit, and building another corn hole set, since it was one of the most popular games they had. About an hour before the meeting, he headed upstairs to shower and dress.

As he stepped into the hallway, Mel was coming out of the bathroom, fully dressed in a skintight black pencil skirt and a black-and-white striped blouse and had her long dark hair braided and lying over her shoulder.

He'd never seen her look so good. He pulled her into his arms and kissed her and told her just that. She slapped him playfully.

"You smell." She pushed him away. "You're going to soil me." She laughed. "You'd better hurry up and shower. I'm going to finish getting everything ready for the meeting."

"I thought we were just going to stand up there and talk about what we want to do," he said with a slight frown.

Her eyes narrowed. "Leave this to me. It's what I went to school for."

He shrugged. "If it makes you happy"—he waved his hands—"take it." Then he kissed her once more before she shoved him towards the bathroom.

"Shower. I laid out your dress clothes and ironed your shirt." She narrowed her eyes. "Don't wrinkle it."

"Yes, ma'am." He smiled at her as he started to slowly peel his clothes off. He saw her eyes heat as she watched his slow striptease.

After tossing his shirt onto the floor, he reached for his

jean buckle. Her tongue darted out and licked her lips, which she'd painted a deep red color. He had smeared the lipstick slightly by kissing her.

Her eyes followed his hands, and he could have sworn he heard her heartbeat from where he was. When his pants dropped to the floor and his desire for her sprang free, she jumped slightly, then turned and rushed down the hallway.

"No time to play." She shook her head.

"There is always time to play," he said softly. He reached for her, only to have her dash out of his reach and rush towards the doorway.

"Shower!" she called back. She stopped at the end of the hallway and glanced over her shoulder. "I'd suggest you use cold water." Her eyes traveled slowly back down over his body, and she swallowed before quickly turning around and leaving.

"Well, hell." He stepped in and stood under the cold spray and tried to get the image of her in that outfit out of his mind.

An hour and a half later, he was standing in front of a room full of townspeople, feeling ready to barf. Thankfully, Mel came through for him as she'd said she would.

From the moment they had called on them, he'd felt tongue tied. He was sweating profusely and was positive that if he was forced to talk, he would vomit instead.

"Good evening," Mel said in a calm voice. She turned towards him and, after running her eyes over him, nudged him back into his seat. "I've got this," she said softly.

For the first few moments, his ears were still buzzing, and he missed the opening lines of her speech, but when he heard the room burst out in laughter, he shook off the nerves and focused on what she was saying.

"Now, if you'll all agree, times are changing, and Haven needs to upgrade to draw in more tourists. I doubt Mom and

Pop are going to come all this way to take their kids to one of our fine strip clubs." More chuckles.

"Well, they are pretty good strip clubs," someone called out.

"True." Mel nodded. "But what about the kids?" She tilted her head slightly. "Haven is surrounded by so much beauty. Beauty that families should get to enjoy." It was then that he realized she'd handed everyone in the room packets. He reached down and looked at the one she'd set in his lap. She'd even set up a slideshow on the projector. How had she done that without him noticing? He turned slightly to see a few pictures of his land with the mountains surrounding the town. The picture was… breathtaking—the bright green of the fields, the beautiful colors of the trees on the hills, the crisp white snowcaps against the perfect blue sky. "And we can all agree that it's one of the best views in Montana."

"In the States," someone called out.

"Okay, I'll agree with you on that." Mel flipped to a picture of the Hard Way. The land behind it filled the screen now. "And I think we can all agree that the Hard Way has recently earned its title as best bar and grill in Haven." There were several cheers. "So why stop there?" The screen filled with another image of the land behind the main building from overhead. Next to it was a computer drawing of what they had planned. He had seen the image that Mel had created before, but it hadn't been as detailed as it was now. It clearly showed the thirty-five RV spots, the bigger building housing the bathrooms and laundry facility, and the swimming pool. Then she flipped the button again to show a slide of the two images combined.

"We're proposing thirty-five private deluxe RV parking spots to begin with, all with thirty- and fifty-amp power, water and sewer hookups, and cable television. Each spot will have their very own picnic table, firepit, and barbeque grill. There will be a community swimming pool and pool house, private bathrooms with family showers, laundry facilities, and a community outdoor dining area." She flipped to another screen and showed a beautiful gazebo with a young couple dressed in wedding attire. "The grounds will have several choice spots for special events, both local and those for out-of-towners." She flipped through a few pictures of outdoor parties, and he noticed a few pictures from the back deck of the Hard Way with families such as the McGowans enjoying the space they'd built. Then she showed a picture that she'd taken from the back of the land, overlooking the field, with the Hard Way nestled in front of the mountains. He felt a wave of pride wash over him. This was his. He'd done this. He and Mel. "Haven has so much to offer," she continued, showing more images of the small town, including the Dancing Moose, the grocery store, the schools, the state park, and a few more small shops in town. "Help us share it with others." She finished off with the image of the RV park transposed over the current land, but this time a large logo sat at the top that read Haven RV Park and Event Center.

There was a moment of silence, and then everyone burst out clapping and cheering.

Martha Brown, mayor of Haven, hit her gavel on the desk loudly and then held her hands up to quiet everyone down.

"I think we can safely switch to the voting portion of the night, so that we can all approve Brent and Mel's permit," she called out.

Brent sat there and watched every single hand raise in the room when the vote was called out. Just before Martha hit the gavel to the table, the door burst open.

"I object." Everett stormed into the room, closely followed by his two sons.

"You're too late," Martha said. She slammed her gavel

down. "The motion carries. Haven RV Park and..." She turned to Mel.

"Event Center," Mel said with a smile as Martha nodded.

"Are approved." Martha slammed the gavel down again. "Now, we can move on—"

"I object," Everett yelled out again.

"Mr. Phillips, as I mentioned before, you are too late. The motion has already been voted on and approved by the committee." Martha waited a beat. "If you wish to file a complaint..."

"Yes, I do," Everett said.

Martha's eyebrows arched. "Then you can file a complaint at next month's meeting."

"That's bullshit," Everett barked out.

Martha's shoulders straightened. "I've tolerated you coming into my office for the past few months to complain about the Hard Way's goings-on because it's my job to listen to this town's constituents, but let me make it perfectly clear. This committee, no, this town has just approved Brent and Mel's plans for *their* property." She narrowed her eyes. "No amount of squabbling over what might have been is going to stop this project from moving forward. Your family sat on that piece of land for over a hundred years and didn't do squat with it. Your son gambled it away and *lost* it. Now all of a sudden you decide you want it back and it's the most important thing in the world to you. Everyone in town knows you have no legal right to that property any longer. So unless you get over it, my office will no longer be hearing any of your complaints." Martha slammed the gavel down again when the entire town busted out in cheers.

Then Martha nodded to Dale and another officer, Chris, who were standing at the back of the room.

"The Phillipses are done here," she said clearly.

The two men walked over and started talking to the

Phillips men quietly. In less than a minute, Dale grabbed the father's arm and started pulling him out of the building while the sons yelled and argued with Chris.

When the room quieted down finally, Martha continued.

"We did it," Mel said quietly as he took her hand.

"You did it," he corrected and, not caring who saw them, pulled her closer for a kiss.

When the sounds of cheers broke into his thoughts, he pulled back and laughed. The entire room had turned their attention on them.

Once again, Martha banged her gavel down and looked over her reading glasses at them.

"I think it's safe to say that we are done with you two tonight." She smiled. "You are excused."

Brent laughed and then nodded. "Thank you." He took Mel's hand and pulled her towards the door.

"Wait, my purse." Mel laughed and rushed back to grab her things while everyone in the room laughed along.

When they returned to the Hard Way, they were greeted with cheers.

"Obviously, the news has reached everyone in town," he said sarcastically.

"Congratulations." Jamie walked over and handed each of them a shot of something, which they held up in salute, along with everyone else in the place.

"To Haven's very own RV Park and Event Center," he called out and then drank after the cheers.

Then he took Mel's hand and pulled her towards the stairs as the room burst into normal conversation.

They barely made it through their private door upstairs before he fused his mouth to hers. Then he pinned her to the door as his hands roamed over that tight body of hers, enjoying the feeling of the soft fabric she wore and the even softer skin underneath.

Her clothes hit the ground, followed by his. Movement was a blur, their heartbeats matched beat for beat. Their breath mixed as they moved as one. He thought that a little of the desperation would fade when he plunged into her, but instead it intensified.

"More," he growled, running his mouth down the pale column of her neck. "I want to hear you say it." He stilled, embedded deep within her.

Her eyes locked with his. "I love you," she said, gripping his hair as she tried to pull him closer.

"I love you." He started to move again only to lose himself once more in her.

"I can't move," Mel said sometime later. He was still pinning her to the heavy door, his face buried in her hair, which he'd pulled loose from its braid.

The sexy outfit she'd worn was now wrinkling on the floor at their feet, next to his good shirt, his jeans, and his shoes. The fact that he was using the door to stay upright had him smiling.

"Me either," he admitted.

"So, we're going to sleep here then?" she asked. He laughed.

"I might be able to move in a moment." He felt her body brushing against his. "If you keep doing that, I'll be doing more than moving in a moment," he said with a groan.

She stilled. "Take me to bed first," she whispered into his ear.

He didn't have to be asked a second time. He hoisted her up gently in his arms and carried her down the hallway and into their room, being careful not to trip on the discarded clothes.

Later, he fell asleep once more with Mel wrapped around him. His future was looking so bright that he had to keep reminding himself that life wasn't a dream.

With all the hell he'd been through in his life, he deserved to be happy like his sister was. Mel deserved happiness too. They'd both lived through hell and had still somehow found one another.

He had just fallen asleep when he heard her phone ring. She rolled over and answered it, and he knew instantly that something was wrong when she sat up.

"What do you mean they're missing?" she asked.

CHAPTER 26

"*I* mean they haven't returned from their weekend visit to their cottage," Brax answered her.

Brax Miller was her parents' long-standing butler or house manager. The older man had basically run the house when she was growing up.

Brent reached over and turned on the bedside lamp.

"Problems?" he asked.

She blinked a few times to wake up. "My parents are missing." She felt her heart jump in her chest. Then she turned back to the phone and asked Brax, "When were they due back?"

"This morning," the man answered.

"Have you called them?"

"Several times." The man's calm tone had never wavered in all the years she'd known him and didn't even now. "They haven't answered or returned any of my messages."

"Are you sure they were due back today?" she asked, her eyes locking with Brent's.

"Yes, ma'am," Brax answered. "I hate to bother you, but

your parents made it clear that if something were to go wrong, to contact you."

"Yes, I'll…" She looked to Brent.

"We'll go there," Brent said firmly.

She nodded. "We'll head there. If anything changes, give me a call. Have you called the police?" she asked, her heart skipping.

"No ma'am. My orders…" he started.

"Good," she responded. "We'll be there soon. I'll text you with our ticket information when we have it."

She hung up and turned just as Brent got off the phone with his brother-in-law.

"Trey has his pilot's license and a plane. He's going to fly us to Seattle," Brent told her. "We're going to meet him at the Haven airport in an hour."

She tried to hide her concern and fear, but Brent walked over and wrapped his arms around her.

"They're okay," he assured her. "I'm sure they're okay." He kissed the top of her head.

She held onto him for a moment before pulling away and looking up into his eyes.

"I'm not sure what will happen when I return. Ethan still has friends in high places," she said, feeling her stomach roll.

Brent surprised her by smiling. "So do I. Trey is having his brother contact some friends in the Seattle area. I was thinking of giving Dale a call too and see if he has any connections up there as well."

She nodded, not trusting her voice. Then he nudged her.

"Better pack some clothes." He motioned to the bag he'd tossed on the bed.

For the next few moments, she blindly threw clothes in the bag and stuffed her makeup kit, toothbrush, and other toiletry items in as well.

As they drove to the small airport that she hadn't even

known Haven had on the outskirts of town, she stared out the dark window and dreaded what was to come. She watched as Brent sent TK and Jamie messages telling them that they'd be out of town for a few days and to let him know if they needed anything.

Both women responded that they would let them know and to be safe.

It was strange. Not once since she'd received Brax's phone call had she worried that her parents had been involved in an accident of any kind. There was no doubt in her mind that Ethan was behind their disappearance and the crazy part was, she knew exactly where they were.

When she'd been eight, her parents had bought a small cottage on an island in the San Juan Island chain. Well, it was small in their book with five bedrooms, four baths, and five thousand square feet. The three-plus-hour drive from her parents' main home south of Seattle on the coast of Puget Sound was just long enough for her parents to consider it their summer getaway place.

The five-million-dollar home sat directly on the water with its own private beach and Olympic-size swimming pool. It had practically been her second home growing up. She couldn't remember a summer they hadn't spent at the massive cottage built of glass, stone, and wood.

If they went up there and hadn't returned, she was positive it was due to Ethan. After all, her ex had sworn to her that one day he'd get his hands on the gorgeous place himself.

Her father and Ethan had spent many summer fishing weekend trips at the place, enough that Ethan knew every inch of the home. It was the perfect place to hole up, with its full walls of windows and the single-lane road leading to the place. The fact that it was surrounded by thick trees on one side and wide-open water on the other made it almost a fortress.

She was surprised to see Dale standing with Trey in front of a small plane, waiting for them.

Brent shook both of their hands. "Thanks for putting everything aside for us," Brent said.

Trey nodded. "That's what family does." He turned to her. "How are you holding up?"

"Okay, for now." She turned to Dale. "I didn't expect you to come along."

Dale smiled. "When I called my old army buddy who works for the Washington State troopers, he suggested I head his way."

"You called the cops?" She felt her heart skip.

"No," Dale assured her. "Nolan assured me he's keeping this off the record. For now."

She nodded, feeling slightly better. The four of them settled in to the dual engine plane, and she held onto Brent's hand as they took off and headed west into the darkness.

She must have fallen asleep and woke when the sound of the engine changed.

"Easy," Brent said. "We're coming into Seattle now."

"What time is it?" she asked.

"Just past three in the morning," Trey answered for her. "We made good time," he said over his shoulder. "Good winds."

She was too tired and too worried to calculate how much time had passed since Brax had called her. Instead, she focused on the row of lights on the ground that they were heading towards. Was Brax already there?

She checked her cell phone for messages, hoping for word from her parents. Instead, she had a message from Brax assuring her that he would be there at the airport to pick them up.

The landing was as smooth as the takeoff had been. They taxied into a private hanger, and Trey cut the engine. She looked out the window and saw Brax standing beside her silver BMW and her parents' larger black Porsche sedan.

The man hadn't aged a day since the last time she'd seen him over a year ago.

She knew better than to rush to him and wrap her arms around him. How many times in her youth had he berated her that one simply doesn't manhandle the help? Still, she had to fight the urge to reach out to him as the four of them stopped in front of the car.

"Thank you for meeting us," she said in a calm voice. Brax nodded. "Brax, this is Trey McGowan, Dale Alaqua, and Brent McCaw." She motioned to each of them. "Brax Miller, my parents' house manager."

"I've arranged a car for you." He motioned to the BMW behind him. "If you wish, I'll take your things back to the main house." He motioned to the larger sedan.

"Trey, you should head back with Brax," Mel said, turning towards him. "Thank you for flying, but I can't ask you..." She shook her head. "I won't let you get involved in what is going to take place next. Not when you have a newborn at home."

Trey opened his mouth to argue, but Brent stepped forward. "I agree."

"Me too," Dale added. "We've got this." Dale laid a hand on Trey's shoulders. "You can rest up and fly us all back when this is over," he said with a smile.

"Brax, please make sure that Trey is comfortable until we return," Mel said. Brax nodded slightly, then motioned for Trey to follow him. He took Trey's bag from him and put it in the trunk of the Porsche.

Mel walked towards the BMW, tossed her own bag in the trunk, and waited for Brent and Dale to do the same.

"I'll drive," she said when Brent reached for the driver's door. When his eyebrows arched, she smiled. "It is my car, after all."

"This is yours?" he asked her.

She chuckled. "Given to me on my twenty-second birthday." She slid behind the wheel. She'd missed the power of the car.

"This sure beats your beat-up truck," Brent said as she pulled out of the airport, her tires squealing as she gassed it and headed towards Orcas Island.

"How long before we get there?" Dale asked from the back seat.

She added the destination into the car's GPS, which calculated that they would be there in just over two and a half hours. "At this time, with no traffic, I bet I can cut half a half hour off that time." She punched the gas pedal when she hit the open road of Highway 5.

"Don't let me see the speedometer," Dale said from the back seat. "Just keep it under a hundred. And drive safe."

"I'm always safe," she said, glancing over at Brent.

"Where's your friend?" Brent asked Dale.

"He's going to meet us up at the ferry to the island. I'm sending him a text now telling him when we'll be there," Dale said.

For the next two hours, she was completely focused on driving and getting to the ferry that would lead them to the secluded island.

"That's Nolan," Dale said, leaning forward.

Mel saw a tall man leaning against a pickup truck. The man was built like the Mountain from *Game of Thrones*, and she thought that there might actually be a chance they could beat Ethan. He had dark skin and pitch-black hair like Dale's, assuring her that he too had some American Indian blood.

They pulled the two vehicles onto the ferry less than

fifteen minutes later, and they all hung out below deck and talked about what was about to go down.

"What can you tell us about the situation?" Nolan asked Dale. Dale turned to her.

"Give us a brief layout of the place," Dale asked her.

She pulled out her cell phone and showed them pictures of the place. "It's made of glass. It's secluded. There is a dock and a boat house, but my parents sold the boat when I graduated, as they decided they didn't use it as often as they used to when I was younger. There are three bedrooms in the walk-out basement, with a wall of windows facing the water, the boathouse, and the pool. The hallway connecting the rooms runs along the back side, with the bathrooms between each room. There's a theater room at the end." She thought about the place. "Two bedrooms and the main living area are all upstairs. The setup is pretty much the same upstairs—a long hallway along the front of the house leads to each bedroom. The house is shaped like a bent L. The main living space, kitchen, and family rooms and my father's study are on the shorter side. The moment we drive up the driveway, he'll know it. My parents have a state-of-the-art security system. How are we going to sneak all of us onto the property?"

"Leave that to me," Nolan said, holding up his hand. Then he cracked his knuckles and smiled at them.

"Nolan was our tech guy," Dale added.

"I can usually remote into the system and disable it." Nolan said easily.

"Okay," Mel said slowly. She glanced around him. "Ethan is a cop. Which means he will most likely have several guns." She glanced to Brent. "I can't ask you to—"

"You don't have to," he said, taking her hand.

"We're all in this," Dale agreed. "Family first," he added. "We'll get your family back safely. Besides, we're not technically breaking any laws. We're just... checking on some family members. Until either of us"—he motioned between him and Nolan—"technically see anything illegal, we're just concerned friends coming along for the ride."

Just then she felt the ferry start to slow down.

"We're here." She looked up and saw the lights from the docks on Orcas island.

"How far is the house?" Brent asked her.

"Ten minutes," she answered as she climbed back into her car.

"How far is it from the water?" Dale asked, looking over at the other smaller boats at the dock.

"Five minutes," she said with a smile.

A few minutes later, they drove away from the docks just as the sky was starting to lighten with daylight.

Dale and Nolan had rented a boat and after she'd given them directions on his phone, they headed out towards her parent's property. Her first job was to make sure that the security system was disabled after walking inside so that they could sneak onto the property from the shore. They would have to figure something else out for Brent.

As she and Brent drove towards the house, she tried to stop the nerves that were causing her hands to shake. After all, there was a slight chance that Ethan and her parents weren't there. What would they find? Were her parents okay? She doubted Ethan would harm them. After all, he was a police officer. He knew the consequences of those actions. Didn't he?

"When I turn this corner, he'll know we're here," she said.

"Then pull over and stop. Let me out here," Brent said. "I'll sneak up to the house on foot. He will only be expecting you. Make sure to disable the alarm, like we said."

She pulled over and put the car in park. "I will," she agreed. Without another word, she went into his arms. The kiss was quick yet deeper than any other she'd ever experienced.

"Be careful," he said to her. She nodded.

"You, too. The house is that way." She motioned towards the property."

He nodded. "I love you."

"I love you too." She watched him slip into the dark trees.

Just as the sun rose fully in the sky, she parked besides her parents' small sports car. The fact that it was sitting outside assured her that Ethan's car was parked in the garage, out of sight.

Her father always parked his classic cherry red Corvette in the garage. Always.

There would be no hiding in the darkness now. The cloudless blue sky shone overhead, signaling that it would be another perfect late-summer day.

She climbed out of the car and straightened her shoulders. She knew without a doubt that she was being watched. She'd always gotten that itch between her shoulders every single time Ethan had watched her.

Taking her time, she walked towards the wooden double front doors, knowing he was assessing her from somewhere inside the house. She'd learned how to walk to please him and made a point to do so now—toe, heel, toe, heel—adding an extra sway to her hips, as every woman should, according to him.

She hated the fact that she was still dressed in the clothes she'd hastily pulled on last night in Montana. She knew Ethan would assess the simple worn jeans and sweatshirt and judge her for them. She needed him in the proper mindset if she was going to pull this off. Everything had to be perfect. She had to be perfect.

"Mom? Dad?" she called out cheerfully after unlocking the door and turning off the alarm like they'd agreed she would do. "Are you here?" She tried to keep her voice casual, as if it was the most normal thing that she would show up after being gone for months.

She was greeted with silence and tossed her purse down on the entry table like she'd done a million times before. Thankfully, she'd tucked her 9mm in the back of her pants. Ethan didn't know she owned one. Not even her parents did. He also didn't know that she'd learned to shoot and fight since the last time they had sparred.

She walked down the brightly lit entry hallway with its overhead sky lights and headed towards the living room as she called out once more.

"Mom? Dad? Are you here?"

"I… in here, dear," her mother called out.

Pasting on a smile, she passed by her father's office, walked through the kitchen and past the formal dining room, and stepped into the large living room. She stopped, her heartbeat jumping in her chest as she held in a scream.

Ethan stood over her parents, who were each duct-taped to their matching expensive leather recliners. The fact that it appeared that they had been there for days made her seethe. She could see that both of her parents' clothes were soaked with sweat and urine, as if the only way they'd been allowed to relieve themselves was to do it where they sat. She could smell them from across the room.

Her heart skipped at the sight of Ethan smiling at her.

"Hello, dear," he said as he cocked the gun that he held at her father's head. Without giving her a moment to speak, he fired.

She watched in horror as the side of her father's head exploded. Both she and her mother screamed at the same time.

Before she could recover, Ethan moved towards her mother's chair. Another shot rang out, only this time, Ethan's neck exploded with blood as he flew face forward into the coffee table. The glass table exploded as he fell onto it, sending sharp shards of glass flying everywhere.

Her mother was still screaming and crying out for her husband.

Mel continued to look at her dad, as if willing him to move. To cry out to her. To yell at her. To say he was sorry once more. Instead, his eyes stared blankly towards her.

Mel was rooted to the spot as memories of the last time she'd seen him, his last words to her, played over and over in her mind.

She would have stayed, locked in her mind, if she hadn't seen Ethan starting to get up out of the corner of her eye.

Then she let her instincts kick in as she flew towards the man who had just taken away the first man she'd loved in her life.

CHAPTER 27

Brent was moving as quickly as he could towards the house and stood just outside the large glass doorway to a bedroom when he heard the first shot.

Without thinking, he picked up the largest rock he could find and crashed through it just as a second shot sounded out.

Pushing through the large shards, he rushed through the massive bedroom, down the hallway, and towards the sound of screaming.

He entered the living room just as Dale and Nolan rushed through the broken glass doorway on the back of the house.

He watched in horror as Mel tossed a very large blond man in a police uniform down a set of stairs. The man broke a few of the stair's glass railings along the way as he fell downwards.

He expected Mel to stop, to rush to her parents. Instead, she rushed towards the stairs, pulling out the gun from the back of her jeans as she went.

"I'll kill you," she screamed.

"Stop her," Dale said to him. He rushed over and grabbed

Mel's arm, pulling her into his arms, making sure to take the weapon from her hands as he did so.

"He killed him," she cried into his chest. "He killed him."

"Roy!" Belinda cried over and over again. That's when Brent glanced over and noticed Mel's father. Turning his body, he tried to shield Mel from the sight, then realized that she'd probably witnessed the entire thing firsthand.

"Easy," he said, glancing down the stairs. "Get him." He motioned to Nolan, since Dale was helping cut the duct tape from Belinda's body.

Nolan was halfway down the stairs when another shot rang out. Going with his instincts, Brent pushed Mel down to the ground as two more shots sounded.

He heard Nolan fall the rest of the way down the stairs and guessed that the man had been shot.

"He still has a gun," Mel said to him. Then she tried to take the gun from his hands. "Let me," she said.

"Melinda, what have you done?" someone called from the basement. "Why have you killed your parents?"

Mel stopped. All of the fight died in her, and Brent saw her face pale.

"He's going to try and pin this all on me," she whispered.

"Now you've gone and killed… whoever the fuck this is." They heard another shot and then a laugh that had Brent's skin crawling. "Damn if the man won't die."

He let his guard down for just a split second, and that's all it took for Mel to twist free of his hold. He watched in horror as she yanked her gun back out of his hands. Instead of darting towards the stair, she ran towards the back door and was outside before he could respond.

He listened, unsure of what to do, as they heard a few grunts from the basement. He could only assume that Ethan was kicking Nolan, playing with his prey before he dealt the final blow.

"Talk to him. Stall him," Dale said quietly and then followed Mel quickly out the back door. He'd stopped cutting the duct tape on Melinda and the woman was still tied to the chair, crying for her husband.

Brent crawled on his stomach towards the stairs, trying to think of anything that would stall a killer. Then he remembered Mel's conversation about how Ethan was a true patriot.

"Do you know who that is?" he called out. "He's a state trooper."

"The fuck he is," Ethan called out. "No one would hire an Injun as a cop." He heard another grunt.

"It's true," Brent called out. "If you kill him, you're killing one of your own."

"I'm no Injun lover," Ethan called out. "Besides, it's not me doing all the killing. It's my deranged mentally ill wife."

"Ex-wife," Brent called out, causing Ethan to laugh.

"No, Melinda's still my wife. You see, because of her mental instability, I had the divorce cancelled. Everyone has known for years she's been sick." The more he talked, the louder he got, and the surer Brent was that the man had lost it. "Where are you, sweetie?" Ethan called out. "It's time we ended this game of cat and mouse."

Brent could see the man now through the broken glass. He was standing over Nolan, the gun pointed at the man's head. There was a large red pool underneath Nolan's shoulder and leg, but the man was glaring up at Ethan.

He opened his mouth to say something more, but then he saw a grey blur rush from behind Ethan, tackling him away from Nolan's body. When he realized it was Mel, Brent rushed towards the stairs, watching in horror as Mel kicked out, knocking the gun from Ethan's hands. Then she punched him in the nose with an impressive right hook, which sent the man back two full steps. Brent was at the base of the stairs when Mel twisted around and put Ethan in a chokehold that rivaled those from any MMA fight that he'd ever witnessed.

"You bastard," Mel said, holding onto Ethan's arm and neck, using her thighs to choke the man out. "You killed him," she said over and over again. "I'll kill you with my bare hands."

Dale rushed in through the unlocked basement door and, after taking a look at Ethan's blue face, rushed over and tried to untangle Mel from the unconscious man.

"Help," Dale called out to him. Part of Brent wanted to let Mel get her revenge, but then he understood that Dale wouldn't allow it. Nor could he live with himself if he allowed it.

Brent rushed over and pulled Mel away from Ethan's unconscious body while Dale moved over to help Nolan.

"Damn, I guess we'd better call this in," Nolan said, his voice laced with pain. "We'd better come up with a good reason why we're here."

"We were having a fun weekend, enjoying the sun," Brent suggested as he held onto Mel as she cried. He'd gotten the idea when Mel had mentioned her parents selling their boat. "Then Mel's crazy ex broke in, tied us up, killed her dad." Mel cried out again and laid her head on his shoulder. He held onto her and glanced towards the stairs where her mother was still crying softly upstairs.

"We'd better get our luggage inside before backup shows up then," Dale suggested, holding pressure to Nolan's wounds.

"I'll go get it after I untie Belinda and take them into another room." Brent stood up and helped Mel stand too. "We should tie him up too," he said, glancing towards Ethan. Mel stilled and then stepped out of his hold. He almost stopped her, but then she walked over, yanked a lamp from the wall, and proceeded to hog tie Ethan with the cord. He watched as she tied the cord tightly around his neck.

"Not too tight," Dale said. "We want him to live so he can go to trial for murder."

"Right," she said dryly with tears still streaming down her cheeks. Then she stood up, dusted off her hands, cocked back her leg, and kicked the unconscious man once, very hard, in his balls. All three conscious men winced, including Nolan, who had just been shot twice.

"Low blow, but I'd say he deserved it," Dale said. "Hurry, cops are only a few minutes out," he said holding Nolan's phone.

He and Mel rushed up the stairs to help her mother. It took both of them to hold the woman still while he cut the rest of the duct tape from her. Then Mel helped her walk down the hallway into what he could only presume was the main bedroom.

"You get the bags. Put ours in the room downstairs, the one with the open door, and put Dale's in the other. We'll have to explain that Nolan was just visiting for the day when it all went down."

"What about..." He motioned towards the chairs. It was obvious that her parents had been tied up for more than a few hours.

"We'll just..." She shook her head. "Mom, do you think you can change? It's important."

"He's gone. My whole life is over," her mother cried.

"Go, I've got this," Mel told him. "My keys are on the entry table."

"Your gun?" he said, motioning to where she'd stuffed it back in her jeans.

She reached back, handed it to him. "Put it in my purse. It's registered." She nodded. "I didn't use it."

"Right." He nodded and rushed out of the room, leaving

Mel to convince her mother to clean up a little so they could cover their tracks for Dale's and Nolan's sakes.

"The alarm code is seven-nineteen," Mel called from the hallway. "Better set it off while you're at it." He punched the code in and hit the emergency button before he shoved her gun back into her purse, making sure to zip her purse up again. Then he took the keys and rushed to the car. In one load he grabbed all three of their bags and raced back into the house and down the destroyed staircase, making sure to avoid the large shards of glass. He could already hear the police sirens when he tossed Dale's bag into the other room.

Taking a moment, he opened his bag, tossed a few shirts around the room and then did the same to Mel's bag, taking a second to put her makeup kit into the bathroom attached to the bedroom.

If this didn't convince them, then nothing would.

He returned upstairs, a stream of sweat rolling down his back, just as two uniformed police officers rushed in the open front door.

"Freeze," they both shouted. He lifted his hands quickly.

"Downstairs. They're downstairs." He made a point to keep his hands up. "Help him. He's a trooper. He's been shot."

Both men jumped into high alert. One raced down the stairs while the other continued to hold the gun on him.

"Mel? Belinda? Are you okay?" he called out towards the bedroom. "They're in shock. They're just in there. I didn't want them to wait in there. He killed Roy, my fiancée's father." He motioned towards the living room.

Just then, two more police officers rushed in and he and the other cop relaxed a little.

Over the next two hours, Brent sat beside Mel and Belinda while everyone retold the story that they had hastily come up with, all while they waited on word of how Nolan was doing and waited for the coroner to come and take Roy's body away.

Ethan's unconscious body was taken away by medics, handcuffed to the gurney. He had yet to open his eyes, but they had been assured that he was still breathing.

Every room in the entire house was photographed. Every spent bullet casing was collected and marked as evidence.

He'd never really watched the process firsthand but had watched enough shows to understand the procedures.

Thankfully, Mel had added a little tidbit about them returning from the mainland that morning, after missing the ferry the night before when they had gone to the mainland to shop and have dinner. He hadn't thought of the fact that they would have been seen riding the ferry first thing that morning. Thankfully, she had.

"I don't want to stay here," Belinda said when the police were wrapping up. "Please, take me home," she said, looking into Mel's eyes.

"Of course, Mother." Mel held onto her mom. Her eyes met his and he nodded.

Almost four hours after they'd arrived on the island, Dale traveled with Brent in the shiny red Vette as they followed Mel and her mother in her BMW.

"I've always wanted to drive one of these," Dale said as they sped down Highway 5, heading back towards Seattle.

"You're too tall," Brent said, motioning to how squished he was behind the steering wheel. Dale had a good three inches on Brent. As it was, Brent had to squish down to see the mirrors and not bump his head on the top of the car.

"Yeah, shame," Dale commented. Just then he got a call and Brent listened while he talked to Nolan. When he finally hung up, Dale was smiling. "That man is made of stone." He shook his head.

"Is he okay?"

"Yeah, he's already trying to check himself out of the hospital." Dale chuckled.

"Damn." Brent shook his head.

They had gathered their belongings from the rooms downstairs before leaving. He didn't know how long he and Mel planned on staying in Washington, but he figured Trey and Dale could head back to Haven once they reached Mel's parents' other house.

The police were done with them. It was the word of two decorated officers against the word of one who had been relieved of duty two months previous, by his own father, nonetheless. Having Belinda and Melinda Hawk as witnesses helped as well. Every single one of the police officers who had shown up had known instantly who the family was.

"You'll be heading back to Haven tonight?" he asked Dale.

"Yeah, I see no reason for us to stick around. The police are done with us. They have our information if they have any more questions," Dale answered. "Hopefully, Trey got some rest so he can fly us back. If not, as soon as he's up to the fly, we'll head back."

They were silent for a while.

"Nolan wanted to shoot the bastard the moment we saw him holding the gun to her dad's head." Dale glanced over at him. "I stopped him. I wish I hadn't." He sighed. "Her dad would still be alive."

"It's not your fault. None of us could have known he'd shoot the man," Brent said.

"No," Dale agreed with a sigh. "Still, I wish it had been me beating the shit out of him."

"Ditto." He smiled slightly remembering how Mel had taken the larger man down. "Still, I'm glad Mel got her chance. For all the shit he put her through in the past, she deserved the opportunity to do it first."

"Yeah," Dale agreed, then he chuckled. "It's kind of scary,

knowing what a woman that small can do. I mean, did you see her right hook?"

He chuckled. "Forget her right hook, that kick..." They both winced and Dale grabbed his own jewels.

"You'll have to watch that one. If I were marrying her, I'd make sure I never pissed her off. Not after seeing what she can do to a man."

"Trust me, I have no intention of ever pissing her off," Brent said with a smile.

"Smart man." Dale slapped him on the shoulder.

It took less than a week for them to bury her father. Standing next to her mother and watching the black casket being lowered into the ground was the second hardest day of her life.

She'd been a rock. She'd had to be, for her mother's sake. Her mother seemed to sink further into depression and denial about the entire ordeal.

When Mel overheard her talking to the same pastor that her parents had hired for her marriage counseling, she yanked the phone from her mother's hands and verbally threatened the man with a lawsuit if he ever contacted her mother again.

The day after her father's funeral, she heard that Ethan had sat in front of a judge and had been refused bail, as the judge had considered him a flight risk.

It was all over the news that the son of the chief of Auburn's police had been arrested for murdering Roy Hawk, CEO of RIC. Ethan's father was asked to step down from his position and had complied less than twenty-four hours after official charges were brought against his son.

Every single time they turned on the television, her family's photos were on the screen. There were pictures of her and Ethan's wedding day and pictures of Ethan and her father on a fishing trip. They had pictures that she hadn't even known had been taken.

No matter what happened now, Ethan was never going to be a free man. He'd killed a king in the eyes of Seattle, in the eyes of the world.

The fact that the fourth richest man in the States had been taking down by his ex-son-in-law hadn't sat well with the media.

Reports even surfaced about how Ethan had abused her. All the police reports that he had buried or had dismissed suddenly were found and highlighted, and people were finally able to see that he had convinced everyone to believe Mel had mental health issues. Everyone who had worked with him had believed his stories, and they were coming out of the woodwork to expose his lies.

Even the photos of her bruised body when Ethan had broken into her apartment were leaked and flashed on the screen for the entire world to see.

One reporter, the same woman who had verbally attacked her that day at the Hard Way, did a piece on Mel's new life. The image she'd taken of Mel sitting behind her desk in her office with a very protective Brent standing next to her filled the screen. The woman, a Gabby Collins, went on to tell how she'd been the one to find Mel's hiding place and how Mel had tried to move on after living such a tragic life with Ethan. She talked about her new life in Haven Montana and even mentioned the Hard Way Bar and Grill and how Mel was now engaged to Brent McCaw, the owner.

As they listened to the reporting, Mel had to admit that she was happier about this piece than all the others. Especially since the woman took the last few moments of her report to apologize for her own assumptions of Mel's guilt.

They'd heard Nolan had been released from the hospital the day after he'd been admitted. She'd seen him at her father's funeral, standing in the distance at the cemetery.

When she'd started across the grass to talk to him, he'd disappeared quickly into the crowd of mourners. Brent had mentioned that Nolan had talked to him and said that he felt guilty about her father's death, since he'd chosen not to take out Ethan when he had a chance.

It wasn't until the day they were set to return to Montana that she'd seen the man again.

He showed up on the doorstep to her parents' home. Just seeing him standing there, she melted. Without saying a word, she wrapped her arms around the man and held onto him.

"Thank you," she said as tears rolled down her cheeks. "Thank you."

She felt the man's iron body shake and glanced up to see a single tear roll down his cheek.

"I should have…" he started to say, but she shook her head, stopping him.

"You saved my mother's life. You save my life. That's all that matters." She reached up on her toes and placed a kiss on his cheek. "Thank you," she said again.

"I came here to apologize." He looked down at the flowers he held, which she'd crushed when she'd hugged him. "To tell you that I should have…" He shrugged.

"Come in." She took his hand and tugged the giant man inside. You couldn't even tell he'd been shot only a few days ago, which made her smile. She didn't think she could bear it if he'd been seriously injured. "My mother wanted to thank you herself." She smiled.

They sat in her parents' formal living room, a room they

had only ever used for special guests, while her mother cried on Nolan's shoulder and thanked him as much as Mel had.

She and Brent had tried to convince her mother to return to Montana with them, but she'd turned them down, claiming she had too much there to deal with. She'd talked about selling the house on the island, about getting rid of some of her father's things, and how she was even thinking of selling RIC, since it had been her father's baby. She'd told them that in the past few years, he hadn't really taken a part in the business anyway.

Mel had been shocked to find out that her father had left half of everything to her and the other half to her mother. Even through everything they'd been through, he'd never removed her from his will.

She hadn't wanted the money and would have gladly given it all back for a chance to reconcile with her dad. Had he realized he'd been tricked? Had he felt sorry? She tried not to think about his face moments before Ethan had taken his life, but the fact was, there had been tears and regret behind his eyes. Even in her sorrow, she knew the answer to those questions was yes.

"Will you be okay?" she asked her mother as they stood in the entryway the next morning as they were getting ready to head back home.

"Yes." Her mother smiled. "I'll be fine. What about you two? Are you sure you want to drive all that way?"

Mel smiled. "I've missed the silver bullet." She motioned towards her BMW. "Besides, this will give Brent and I some downtime we deserve before we start the RV park."

"Right." Her mother chuckled as she shook her head. "I still can't believe my daughter is going to run an RV park. In the middle of Montana."

"Don't be jealous," Mel joked and hugged her mother.

"What are you going to do with all this?" she asked, motioning to the house.

Her mother glanced over her shoulder and sighed. "I think it's about time I downsize." She shrugged. "Your father was the one who liked to show off our wealth. Besides, Teresa has been begging me to come stay with her in Arizona for a while. Who knows, I may like it." Her aunt Teresa had arrived the day after they'd returned from the island. Even now, the woman stood by the car, waiting to give Mel a hug goodbye.

"You know where we'll be," Mel told her mother with a smile.

"I do." Her mother hugged her again. "I'm so sorry," she said quietly, "for… everything. For not believing you." She pulled back and then turned to Brent and pulled him in to join the hug. "Don't make my daughter use her new skills on you," she warned Brent. "You've seen what she's capable of."

Brent chuckled. "I wouldn't chance it," he agreed. "You'll be there this fall for the wedding?" he asked. "Both of you?"

"I wouldn't miss it," her mother answered.

"I'm bringing the entire family," Teresa said with a smile. "That's a warning, not a promise," her aunt joked.

Brent took Mel's hand as they walked out the door for the last time. As she pulled out of the gated driveway, she took a moment to glance in the rearview mirror at her childhood home and knew that it would be the last time she'd see it. The funny thing was, it didn't sting like it had the last time she'd left there.

"Ready to go home?" Brent asked her.

"Yes, let's go home," she agreed, and she punched the gas.

Four months later, Mel stood on the side of the hill, overlooking their land as a fresh blanket of snow drifted over the white field beyond.

Four large wooden beams jutted out of the cold ground, marking where the corners of their soon-to-be home would sit.

There were several RVs parked in the distance. It was their first official week of being open, and all of the spots that were currently available were booked solid for the next few months. More spots were set to be finished in the coming weeks, if the weather held up, and she knew that those too would be snatched up.

Even though the pool had yet to be completed, the restrooms, laundry room, and pavilion had been. Word was spreading that it was the best campsite in the entire state.

They had gotten a lot of promotion from the one reporter's story, and it now appeared that everyone had heard about the Hard Way Bar and Grill.

"Happy?" Brent came up behind her and wrapped his arms around her. "Wife?"

"Very, husband." She held onto him and relaxed back against his chest and his warmth. She thought of everything she'd gone through to get to this very moment. This very spot. How much she'd sacrificed to finally find happiness.

"Merry Christmas," he whispered into her ear.

"Merry Christmas," she replied.

"You're cold," he said when she shivered. Then he stepped away and picked up the blanket he'd packed for their picnic lunch and wrapped it around her shoulders. "There."

She wanted to tell him she wasn't cold, but the extra warmth felt too good. Then his arms were back around her and she melted against him.

"It really is perfect, isn't it?" She sighed.

"Yeah," he said, resting his chin on her shoulder. "You're pretty perfect yourself."

She smiled, then turned in his arms. "Will you still say that in, oh, about six months when I'm bloated and fat?" she asked, waiting and watching for his reaction.

He frowned down at her and then his eyes got really large. "You're…"

She nodded, smiling, and laughed when he pulled her off her feet and spun her around.

"When? How? I mean, I know how, but when? What?" Brent asked, causing her to laugh even more.

"The end of June. You know how." She wiggled her eyebrows. "As for what?" She pulled out a small black-and-white photograph and handed it to him. "We'll just have to wait until tomorrow to find out."

"Tomorrow?" He frowned looking down at the dark spot on the image from the ultrasound.

"Yes, first thing in the morning we can go in and find out what sex our first child will be."

Brent's smile grew and then he was hugging and kissing her again as the snow started to fall in bigger flakes over them and their land.

"Best Christmas present ever!" he shouted as he spun her around.

Sweet Surrender

Second Chances

Entangled Series – Paranormal Romance

The Awakening

The Beckoning

The Ascension

The Presence

The Calling

The Chosen

Haven, Montana Series

Closer to You

Never Let Go

Holding On

Coming Home

The Hard Way

Pride Oregon Series

A Dash of Love

My Kind of Love

Season of Love

Tis the Season

Dare to Love

Where I Belong

Because of Love

A Thing Called Love

First Comes Love

Someone to Love

Wildflowers Series

Summer Nights

Summer Heat

Summer Secrets

Summer Fling

Summer's End

Summer's Wish

Distracted Series

Wake Me

Tame Me

Stand Alone Books

Twisted Rock

Hope Harbor

Raven Falls

For a complete list of books:

http://JillSanders.com

ABOUT THE AUTHOR

Jill Sanders is a New York Times, USA Today, and international bestselling author of Sweet Contemporary Romance, Romantic Suspense, Western Romance, and Paranormal Romance novels. With over 55 books in eleven series, translations into several different languages, and audiobooks there's plenty to choose from. Look for Jill's bestselling stories wherever romance books are sold or visit her at jillsanders.com

Jill comes from a large family with six siblings, including an identical twin. She was raised in the Pacific Northwest and later relocated to Colorado for college and a successful IT career before discovering her talent for writing sweet and sexy page-turners. After Colorado, she decided to move south, living in Texas and now making her home along the Emerald Coast of Florida. You will find that the settings of several of her series are inspired by her time spent living in these areas. She has two sons and off-set the testosterone in her house by adopting three furry little ladies that provide her company while she's locked in her writing cave. She enjoys heading to the beach, hiking, swimming, wine-tasting, and pickleball with her husband, and of course writing. If you have read any of her books, you may also notice that there is a love of food, espe-

cially sweets! She has been blamed for a few added pounds by her assistant, editor, and fans... donuts or pie anyone?

facebook.com/JillSandersBooks
twitter.com/JillMSanders
amazon.com/Jill-Sanders/e/B009M2NFD6?tag=jillmcom-20
bookbub.com/authors/jill-sanders